owers

razielreid

PENGUIN TEEN

an imprint of Penguin Random House Canada Young Readers,
a Penguin Random House Company

Published in hardcover by Penguin Teen, 2020

1 2 3 4 5 6 7 8 9 10

Manufactured in Canada

All emojis courtesy of JoyPixels/EmojiOne v2 covered under the Creative Commons license

Library and Archives Canada Cataloguing in Publication

Title: Followers / Raziel Reid.
Names: Reid, Raziel, 1990- author.
Identifiers: Canadiana (print) 20190144602 | Canadiana (ebook) 20190144610 |
ISBN 9780735263802 (hardcover) | ISBN 9780735263819 (EPUB)
Classification: LCC PS8635.E435 F65 2020 | DDC jC813/.6—dc23

Library of Congress Control Number: 2019945231

www.penguinrandomhouse.ca

Penguin
Random House
PENGUIN TEEN CANADA

Patrick Paley

Whitney Paley

Hailey Paley

Lily Rhode (rumored Season 2)

Jessica Strom

Kathy Strom

Joel Strom

Greta Strom

Luis Leon

Gloria Leon

Valeria Leon

Christoph Johnson

Shondra Johnson

Sean Johnson

Ghalib Morcos

Nadia Morcos (Season 1 only)

Yasmin Morcos (Season 2)

Idris Morcos

L.Y. Cadogan

Morgan Cadogan

Brandon Cadogan

Conrad Cadogan

Olympia Miller (Season 1 only)

Bea Getty

Fortune FitzRoy (recurring)

⬭ **paleyhailey**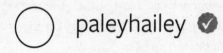

1m followers

itsyouesme Queen 👑

maya.mcelvoguex @mellochlen she's goals 👌 🔥 💯

alek_thapamgr @paleyhailey You're a role model for my daughter! Our favorite on the show by far!

erikzathiz Ich wunschte nicht Euch irre zu fuhren

dawnbat 🐌🐌🐌🐌

agatha_malik_1d not everyone is jealous of you

bpriscinessm How many of those mil did you buy sis? 😂

H ailey Paley takes a poolside selfie and uses an airbrush app to smooth out any discrepancies. Not that she really has any. Her phone case says "Social media seriously harms your mental health™" and has a photo of a pill bottle with a label that says:

LIKES

LONELINESS RELIEVER

DEPRESSION REDUCER

She posted a group shot of the teen cast sitting around a bonfire on the beach. Hailey's strategically placed next to Joel Strom. And it's the comments that have pushed her over the edge. Everyone's wondering if she and Joel finally get together on the new season *of Platinum Triangle*.

Hailey is lying on her stomach on a chaise lounge by the pool of the Stroms' Mediterranean mansion in gated Beverly Park. The sun reflects off the interlocking *C*s on her hot-pink Chanel bottoms.

"Okay," Hailey says, "confirmed sponsors for the party tonight include Flat Tummy Co., Girly Curves, Cocowhite, Fit Tea, Hairburst, Natalie's Orchid Island Juice, Nip + Fab . . ."

Greta Strom does a back dive off the springboard in a Moschino bra. Bea Getty, sitting with her feet in the water, protects the screen of her phone from the splash.

Hailey sits up and adds tanning oil to her legs.

"Oh, and Loving Tan. They just DM'd me."

Greta climbs out of the water and wraps a towel around her waist, joining Hailey over at the chaises.

"Gee, Hails. How will you have any time to do coke and sleep with your dad's co-stars if you're posing with sponsors all night?"

Hailey gives Greta a look. "You're beyond."

"Like throwing a million-dollar party for reaching a million followers?" Greta asks, laughing.

Hailey plays "A Milli" by Lil Wayne off her phone.

"You guys," Bea says. "Brandon's live on Insta from Hong Kong!" She comes over from the pool with her phone to show them.

"What's he doing in Hong Kong?" Greta asks.

"He was really craving dim sum."

Bea sits on the end of Hailey's chaise lounge as they watch Bea's boyfriend Brandon Cadogan's video. He's in the back of a car driving through a seedy area of Hong Kong. The driver is shouting in Chinese and frantically waving his hands.

The caption is: *Legit driving in circles, lost AF, in Hong Kong with a driver who speaks no English!!*

The girls laugh. They're all on their own phones now. Greta gets a ping.

"Hails, have you seen this?" She flashes Hailey her screen. "It came up with my *Platinum Triangle* alert."

It's a *Hollywood Life* article with the headline "Hailey Paley's Cousin, Lily, 16, arrested in Malibu—Pic." At the top of the article is Lily's mugshot.

"Lily Rhode, cousin of *Platinum Triangle* breakout star Hailey Paley, was arrested last night for a burglary in Malibu following a high-speed chase down the Pacific Coast Highway . . ." Bea reads the article over Greta's shoulder.

"I can't believe how many Shares it's getting," Greta says, lowering her phone.

With a sigh that would be worth at least 10k in a Rodeo Drive display window, Hailey slides on a pair of ivory cat's-eye sunglasses and leans back in her chaise.

"You don't reach a million without enemies," she says.

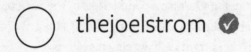

thejoelstrom ✓

1.8m followers

brittoni99 My future husband

yourchallengevideo Get out the Illuminati it's not good bruh I'm telling Jesus don't want you to worship Satan why you got time get outta Hollywood bruh that's bad bruh

pjalicee بسم‌الله خوش لگ شدی امشب

braydyn.anderson Man your just a gift from god

lori.tho I just want you to know that you're really cute and I stalk you all the time 💋💋💋

Joel Strom pulls into the driveway in his blue Porsche 911 Targa with a surfboard strapped to the top. His sun-kissed face is beaming through the open window at Valeria Leon, leaning against a parked BMW.

"Almost lost your boyfriend to a double overhead today!" Joel flashes Valeria a wide smile as he steps out of his car wearing a Thrasher hoodie and swim trunks.

"Sean's not my boyfriend," Valeria says. "He's my relationship status."

Joel takes off his HUF hat and runs a hand through his shaggy blond hair, frizzy from the day at Zuma Beach.

"What're you doing out here by yourself?" he asks.

"Hails and Bea are out by the pool with your sister planning an impromptu million-dollar party in honor of Hailey reaching a million Instagram followers. I couldn't bring myself to go in."

Valeria has more than three million followers because of her acting career, and Joel has more than a million because he sold his soul on YouTube when he was, like, five. Neither of them cares.

Joel puts his hat back on and pulls the rim lower, casting a shadow over his American-money-green eyes. He motions for Valeria to follow him inside.

The TV is on in the living room when they step into the house. Joel's mom, Kathy, is watching the just-released trailer for *Platinum Triangle*. The season 2 premiere is a month away. Joel knows his life is about to turn upside down.

Platinum Triangle revolves around the lives of several affluent families who live in the Bel-Air, Beverly Hills, and Holmby Hills neighborhoods of Los Angeles. The real stars are the family matriarchs, who are held together by Juvéderm and rosé. The teens have their own storylines.

For example, Valeria's currently in a hot new romance with Joel's best friend, Sean Johnson. There's even a feature about it in the new issue of *People* magazine.

Q: When did you know he was the one?

A: When my publicist told me he was.

Actually, Valeria's answer was something sweet. Something like "We fell in love at San Vicente Bungalows, a private club-house. You're not allowed to take photos. We were able to create something real, totally off camera. Something that's just ours."

Something everyone follows.

As they walk past the entrance to the living room, they

overhear the most heated part of the trailer, when Joel's mom and Hailey's mom, Whitney Paley, are at each other's throats. It's petty AF. Whitney and Kathy are best friends who don't really like each other at all. Kind of like Hailey and Greta.

"Let's talk about *your* fake fucking life," Kathy yells on-screen. "Let's talk about *your* marriage. How many times has Patrick cheated, Whitney?"

"At least my husband didn't marry me so he could wear my clothes!" Whitney screams back.

Joel cringes. He's been avoiding the trailer. He quickly leads Valeria out the back door of the house. She reaches over and gives Joel's hand a quick squeeze before pulling away.

It's going to be hard to get through the new season. It shows everything. His dad moving out, the transition . . . Joel's handling the changes in his family better than his sister. Greta is self-destructive. On the first season of *Platinum Triangle*, she slit her wrists in front of the camera. Their parents threatened to sue the network if they aired the footage. Greta was disappointed—that had been the whole point!

They cut across the yard toward the pool, where Greta, Hailey, and Bea are hanging out, stoned and starving.

"Hey, Greta," Joel says. "How many times has Mom watched the trailer?"

"Oh, I'd say at least a million." Greta shoots a look at Hailey.

"Are you coming to my party, Joel?" Hailey lowers her sunglasses.

"A milli," Joel says. "Quite the accomplishment."

"Careful, Hails," Valeria says. "It's not all VIP access, gifting suites, and retweets. There's a dark side to Hollywood. The trolls, the users, the stans, the—"

Follow

Foll

"—embarrassing press about your cousin from the Valley," Greta finishes. She holds up her phone for Joel and Valeria to look at the *Hollywood Life* story.

"Who's Lily Rhode?" Joel asks.

"Hailey's trailer park cousin," Greta answers. She turns to Hailey. "Does she have a fat family? I see a spin-off!"

Bea shrieks with laughter. "Can I please be there when you pitch it?"

"She looks like you, Hails," Valeria says, looking at Lily's mugshot.

"Yeah." Greta smirks. "Just not as apathetic."

Joel glances at the mugshot. Hailey must be mortified. Lily is something she can't control. Hailey once got rid of a family dog because she thought its bark was "indiscreet."

Hailey pushes her glasses up her new nose. According to her posts, she's been in Côte d'Azur most of the summer, but the photos were all plagiarized. Joel knows she's actually been locked in her room, recovering from the surgery.

"Literally everyone is trying to get on the list for my party," Hailey says, checking her phone.

"Enjoy it while it lasts," Joel says. "Viral is obscurity buying its time."

lily rhode

no results found

After a night in jail, Lily, handcuffed, is guided by a uniformed police officer down a corridor in the Malibu/Lost Hills Sheriff's Station.

She's brought into a meeting room where a lawyer is sitting at a table, a folder open in front of him with Lily's mugshot sticking out. It's the first time Lily has seen it and it shocks her. It's like looking at someone else. That can't be her. It's like when she sees her Aunt Whitney or her cousin Hailey on *Platinum Triangle*. They're so familiar and yet she doesn't know them at all.

The lawyer barely glances up at Lily as her handcuffs are removed and she takes a seat across from him.

"Lily Rhode, I'm Stan Yates. I'll be your public defender." He passes Lily a box. "Here are your personals."

Inside is Lily's phone, her ID, the keys to the trailer where she lives in a mobile-home park in Van Nuys, and the Tiffany charm bracelet she was wearing when she and Chris were arrested. She reaches in to touch a heart charm and traces it with her finger.

"The stolen property is valued at over a hundred thousand dollars, which makes it grand theft." Stan glances up at Lily from his file. "How would you like to plead?"

"Guilty." Lily reaches for her phone and turns it on. "Of FOMO."

Lily can't believe that the sheep Chris stole is worth more than a hundred thousand! It's a Lalanne, apparently. She had been so naive to think that he was actually taking her to a party at a beach house off the Pacific Coast Highway. She'd built up the scene in her mind on the drive from Van Nuys, imagining a bonfire on the beach, like the photo Hailey posted . . . the illusion had quickly popped.

No lights had been on in the yacht-like beach house when they pulled into the motor court in Chris's black Camaro.

"Where's the party?" Lily asked.

"I know the guy who lives here," Chris said. "Well, I follow him." Chris showed Lily the guy's feed. Champagne bottles popping over exposed breasts, designer labels, money-clogged toilet bowls, videos of bikini-clad girls being thrown off the roof of the beach house into the pool. According to his most recent Story, he's out of town, partying in Palm Springs.

"You won't believe his art collection," Chris said, staring through the front windshield up at the dark house.

It happened so fast. Lily was kind of buzzed from the roadie. It was supposed to be a good night. It was supposed to be her escape. As they drove along the coast, Lily pretended she deserved nice things.

"Where are you going?" Lily asked when Chris stepped out of the car. He just slammed his door shut and she watched him disappear around the side of the house. Lily switched off the stereo, waiting. Then she heard glass break. Followed by the house alarm ringing. Lily jumped out of the car like she was trying to jump out of her skin. Chris came running back, moments later, with a life-size furry sheep sculpture in his arms.

"Are you crazy?" Lily yelled. "What the hell is *that*?"

"Your ticket out of the Valley," Chris said.

It struck Lily, the way he said it. It was like time stopped. Just for a second. Then in the chaos of it all, Lily found herself getting back into the car.

Chris shoved the sheep onto Lily's lap as they sped out of the motor court and down the PCH. He was driving like a crazy person, weaving between honking cars. When she heard police sirens, Lily panicked. She tried to shove the sheep out the passenger's window but it wouldn't fit. Chris leaned over and pulled her back, losing control of the wheel.

The Camaro careened into garbage bins at the end of a driveway and crashed straight into the garage door of a beach house. The cruiser pulled up behind them and two officers jumped out, guns drawn. Chris's face had hit the steering wheel and his nose started gushing blood. Lily was spared from the brunt of the impact by the sheep, which acted as a sort of airbag.

"Since you don't have a record, and the other defendant is over eighteen, we'll fight to get the charges reduced to a misdemeanor."

The sound of Lily's lawyer's voice snaps her out of her flashback. Stan looks down at his paperwork and back up at Lily. "Do yourself a favor, kid. Drop the loser. You can do better. I have a daughter about your age. You know what I tell her? Shoot for the moon. Even if you miss, you'll land among the stars."

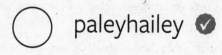

paleyhailey ✓

1m followers

paleyhailey #ad Celebrating reaching a milli with something sweet... These @flattummyco Appetite Suppressant Lollipops literally taste as good as skinny feels! 🍭

benmsomn__ JAILEY 😍😍

trendyxsavs Imma kill her

cariseazares fake inside and out

The infinity pool in the backyard of the Paleys' modern house in Trousdale Estates in Beverly Hills spills open to the sunny L.A. skyline all the way to the Pacific Ocean in the distance. The property is bustling with activity as Hailey's party is being set up.

Bartenders who all model for IMG stock an outdoor bar; a selfie wall made of white roses borders the yard; lights are strung around palm trees; a pink VIP tent is being erected; and a red carpet is unrolled in front of a step-and-repeat featuring all the sponsoring brands, the *Platinum Triangle* title, and the spiral logo for MKTV. Valeria doesn't even get this much sponsorship! The world is predicting big things for the spawn of movie star Patrick Paley.

"Is that Grey Goose?" Hailey snaps at one of the models at the bar, pointing to a bottle of vodka. "I only drink Belvedere." Hailey's mom says you don't get a hangover from Belvedere, and she would know.

Celebrity event planner Kevin Lee is strutting around as he organizes the setup. He's the most extra person ever and a living legend. Kevin did Brad Pitt and Jennifer Aniston's wedding. He's wearing a skintight pink suit with rhinestones and rose-tinted sunglasses as Hailey greets him with a double-kiss.

"Kevin, you've outdone yourself. I can't believe you pulled it off so fast!" When Greta and Bea were more interested in gossiping about Lily than helping her plan the party, Hailey knew she had to call in the big guns.

"Beverly Hills, darling! Chi chi chi chi chi!" Kevin puts an arm around Hailey's shoulders and leads her across the yard toward the house. "Guest of honor, don't worry about a thing. You just go get dressed. Million-dollar party—lots of bling bling bling bling bling!"

Kevin goes over to supervise the building of the VIP tent just as Whitney steps outside through the retractable glass wall leading into the Paleys' kitchen.

Hailey's dad once told *Entertainment Weekly* while promoting one of his movies that he married Whitney because she reminded him so much of the woman in his favorite painting, *Beverly Hills Housewife* by David Hockney. An icy blond woman frozen in front of a glass-box mansion, elite and alone.

"We may have another guest of honor tonight," Whitney says. She must have heard Kevin's carrying voice.

"Who?" Hailey asks.

"Your cousin Lily."

"The one who won't stop being poor?"

"Don't be so judgy, darling. Lily doesn't have anyone!"

"What about her mom? Is Aunt Erin still selling stories about you to the tabloids?"

"I talked to Erin this afternoon, actually. She's in Reno with her new boyfriend. You won't believe it! They left Lily behind in the trailer."

"Canceled," Hailey says. She whips out her phone.

Her mother's trashy side of the family is too real. Hailey can't imagine growing up in the Valley, never mind in a mobile-home park. Jesus fuck. Hailey used to pity Lily when they were kids but now she's just embarrassed by her. Hailey's glad that Lily's off the grid. She doesn't have an Instagram and has never been associated with Hailey's brand. Until now.

Hailey looks up the *Hollywood Life* story on her phone and stares down at Lily's mugshot. It's a testament to her family's fame how many Shares it's getting.

"Did someone at the police station leak the photo?" Hailey asks. She looks up at Whitney, who just blinks back at her. "Mother, you didn't!"

"Oh, I've had connections in the force since your father's first DUI. I just wanted to create a little buzz, distract from the negative press surrounding the trailer. Lily's arrest couldn't have come at a better time."

"I can think of a better time," Hailey says, indignant. "Like, not during my party! Or never?"

"Erin and I talked after a call I had with *Platinum Triangle* production . . . I'm feeling anxious about the trailer, Hails. I'm worried I went too far in my feud with Kathy Strom this season. People are calling me transphobic!"

Hailey rolls her eyes. "Bots."

"Kathy has all the viewer sympathy because her husband chopped off his dick! Look at the comments."

Hailey indulges her mother by opening Instagram and clicking on Whitney's most recent post.

"Is that my Viktor & Rolf dress?" Hailey asks.

She has to admit as she scans through the comments, Whitney's getting slammed.

> **here2bentertained** Saw the trailer and not watching season 2 bc of you. Your empathy is zero. I'd love to see how you behave with nothing. Yuk.

"And of course I'm the one who first mentions the possibility of Morgan Cadogan faking cancer on camera." Whitney is at the center of every storyline. "Kathy might have run with it, but it came out of my mouth first. How do you think that'll look if she really does have cancer?"

"Well, *I* just reached a million followers," Hailey says, closing Instagram.

"What about you and Joel?" Whitney asks. "Can you honestly say you got the story you wanted for season 2?"

Hailey stares out at the backyard. Joel Strom is her one and *only* failure. This season Hailey and *Platinum Triangle* story producer Sam constructed all of these scenes between Hailey and Joel. Their followers are so loyal. #Jailey. But Joel has been hard to reach. There were a few moments caught on camera that looked like something was building between them, but then Joel would become aloof. Hailey's been friend-zoned, and her brand is all about being desired—so that doesn't really work for her.

"Sam's looking for Lily now. Production wants to shoot some footage with your cousin and introduce her near the end of the season," Whitney says.

"*What?*"

"I was thinking we can do a makeover segment . . . you know, a shopping spree, give Lily—and the audience—the whole Rodeo Drive fantasy. All it'll take is a little fake compassion and our reputations will be restored!"

"You really scare me when you don't eat anything but Klonopin all day and start plotting." Hailey gives her mother a look. "You really want Lily to be on the show?"

"We'll sort out her legal issues, obviously. I mean, Hails, you'll be a role model to this girl. You can have her walk in the Dress for Success fashion show you're organizing at the Beverly Hilton."

Dress for Success is a charity that donates clothes to women for job interviews. Hailey is one of those girls who treats people like shit 364 days of the year and then throws a charity fashion show on the 365th day and calls herself a philanthropist.

"She can stay in the pool house," Whitney says.

"You want her to *live* here?"

"Not permanently. Just until we have enough footage."

Hailey opens her mouth to protest but quickly closes it. Maybe having Lily around *isn't* such a bad idea. It'll mean the cameras will start rolling again, and Hailey will have one more chance to write the perfect ending for season 2. Besides, the press is all over Lily's arrest, and it'll be cute if Hailey saves her.

"Are we literally sucking this girl's blood right now?" Hailey asks.

Whitney tries to arch an eyebrow but she can't because she just came from an injectables appointment.

Hailey pulls up Lily's mugshot on her phone.

"Welcome to Beverly Hills, darling," she says, her voice becoming increasingly ominous. "Chi chi chi chi chi . . ."

lily rhode

no results found

L ily's phone pings repeatedly as she steps out of the sheriff's station. Her mugshot is all over the internet. Lily's trying to keep up with all the incoming messages from her friends who have seen her in the press and can't believe she's related to the Paleys. Half the messages are from Lily's best friend from school, Mia, who is freaking TF out. She watches *Platinum Triangle* religiously and she feels personally betrayed that Lily never told her that she's one degree of separation from the hottest show on TV.

It's not just Mia. Lily hasn't told *anyone* about her famous relatives. She tries not to think about the Paleys because she knows the thoughts will spiral—thinking about them will turn into comparing herself to them.

Lily looks up from her phone, across the vacant parking lot. Where to now? There's no one waiting for her at home.

Lily's about to call an Uber when a black SUV pulls up to the curb in front of the station. A woman in her early thirties, dressed all in black with her hair in a messy bun, jumps out of the back.

"There she is!" She strides right up to where Lily is standing. "Quite the debut! What's next, a sex tape?" She leans in and lowers her voice. "I can help you slide into the right DMs, if you'd like."

"Excuse me?" Lily asks.

"Joking! Totally joking. You're only sixteen."

"Do I know you?" Lily gives her a weird look.

"Sam Dresner, story producer on *Platinum Triangle*." Sam puts out her hand. Lily reluctantly shakes it. "Your Aunt Whitney sent me to find you."

"My aunt?" Lily looks past Sam toward the SUV. "Is she here?"

"No."

Lily looks back at Sam, who winks.

"But she sent a camera!"

realvalerialeon

3.3m followers

tanya_emily @anevae_19 she's a hoe who keeps bringing up drama about Sean so she needs to get over herself

anevae_19 Excuse me she's not a hoe u r 🙄 but that's ok bc I still love u bc your my little mini me 😂 @tanya_emily

blue2380 @tanya_emily what drama does she bring to Sean?

tanya_emily blue2380 LMFAO we weren't even talking to you 😂 😂 🖐 get tf out 😂😂😂

blue2380 @tanya_emily @anevae_19 but I am talking to you since you're on my faves page talking reckless on a subject you don't even know about! AGAIN how tf is she a hoe?

anevae_19 @blue2380 lmaooooooo nigga you funny I wasn't calling her a hoe I was calling my FRIEND a hoe read the friken comments before you say stuff Oml go get a life and stop saying stuff until you read it correctly now you can get tf out

blue2380 @anevae_19 girl bye 🖐 if you love her like you claim, you wouldn't be up here calling her a hoe!

bellvwyckoff Shut up @anevae_19 @tanya_emily @blue2380 why u fightin

blue2380 @anevae_19 1. Don't call me no nigga. 2. Bitch I can read 3.youre ignorant as they come

anevae_19 @bellvwyckoff we aren't fighting 😂 👏 we do this everyday

Valeria's old movie star posters are hanging on her bedroom wall. The *Barney and Friends* movie. The first live-action *Dora the Explorer*. She'll never forgive herself for not being cast in *Dora and the Lost City of Gold*. But the poster that makes her mouth go dry is Dr. Seuss's *Did I Ever Tell You How Lucky You Are?* starring Valeria and Patrick Paley.

Valeria rummages through her closet, choosing an Alice + Olivia off-shoulder white lace boho dress, and she sprays herself with Miu Miu perfume (*No one can resist my Twist*) before checking her reflection in the full-length mirror. She's cute and hateful.

When she gets downstairs, the TV is on in the family room. Valeria's mom, Gloria, is watching *Daily Pop* as she holds Valeria's baby brother, Leo, and tries to tidy up the kitchen counter. Valeria's six-year old sister, Sophia, is jumping on the couch.

". . . sources reveal Hollywood may be bracing for another sex scandal," the host is saying. "The allegations are against an unnamed actor of a major studio franchise and involve sexual misconduct on film sets spanning nearly two decades . . ."

Leo is crying and Gloria is shaking him, a little too roughly, trying to soothe him. She reaches for a bottle of Klonopin on the kitchen counter and swallows a capsule with a sip from her Starbucks cup.

Valeria used to be on the same anxiety pills to help her get over her nerves before auditioning. She was also on Adderall to keep her energetic on set, and Ambien to help her sleep. Her mother referred to Valeria's decision to stop taking the pills as her "teenage rebellion," but Valeria just wanted to feel again.

"Sophia, cut it out!" Gloria says sharply.

Gloria tries to give Leo a pacifier but he spits it out onto the floor. His sobs turn hysterical.

Valeria takes him from her mother's arms. He instantly calms down. Leo is Valeria's favorite thing in the world. She loves him more than anything. And the feeling is mutual. He actually smiles at Valeria as a last tear streams down his chubby cheek. Gloria's too relieved to be offended.

"Want me to put him down before I go?" Valeria asks.

"Sophia!" Gloria snaps. Sophia immediately stops jumping. Leo's lip trembles like he's about to start wailing again, but Valeria manages to rinse off the pacifier and get it in his mouth just in time.

"I'll put him down," Gloria says. "You're late enough as it is. I hear *Platinum Triangle* is shooting the party. Leave it to Whitney to get production running again just for her. I want you featured with the long-lost trailer trash cousin, if you can. And make sure you're seen with Sean!"

"Fine. Whatever."

"Not *whatever*. His dad played for the Lakers, Valeria."

Valeria shrugs. "Christoph Johnson's kind of a crackhead now."

Gloria picks up a stack of mail next to the pill bottle on the counter and waves it around. "Having you linked with someone so high profile is good for publicity. In case you haven't noticed, these aren't fan mail. They're bills."

Sometimes Valeria thinks her mother derives pleasure from hurting her.

"God knows my *Platinum Triangle* salary isn't going to cover them. They think they can pay us with attention."

"Because they can," Valeria says.

Gloria gets competitive. "I'm more in demand than *you* these days. And it's not like we can count on your father. He's in Vegas cracking eggs his golden goose hasn't yet laid."

She takes Leo back from Valeria's arms, giving Valeria a once-over.

"Is that what you're wearing?"

"What's wrong with it?"

"I repeat, *the show*'s filming. Put on something that shows a bit more skin."

Sophia figures she's stopped for long enough and resumes jumping on the couch. Gloria sighs.

"Go look in Sophia's closet."

Valeria rolls her eyes and turns to go.

"Oh, and Valeria?"

She stops and looks back.

"He wants to see you tonight. At the Montage Beverly Hills."

lily rhode

no results found

L ily sits across from Sam in a red leather booth in Formosa, the famous Old Hollywood café on Santa Monica Boulevard where the stars used to go after the day on set. It's dimly lit and designed with a Cantonese theme, framed photos of Hollywood stars lining the walls. Frank Sinatra, Lana Turner, Humphrey Bogart, James Dean . . . The waiter brings them each a mai tai, which Sam swears all the stars used to drink when they'd meet at Formosa.

"So what is it exactly that you do on *Platinum Triangle*?" Lily asks. She takes a sip of the drink and immediately feels her shoulders relax. She's exhausted. Last night catches up to her all at once. She didn't sleep in her cell.

Sam finishes sending a text and places her phone on the table. "I'm a story producer. I work with the cast and crew to create a narrative around the footage we're shooting."

"So it *is* scripted?"

"Everyone thinks that, but no. It's not. I don't create stories, I just sort of"—Sam smirks—"herd them."

Lily takes another sip. A generous one. Old Hollywood style.

"I don't know anything about the show. My mom and my Aunt Whitney got in a huge fight way back because my mom was selling stories to the tabloids about Whitney after she married Patrick Paley. They haven't really talked since."

"Well, they spoke this morning. Your aunt called your mom after she heard that you'd been arrested. Whitney's worried sick!"

"She is?"

"I understand your mom's not currently living in L.A.?" Sam asks.

Lily shrugs. "She's a free spirit."

Something in Lily tells her that she's auditioning. She takes another sip of her drink and leans back in the booth. It feels like she's giving a confessional.

"I came home on the last day of school and there was a note saying she was out and didn't know when she'd be back. She wrote it on the cover of one of her tabloids. She used to draw devil horns on Whitney and Patrick posing on the red carpet."

"Tragic." Sam stares at Lily. "How are you getting by?"

"I got a job lifeguarding this summer so I can pay rent on the trailer. At Zuma. A world away from the Valley." Lily doesn't disclose that when she got hired as an L.A. County lifeguard, she requested Zuma Beach because it's featured so much on *Platinum Triangle*. She just wanted to feel the warmth of the sun that always seems to shine on TV.

Sam's eyes light up. "The lifeguarding angle is *so* relatable . . . and the fact that you've been forced to take care of yourself because of your mom's abandonment. . . . Everyone loves a little family drama."

"There's always been drama with the Rhode sisters. My mom is jealous of Whitney. I guess they were a lot alike growing up.

They both went for tall, dark, and bad. My Aunt Whitney just went for tall, dark, bad, and *famous*."

Lily looks up at a framed photo of Spencer Tracy hanging on the wall. "I wonder what it would be like to grow up with a dad like Patrick Paley."

"Where's your dad?" Sam asks. "If you don't mind me asking? Did you contact him when your mom—"

"Ran away to Reno with some guy she met on Tinder?" Lily laughs. "My dad's never been in the picture."

"Got it. Moving on. Do you watch the show?"

"No. At least I tried not to. I didn't even tell any of my friends that I'm related to the Paleys."

"Why not?"

Lily spins her mai tai on the tabletop.

"I guess I just didn't want to be compared to them. I didn't want to compare *myself* to them." She sighs. "It's been a lonely summer. After my mom left . . . I found myself binge-watching the show, one episode after the next. I saw the trailer for season 2 last night. Which is what led to me being arrested."

Sam chokes on her drink. "Not the first time the show has been blamed for that!"

"I went out with this guy. He's been trying to get with me forever. Chris. He's a senior. He said we were going to a party in Malibu but it was really the house of some guy he follows on Instagram and wanted to rob."

"How very *Bling Ring*," Sam says. "Is Chris cute? He'd better be cute if you got a mugshot over him!"

Lily stares back up at the wall of movie stars.

"He's one of those Hollywood Chrises, you know? A generic superhero hunk. And that's what I wanted. A co-star. I wanted to pretend I was going to the kind of party they go to on the show." She blushes. "I have escapist tendencies."

Sam breaks into a big grin. "Then I know just the place for you!"

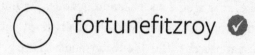

fortunefitzroy ✓

140k followers

tinapoplawski Gorgeous!!! Love the faux fur 🖤 🖤 🖤

sasha6asl16 Wow crazy nails 😶

mollybachmann I feel we could be besties 😙

zombieatletier @fortunefitzroy GIRL. GIRL! You probably look absolutely stunning when u cry like for u it's probably diamond dust infused tears 😭 💖 😍

ap_jid This is who I want to be.

"Yasss, henny! That Alexis dress is *everything*." Fortune FitzRoy air-kisses an arriving guest. "Obsessed."

Fortune doesn't mind working the door for Hailey's party. This way everyone has to give him attention.

"Do you do your own makeup?" the girl asks. Fortune can't remember her name even though he just looked it up on the list. "And I *love* the faux!" she squeals.

"Just a li'l something I pulled out of the closet." Fortune does a twirl in his Matt Sarafa FAKE collection coat, almost knocking off his headset. The lining is a black-and-white satin fabric covered in the "fake" graphic. Fortune's clothes tell you everything you need to know about him.

"Don't forget, the step-and-repeat is to your left when you walk out back," he says.

Fortune is like an angel; he's so androgynous. Definite Slytherin. He's tapping his @sealedwithakrisnails on a clipboard. Fortune just appeared on feeds one day, and because he's so shameless, it was like he was always there.

A lime-green Lamborghini Huracán Coupè pulls into the Paleys' motor court. Idris Morcos is behind the wheel, wearing an iridescent Gucci logo tee. According to Idris's dad Ghalib Morcos's Wiki, the Morcos family are descendants of Daher Al Omer, Prince of Nazareth and the Sheikh of Galilee. The Lambo lurches to a stop and Greta lifts her head from Idris's lap, wiping her mouth with the back of her hand. Fortune watches through the windshield as they make out.

Idris steps out of his car and adjusts the bulge in his shredded Dsquared2 jeans. His arm is around Greta's shoulders as they cut across the parking lot toward the front door.

"You look amazing!" Greta gives Fortune a double-kiss. "As always."

"Aw, thanks, sis! I love your lip gloss!"

"What's up, Fortune? Looking fly, bro." Idris fist-bumps Fortune. Sealed with a fist.

"How's Hailey?" Greta asks. "She sent me a frantic text. Something about her cousin?"

Fortune is *living* for this. He leans in conspiratorially, his fur draping off his shoulder.

"Moving into the pool house," he says. "*And* she's going to be on the show."

"Woah. I better go find Hails and keep her away from the dessert table," Greta says. "She doesn't handle change very well.

Remember when she thought Anna Wintour was leaving Condé Nast? She had rampant bulimia for weeks . . ."

Greta disappears into the house, leaving Idris trailing behind. He steps up to Fortune and pets the collar of his fur coat.

"So, is Hailey's cousin as hot as her?"

"What is it about Hailey?" Fortune asks. "You don't actually believe the vow-of-abstinence scene, do you?" It was an arc on season 1 of *Platinum Triangle*. Fortune thought it had great comedic value. Hailey could get really righteous about the story-line, though, acting like she really *was* a virgin. She and her dad did the whole "purity vows" thing, where she pledged to remain a virgin until marriage, and he vowed to "uphold her purity" or whatever. It was a big deal and they did it at Hillsborough Church, which has become a major Hollywood hot spot.

"Bro, it doesn't matter what's real," Idris says. He leans in and whispers in Fortune's ear. "It only matters what people think is real."

paleyhailey ✓

1m followers

brxxuhh27 @paleyhailey and just what do I with you ? You've been such a naughty girl, I think some on needs to be taken over my in her lingerie and garter belts stockings and given a spanking.Then then after you all done pouting, you come to uncle "B" sit on my lap and give me a big kiss and tell me how sorry about you are for being such a naughty girl.Then we will see what's happens if you behave yourself , maybe you will get a reward? Then again maybe not?

Hailey's sequin dress looks painted on. It glistens like the city lights in the background of the party. She's wearing Milly for her milli party. It's a moment.

Strobe lights on the influencers and the dance floor. The DJ looks like a shirtless Adam Levine. There are swans wearing diamond-encrusted chokers in the pool. The flashing cameras of photographers light up model genes on the step-and-repeat.

A *Platinum Triangle* camera operator follows Hailey as she greets her friends with double-kisses and hateful smiles. She notices her mom over by the selfie wall of white roses, talking on her phone and sipping Champagne. Looks like drama! Hailey leads the camera straight to it.

"If you can't get a groupie slut to Planned Parenthood, then what *is* the point of you?" Whitney is saying. "And as for the so-called exposé in the *L.A. Times*—kill it! This is the *last* thing we need right now . . ."

When Hailey realizes the drama is a little *too* real, she looks at the camera guy and drags a finger across her throat. He immediately goes off to film somewhere else. The production knows to keep the Paleys happy. It's in their contract that if they motion that they don't want something filmed, then the camera has to back off. Patrick Paley won't shoot otherwise, and he's the big ticket. The Paleys are the only family on the show with that much power. Although Kathy Strom came pretty close when she threatened to sue the network for causing Greta emotional distress and capitalizing on her breakdown when she slit her wrists. It was a bold move. Whitney thought for sure the producers were going to drop Kathy for season 2 over it but she got picked up, and with a bigger contract.

Whitney was secretly relieved—what's a hero without a villain?

"I have to go," Whitney tells the person on the phone. She hangs up and turns to Hailey, flashing a smile. Whitney has the sickest style. She's wearing Marchesa, which she loves to tell you she was doing before wearing Marchesa became fashionable again.

"Who was that?" Hailey asks, narrowing her eyes suspiciously at her mother. They're always on the same team, so Hailey knows what she's capable of better than anyone.

"Your father's agent. He has a new script for him."

Whitney checks her phone.

"I heard from Sam. Lily should be arriving any minute."

"About that," Hailey says. "I'm going to need a padlock on my closet. How long is this Beverly Hillbillies story arc supposed to last, anyway? Shall I ask Brandon if we can shoot at his house?"

Brandon Cadogan's dad owns the Chartwell Estate in old Bel-Air. It was used as the exterior shot on *The Beverly Hillbillies*.

Hailey looks across the party at Patrick standing by the bar.

"What does *Daddy* think about Lily?" she asks.

"Besides his appreciation for her taste in modern art?" Whitney chuckles. "He thinks Lily might be a good look for all of us." She sips her Champagne.

"You weren't talking about a new role for Daddy, were you?"

"Of course."

Hailey sighs.

"What is it this time, Mother? More on-set sexual misconduct rumors? How trite. Is *that* the real reason you're so eager to play fairy godmother to Lily's Cinderella? Trying to distract from Daddy's latest scandal, are we? Better start the damage control now; we don't want him to end up in rehab again. He's already been for 'anxiety' and 'exhaustion.' Never for being a raging coke whore, of course. So, what next? Maybe an autoimmune disease? They're *so* in right now. One of those *L* diseases. Lupus . . . or Lyme!"

Whitney raises her Champagne flute.

"Or Lily."

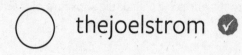

thejoelstrom ✓

1.8m followers

isoldeisolde1101 When greta slit her wrists she probably used your abs 😍😍

that_muse_kid Check out my drawings @thejoelstrom

ventura_artiste Omg I've been following his videos since I was three @realjustinalso

itsericaqueen Did you know? Here in the Philippines you're photo is here everywhere in the barbershop and you're the model 😂😂😂

luna_alix Are you sad??

Joel's Porsche Targa pulls up to the curb outside the Paleys' house in Trousdale Estates. The car was a sweet-sixteen birthday present from his dad. Greta got a car, too, but she refused it. Just like she's refusing to see their dad since the transition. Greta's car is in the garage at their dad's new place in Malibu. A G-Wagon, like Greta's always wanted.

It was Joel who had to tell their dad that Greta wouldn't accept the car. Joel's biggest fear this past year has been that his dad might commit suicide. And he just knows it would be, like, Jessica killed herself? Let's do the show anyway!

33

Joel stays in his idling Targa trying to muster up the will to enter the party. He's anxious. That's trendy.

A ping comes into his phone. @celiadaniz slips into his DMs.

celiadaniz Hi joel!!

celiadaniz How are you

celiadaniz You're so hot

celiadaniz Sent a photo.

celiadaniz Sent a photo.

celiadaniz Sent a photo.

celiadaniz I really want to date you!!

Joel looks at the nudes. He almost replies, mostly out of habit, but then it dawns on him that he doesn't want to. Joel feels sad.

He's listening to a classic rock station. "The Great Pretender" starts playing. He leans his head back against the seat and closes his eyes.

While he was surfing this morning, waiting for a wave, he was flat on his board and his mind became so clear. His pineal gland (his "third eye," according to Sean) was literally cracking open and ripping out of his forehead. Sean says it's the house of the soul, and when he's in the water, Joel's soul is at peace for a change.

Joel finally turns off the ignition and steps out of the car, just as a black SUV pulls up to the Paleys' gate. There's a girl in the backseat. She has blond hair pulled into a ponytail and she's staring out the window. She and Joel lock eyes, and it's like he's back on his board, suspended between the air and the water.

As the SUV glides through the gate, Joel's distorted reflection slides off its sleek exterior.

Joel heads up the driveway, passing Fortune FitzRoy working the door with a line of guests standing behind a red velvet rope. Joel spots the girl standing in the middle of the driveway, staring up at the front of the house. There's something about her, like she doesn't belong here either.

"You here for the party?" Joel asks as he walks up to her.

She keeps staring up at the house. "It looks so different on the show."

"For security reasons. They use the facade of a house in, like, Los Feliz."

"Of course they do."

She turns and looks at him. Joel sees the moment of recognition, and there's this fear/dread thing that overcomes him whenever he's recognized. But she's chill. She just blinks and looks back at the house.

"You wanna head in?" Joel asks.

"I'm supposed to wait . . ." Her voice trails off as they see *Platinum Triangle* crew members coming out of the house.

"Okay, let's get you mic'd!" Sam says. She's with the audio guy, who is untangling a mic pack. "Whitney and Hailey are going to meet you in the living room."

"What?" Joel is taken aback. "Sam, no one said anything about shooting tonight. I'm probably not even staying long. This isn't really my scene."

"You're right," Sam says. "It's not. It's Lily's."

The mic wire drops down the back of Lily's shirt and she jumps. Sam smiles at Joel.

"Your new co-star."

lily rhode

no results found

"Just pretend the camera isn't there," Sam says over her shoulder as they go through the Paleys' house into the living room, where a *Platinum Triangle* camera is waiting for them.

"Not there?" Lily asks. Not only is there a reality-show TV camera pointed at her, but she stops in front of an art piece hanging on the wall—it's a blown-up image of paparazzi cameras by Terry Richardson.

"My PA just texted that she has eyes on Whitney." Sam shoots off a text. "I'm going to go greet her and bring her to you. We good?"

She lowers her phone and looks at Lily, still staring at the picture.

"How much?" Lily asks.

"How much what?"

"I'm assuming my mom had to sign a release if I'm going to appear on the show, since I'm a minor?" Lily turns to look at Sam. "So, what exactly am I worth?"

Sam opens her mouth as if to deny it, but quickly deflates.

"Twenty-five thousand dollars and a Prada purse."

Lily feels like she's just been slapped. Like during the epic fight between Whitney and Kathy Strom in the trailer for season 2. She's not surprised, but it still hurts.

She looks back at the Terry Richardson as Sam heads off to

herd Whitney. There's a switch at the bottom of the frame. Lily flicks it and the piece comes alive, cameras flashing and making clicking noises.

Lily looks straight into the *Platinum Triangle* camera filming her.

It's so disorienting being in this house after seeing it on TV. She's fantasized about this moment. She just always pictured she'd be wearing a Jovani gown when it happened, and not the same tank top and shorts she wore during a night spent in jail.

She hears indistinct chatter and the sound of heels clicking against the floor before Whitney bursts into the living room. Whitney looks so much like Lily's mom it momentarily paralyzes her. But her Aunt Whitney is like the *after* version. She's had so much work done.

Whitney throws her arms around Lily and pulls her into a hug. "It's *so* good to see you, Lily!"

"Hi, Aunt Whitney," Lily says shyly. The clicking of the cameras from the picture suddenly seems so loud her ears are ringing.

"You've had quite the insane twenty-four hours, girl!" Whitney says, pulling back and looking Lily over. "But you look great! Your tan is insane."

"I'm always on the beach," Lily says. "I've been lifeguarding a lot this summer." As she speaks, it dawns on her how little her aunt knows about her.

They sit on a red velvet Jean Royére "L'Ours Polaire" sofa, which Lily recognizes from when Whitney gave a house tour on the first episode of *Platinum Triangle*. The couch is Patrick's baby. He collects modern art, furniture, and DUIs.

The camera operator focuses them in frame, while Sam and a production assistant are standing off to the side. Lily looks over at Sam, who gives her an encouraging nod.

"Why didn't you call me as soon as Erin ran off to Reno?" Whitney asks. "You didn't have to be left alone."

"I didn't want to impose." The truth is, Lily didn't even think of calling her aunt. It's been so many years, and the Paleys have always lived in a different world.

"We're family, Lily," Whitney says. "We have to stick together. Now, as far as your arrest goes, there's no reason to be embarrassed. God knows you're not the first person in this family with a mugshot!" Whitney laughs.

At the mention of her mugshot Lily grows even more self-conscious. She steals a look at the camera. She feels like her words are caught in her throat. How is this going to look on camera? She has to explain that she didn't know Chris was planning a break-in.

Whitney places a hand on Lily's knee to bring Lily's focus back to her.

"Don't look so worried! We're going to get all your legal problems sorted, okay? Who could blame you for falling in with the wrong crowd? Abandoned in the Valley. I'd die!"

Hailey appears at the doorway in that moment, looking like Taylor Swift after digging herself out of a grave and getting a red-carpet oxygen facial.

"Lily!" Hailey squeals. Lily rises from the couch with Whitney as Hailey comes over and gives her a double-kiss. They're barely touching. "It's literally been forever!"

Hailey notices Lily's Tiffany charm bracelet.

"And look, Mom! She's wearing the bracelet I gave her for, what was it, like, your tenth birthday? Has it really been that long?"

Lily shrugs awkwardly.

Whitney claps her hands together. "Just wait till Patrick sees you all grown up!"

imseanjohnson

1.5m followers

_shylapearle You're fly. Stay fly. Stay Zen @imseanjohnson

radicalandrea I love @imseanjohnson @realvalerialeon together!
But she goes through guys like underwear so I doubt it'll last.

youngdog_jay Miss those dope dreads

rennie_loveflirt_miers 🖤 ONLINE SEX AND MASTURBATE ON
WEBCAM WITH ME! 🖤 GO TO MY PAGE 💋

marcosammson911 We're the new generation weak up and pay
attention

Sean Johnson is sitting with Valeria at a table set up in the Paleys' backyard, staring out at the party. Sometimes he feels the most alone in a crowded room, and if there is a connection between him and Valeria, that's it. Maybe it's not romantic. But that doesn't mean it isn't real.

They can hear Greta and Idris over by the pool.

"Get me a swan!" Greta is yelling. "The black one!"

"Yeah?" Idris asks. He pulls Greta in for a kiss. "You want a swan?"

Idris whips off his Gucci tee and tosses it to the side, jumping into the pool as Greta shrieks with laughter. The swans desperately try to flutter away.

The water splashes all the way over to where Sean and Valeria are seated. Sean sees Joel cutting across the party toward them.

"You guys hear about our newest cast member?" Joel asks.

Sean follows Joel's line of vision over to Whitney and Hailey, who are coming out of the back of the house with a blond girl linked in their arms.

"Hailey's cousin," Joel says. "I didn't recognize her at first."

"A second Hailey?" Sean asks. "Yikes."

"You mean a third," Valeria quips. "She already has two faces."

"I don't know," Joel says. "There's something about this girl that seems different . . ."

Sean can *feel* the camera before he sees it. Sean's wearing a Damien Hirst I "Spot" DH tee-shirt. His "spot" speeds up in his chest.

"*Platinum Triangle,* ten o'clock."

The camera is pointed at them.

"Later," Joel says, dashing out of frame.

Sean and Valeria know what to do. Sean stretches his arm around the back of Valeria's chair. She leans in close and whispers seductively in his ear.

"I ate a baloney sandwich for lunch."

Sean tries not to burst out laughing.

"I'm wearing the same socks I wore yesterday," he says.

"Ew!" Valeria cracks up.

Sean kisses her before they have to do another take.

"He gone?" Sean asks.

Valeria steals a glance.

"All clear."

Sean retracts his arm.

"I think I'm gonna sneak out," Valeria says.

"Close-up's in the bag. You need a ride?"

"I brought my car." She kisses his cheek. "Pleasure working with you, Sean."

He watches her walk off, his eyes landing on Idris getting pecked in the face by a swan in the pool, then over at the almost famous people on the dance floor, posing on the red carpet, trying to get in the frame of one of the *Platinum Triangle* cameras shooting the party . . .

Sean pulls out his phone.

imseanjohnson We're all going to die

⭕ lily rhode

no results found

Lily wonders if Patrick still sees himself as he was twenty years ago. The face-lift helped. Or so he seems to think. He looks kind of odd. Lily read in one of her mom's tabloids that Patrick is eating more beets these days and the health kick has done *wonders* for his skin. Lily's mom said it was planted by a publicist and that he actually had plastic surgery. "They always change their hair when they get plastic surgery!" Erin pointed at the TV as they sat in the trailer watching Patrick win an award at the Golden Globes.

Patrick's face wasn't pulled too tight or anything, but there's something eerie about the way he looks. He's partied so hard that his eyes look permanently boiled in water—bulging out of his head, red vessels surrounding those baby blues that can still light up the silver screen and heart chakras.

"This party," Lily says, looking around as she stands with the Paleys. "I've never seen anything like it." But that's a lie. She's seen it on TV. She's dreamed it.

"I'm glad you could make it, Lily." Patrick flashes her a smile. "Sorry that I have to run; you're catching me on my way to set."

"I didn't know you were working tonight?" Whitney pouts.

"Night shoot," Patrick says. He gives Whitney a kiss. "Sorry, babe. But someone has to bring home the bacon. Although I'm just a B-list star around here these days." He winks at Hailey. "Guess who was asked by a pap while hiking Runyon this morning how it feels to be Hailey Paley's dad?"

"I love my stans," Hailey says.

They watch Patrick head into the house, and Whitney swings her arm around Lily's shoulder.

"Well, that leaves you with me and—" She stops and looks beside her. "Now where did Hailey disappear to?"

Hailey is lost in the crowd. Whitney waves it off.

"The hostess is always in demand! Why don't you mingle? Get a drink. I'll go make sure Ana has set up everything for you in the pool house, okay?"

Lily barely manages a nod before Whitney starts walking off. She's left staring out at the party alone. Almost.

The camera stays on her.

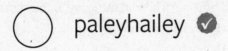

paleyhailey ✓

1m followers

paleyhailey Her heart is a secret garden & the walls are very high… 🏵 🏵 💮 🏵 🏵

The way the pool lights are reflecting off the surface of the water and onto Joel's face makes him look so pretty he pixelates in Hailey's eyes. He's staring across the party, at Lily standing by herself.

Lily isn't alone for long. A shirtless, dripping-wet Idris goes up to her and they shake hands. Good. Let that swine take care of her.

Hailey will take care of Joel.

She comes up behind him and puts a hand on his waist.

"The show's filming," she says.

"I saw."

Hailey smiles. "I didn't think we'd get another chance."

"For what?"

"This."

Hailey takes Joel by surprise when she kisses him, but he doesn't exactly resist.

"It was building between us all season," she says, keeping her face close to Joel's when their lips part. "I hate to be anti-climactic."

"And it didn't happen if it wasn't on camera, right?" Joel asks. He breaks the fourth wall and motions to the camera capturing them from across the pool.

"You don't have to love me, Joel. You just have to love giving them what they want."

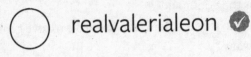

realvalerialeon ✓

3.3m followers

whiteworld_rawmg_544 we kno where u headed... 🔥🔥🔥✌️
good luck!!! I heard its forever there dark, unbareable smell, souls
on top of souls burning tf up non stop screams brimstone nd a
big ass lake of fire... But wait thats fake to huh? U betta rethink
dat shit for real

whiteworld_rawmg_544 u betta get yo mind Right on that one!!!
Can u imagine your whole body burning tf up non stop 🔥🔥🔥
u'll see!!!

I n the elevator of the Montage Beverly Hills Hotel, Valeria takes off the oversize, dark-lensed Max Pittion sunglasses her mother gave her before she left the house for Hailey's party. Gloria came up to Valeria's room as she was changing into something more *in*appropriate.

"I just want to make sure you know what to do." Gloria looked at her awkwardly.

Valeria has always known.

Gloria passed her the sunglasses and told her to try and keep a low profile.

When she knocks on the door of the suite, Valeria pretends that this is the role she's been waiting for. Her big comeback. Valeria is a talented actress—no one can take that away from her.

Patrick answers before the second knock. The top three buttons of his Polo dress shirt are undone, showing off his dark chest hair. She smells liquor and expensive aftershave.

He ushers her inside and looks both ways down the hallway. "Anyone see you?"

"Should I check my Mentions?" Valeria asks.

The door closes behind her.

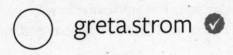

greta.strom ✓

715k followers

voguecelebutantes Your body is just goals 😎

alisha_jusbie These boobs Are definitely photoshopped 😂 👎

febexx I don't like your lips, they're soooo big:/

sinanir Ты прекрасна

dcruise10 you used to do funny pics of funny faces that were so real can you do more of those they're much more approachable

The door opens and Greta and Hailey shuffle into the powder room holding their drinks. The music from the party fades as the door swings shut behind them.

"She's like a stray puppy and I'm, like, I only like teacup Yorkies and only on Instagram," Hailey says, slamming her glass of Belvedere down on the counter. She starts touching up her makeup in front of the bathroom mirror, framed by Martinique banana leaf wallpaper.

Greta pulls her phone out of her Alaïa handbag.

"There's nothing about her online except the press over her arrest. No Insta."

"What does she have to post? Lily's literally from a trailer park. Like, Trump-land."

"Didn't your parents vote for Trump?"

"Not officially!" Hailey snaps.

Greta pulls out a set of keys and a bag of coke from her handbag. She uses the tip of a key to dig a bump and brings it to Hailey's nose. Hailey delicately snorts it before turning back to the mirror. Greta snorts her own bump while looking at her reflection.

"You know me and you don't," she says.

Greta takes a selfie of her and Hailey in the mirror.

"Make sure there's no—"

"Don't worry," Greta cuts her off. "Cropping out the drug paraphernalia. I know you have an image to protect."

"Did you see what she was wearing?" Hailey asks. "And, like, *how* does she already know Joel?" She takes a lime out of her drink and squeezes it between her fingers. The juice runs down the evil-eye clover bracelet on her wrist.

"They were together?" Greta asks.

"Fortune told me he saw Joel and Lily arriving together. This is supposed to be *my* night, not Lily's welcome party."

"So let's bail." Greta dangles the keys.

"Idris's Lambo?" Hailey asks.

"One of the perks of always having my head in his lap is that I'm in close proximity to his pockets." Greta raises an eyebrow. "Where do you think I got the coke?"

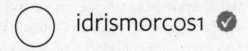

idrismorcos1 ✓

568k followers

phoenixsxinia When I wish I am somewhere new but stuck at work I look on your instagram bro and think where is Idris off to today haha @idrismorcos1

malaik_xh لن تثق إذا كنت أنت مه

maryymohamadi8384 😍😍😍😍🖤

sarahsmithe1111 Such a pretentious prick 🙍‍♀️

"Two whiskey sodas," Idris tells the bartender. He looks back toward Lily and nods his head as she smiles at him. This might be so easy that he doesn't need the GHB, but hey, man, it's a party.

He looks around to make sure no one is watching and unscrews the lid of the bottle, discreetly dumping it into one of the drinks the bartender slides across to him. Idris barely manages to conceal the bottle from Joel Strom when he comes up to the bar. He slips it into the pocket of his wet jeans.

"What happened to *no shirt, no service*?" Joel asks.

"Those swans are savage, bro. I almost lost an eye."

"I hear you, man," Joel says. "If the *Platinum Triangle* cameras don't get you, then the swans will."

Idris turns around and tracks the cameras. He wants to make sure there's no chance he was caught pouring in the GHB. Good thing he's not mic'd. He and Greta made that mistake once. MKTV aired as much of the audio as they could legally get away with, but Idris and Greta like to talk dirty. Joel has barely looked at Idris since the episode aired.

"I thought we were done shooting," Idris says.

The filming schedule is about six months of the year. There's also the "Real Home" footage, which is when a camera crew shows up and shoots for about three hours a day covering whatever goes on in the home of the featured families. And then the producers arrange additional shoots—dinners, parties, charity fundraisers, cast trips. And of course they get the cast "confessionals," where each member of the cast sits alone in front of the camera talking about the scenes.

The confessionals are cut throughout the episodes and usually cause the most drama because of all the backstabbing and gossip. Last season they shot two rounds of confessionals, one before the season aired and then another round about halfway through the season, when everyone had seen enough episodes to know what was being said behind their backs. That's when the gloves come off and the drama escalates for the second half of the season.

"Later, bro." Idris nods at Joel, picking up the drinks from the bar and cutting across the party toward Lily, who's waiting for him.

Idris always lies during confessionals.

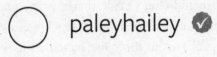

paleyhailey ✓

1m followers

princepaley Notice me @paleyhailey

Sitting in the passenger seat of Idris's Lambo, Hailey clicks on the handle of one of her fans, @princepaley. The page is full of drawings and photos of her. Some of the photos she doesn't even recognize. That's when you know you're famous.

Greta presses all the way down on the accelerator with her Valentino Garavani Rockstud pump. As Hailey scrolls through her phone, she lights a cigarette, a vice she indulges in only when she's anxious and the Klonopin isn't working fast enough and she wants to eat the world and then feel it come out of her, burning like the fiery breath of a dragon.

It's a blur of billboards and broken dreams through the open windows. Hailey flicks an ash over the side. Greta drives through a red light on Sunset Boulevard. She's too busy rapping along to the song blasting through the speakers.

The Lambo speeds ahead, weaving through other cars on the road, tires screeching against the pavement.

They go for drinks at Delilah and end up in Beverly Park. When they pull up to the gate, Greta jumps out and gives the guard a lap dance. Hailey makes a Boomerang.

Beverly Park is eerie at night. They drive past all the fake châteaus and giga-mansions hidden behind gates—it feels more haunted than Hollywood Forever Cemetery. And so empty. Greta must feel it too because she's driving fast; she's driving like something's chasing her. She doesn't slow down as they approach the Strom's estate.

The Lambo comes crashing through the hedges around Greta's house, which is next door to Mark Wahlberg's. They go soaring across the backyard, driving over the garden and setting off the sensor lights. Hailey's hair is thrashing around her head. She can't stop laughing.

Greta hits the brakes and the Lambo comes to an abrupt stop, its headlights shining across the pool. Hailey stops laughing when Greta turns and stares at her with Hollywood vampire eyes.

"Get out," she says.

Hailey knows that look.

"Take the precious!" Greta shoves the bag of coke down Hailey's bra before Hailey jumps out of the car. "And my Alaïa!" She tosses Hailey the handbag.

The engine revs. Hailey hits Record on her phone just as Greta pushes down on the gas pedal and drives the Lambo straight into the pool.

A huge wave of water ripples over the side. The Lambo sinks to the bottom, the surface bubbling.

Hailey watches the water flood in through the open windows. Greta doesn't get out. She stays sitting in the driver's seat. As the Lambo becomes completely submerged, Hailey starts to get anxious. This bitch. Greta doesn't surface. Another minute passes, and Hailey lowers her phone. It wouldn't be the first time Greta's tried to kill herself on camera.

Finally Greta breaks the surface, spitting out a mouthful of water. Hailey's heart doesn't exactly start beating again or anything, but she raises her phone.

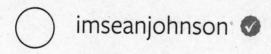

imseanjohnson ✓

1.5m followers

Sean's eyes are closed and he's pressed against the wall in the Paleys' powder room. The bass from the party music thuds through the locked door.

"Imagine, if you will, a world in which the psychic abilities of human beings are proven fact, but powerful cultural forces conspire to keep this knowledge from the masses—fearing what they might become if they knew their true power," Sean says.

Fortune is kneeling on his fur coat in front of him. He looks up at Sean as Sean opens his eyes.

"Isn't that the plot of *X-Men*?" Fortune asks.

◯ lily rhode

no results found

The party is still going strong. Idris Morcos? Not so much. He's stumbling all over the place and can barely keep his eyes open. Lily looks around. Should she be worried? The music is so loud. It might've been more fun watching the Paleys on TV than it is actually being here. A group of girls are obviously talking about her and looking her up and down. She's out of place. Zero glam. And there's been no sign of Hailey all night.

She was grateful when Idris came up to her while she was standing alone, even if she knows what a player he is from watching the show—Lily could never understand why Greta put up with him. But maybe it's like the facade of the Paleys' house: everything on the show has another side to it.

Idris almost falls into the pool. Lily gasps as Joel sweeps in and catches him. Lily was trying to play it cool when she met him before entering the party, *but it's Joel Strom!* He doesn't look real. It's like she's still looking at him through a screen. Lily has to resist reaching out and trying to swipe him.

Joel drops Idris on a floating unicorn in the pool. Idris passes out and floats away with the swans surrounding him.

"He spiked your drink," Joel says, putting his hands in the pockets of his pink distressed hoodie.

Lily stares into her glass.

"I switched them at the bar," he explains.

"Idris Morcos just tried to drug me?" Lily looks back up at Joel. "Isn't he with your sister? Or is that just on the show?"

"Who knows. Greta's just another possession to him. Idris thinks he has it all. He isn't self-aware enough to realize how miserable he is."

They notice a *Platinum Triangle* camera lens pointed at them from across the party.

Joel sighs. "We're supposed to be done shooting this season. But the nightmare never ends."

"I might be to blame for that," Lily says.

On impulse Lily reaches for Joel's hand and takes him to the pool house where Whitney says she'll be staying. He's a bit more real now that she's touched him. Or at least *she* feels more real. Her heart is racing.

Lily slides open a glass door that leads to a bedroom. She knows from the Paleys' home tour that the pool house has an open-plan kitchen, dining area, and living room complete with white modern furniture and a Bettina Rheims coffee table book on an Yves Klein Monogold table. The closet is bigger than her bedroom in the trailer where Lily grew up. There's an en suite with a marble sink that just looks like a slab of marble with a slit in it that drains the water.

The bedroom is pitch-black as she and Joel slip inside. Joel slides the door closed and the music from the party fades. It's replaced by a faint vibrating hum. A blue neon sign on the wall says *Land of Hopes & Dreams*.

Lily and Joel are cast in its blue glow. She feels him staring at the side of her face.

"You really gonna be on the show?" he asks.

"I think I'm already on it." Lily falls to the edge of the bed. "It's so weird being back here. I haven't been to this house since my tenth birthday."

Joel sits next to her. They're not touching but she can feel his own hum.

"I didn't know Hailey had a cousin," Joel says. "Or that you'd been here before."

"We're the same age, but I grew up in the Valley," Lily explains. "Hailey came to my birthday party. She was a diva. She thought the trailer where I lived was horrible. It was . . . but she didn't have to say it like that, not in front of everyone. She called her mom and got her to send a limo to pick us all up and bring us back here. Like, right when we were in the middle of eating pizza. But of course everyone wanted to go to Patrick Paley's house. They wanted to swim in a movie star's pool, and play games in a movie star's yard, and sit in a movie star's home theater watching movie stars . . ."

Lily touches her charm bracelet.

"I don't know if I can do it."

"Do what?" Joel asks.

"Survive in a world where people are made and not born."

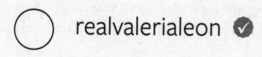

realvalerialeon ✓

3.3m followers

nathalie_fernandess gimme your face ty

tevatsveti עור

favorit3829 You know what are you doing don't you?

allidoisyourmathhomework Follow me! I'll do your Math
Homeworks 100%!!! 🧑‍🦲🏫

heavenlyred3 You're an inspiration to us all 🖤

heavenlyred3 Hollywood trash

"Something to drink?" Patrick asks.

It's like the director whispered in her ear before this
scene started, *Your character can't feel a thing.* Valeria is so
method.

Valeria walks up to the window and stares out at the glowing
city, throbbing with neon and rejection.

"Vodka's your poison, if I remember from that Dr. Seuss shit
we shot together a few years back?"

"*Did I Ever Tell You How Lucky You Are?*" Valeria's reflection
in the window smiles but her face is blank. "No one had to tell
me how lucky I was to be in that movie," she says quietly. "I was
so excited to work with you."

59

Valeria turns to Patrick at the bar. She's breaking character and she knows it. What if she never works again?

"I was working with *the* Patrick Paley." Valeria closes her eyes and remembers how it felt. "I had a poster of you on my bedroom wall."

She takes the drink Patrick hands her. They sit next to each other on the couch. Patrick sips from a tumbler of whiskey. Valeria has the handsomest co-star. Dark brown hair slicked back, streaks of gray at the temples, as distinguished as the light crow's-feet next to his piercing blue eyes, the lines almost designed—like they were purposely left untouched by his plastic surgeon so that John and Jane Fat Fuck America could relate to him on-screen.

John and Jane Fat Fuck America is what Valeria's mother used to call the audience when she was helping Valeria rehearse her lines. "You're boring John and Jane Fat Fuck America!" she'd scream, unhappy with Valeria's performance. "They're heading for the fridge! They're opening a can of Mountain Dew!"

Valeria takes a sip of vodka. She falls back into the couch. Back into character.

"I was nine years old when we worked together. It feels like another Timeline ago. Someone else's Timeline. The thing with fame is that you never expect it to go away. You always expect another moment to come along, and for it to be better than the last."

Patrick traces a finger down her bare arm.

"This moment's not so bad."

◯ lily rhode

no results found

The morning sun shines through the glass sliding doors. Joel and Lily are in bed together, lying over the white duvet fully clothed, the neon sign on the wall above them still glowing.

Lily stirs awake. She breaks away from her dreamless sleep and opens her eyes, into the land of hopes & dreams. Joel's on his back, staring up at the ceiling. He doesn't turn to look at her as she stares at the side of his face; he keeps his eyes on the ceiling. Lily studies his profile. They're stretched on top of the bed, just the skin of their arms touching.

"I found out that my dad is transitioning on Twitter," Joel says. "My mom drinks rosé all day. My twin sister is on the verge of a mental breakdown. And I'm America's golden boy who is just always chillin' shirtless on camera."

He turns his face and looks into Lily's eyes.

"I've never told anyone what's actually happening."

"I've never had anyone to tell," Lily says quietly.

They hold eye contact for a beat.

"I should get home," Joel says.

"Thanks for hiding out with me last night," Lily says, sitting up. "I don't even remember falling asleep."

Joel rolls off the bed and looks down at her. "I never do."

He slides open the door and Lily follows him out to the pool, where Idris is still passed out on the floating unicorn.

"Is that . . ." Lily's voice trails off as she stares at a spot on Idris's bare chest.

Joel cracks up laughing.

"Definitely swan shit! Even the swans know what's up."

After Joel leaves, Lily enters the main house. It's early enough that the Paleys' housekeeper hasn't started work yet. The Paleys haven't had live-in help since Whitney caught Patrick with one of the maids in the laundry room. It came out during a particularly vicious fight between Whitney and Kathy in one of the earlier episodes.

Lily slowly walks through the main house, not wanting to wake anyone. She wants to be alone in the house to process this. It's so quiet without the cameras in the Terry Richardson picture clicking or the sounds of the party outside. The air is so still. Lily's reflection passes in the glass as she steps into the living room. She doesn't know how she ended up here. Is it just because she was in the press? Is that some kind of rite of passage? Do Hailey and Whitney think she's one of them now?

Patrick's Golden Globe is on the fireplace mantle, and there's a Hermès throw on the back of the couch. Lily picks it up and brings it to her cheek. Of course she was blinded with jealousy when she watched the show, and of course she wondered what it would be like to live here. She wished she could be on it.

Lily finds herself walking up the stairs to the second floor. The railing is plexiglass and there are no streaks. Everything in this house is transparent and sparkling. The tall wooden double doors to the master bedroom are closed at the end of a long hallway. Hailey's bedroom door is open. The bed is made and Hailey is nowhere in sight. Lily takes a cautious step inside.

A close-up of Lily's face is reflected in Hailey's vanity, and in a smaller makeup mirror. There's a trifold mirror in the corner of the room. Hailey's four-poster bed is also mirrored. There are so many reflections of Lily's face staring back at her, she's even reflected in the framed pictures hanging on the walls. All shot by @bryant, an Instagram photographer who shoots practically every model and influencer in L.A.

Lily turns the LED lights on in Hailey's walk-in closet. An entire wall is dedicated to Hailey's Judith Leiber handbag collection. It's breathtaking. The clutches are organized in different categories. The food: a French Fries Rainbow clutch, a Couture Cupcake, a Hamburger; the must-have accessories: a Black Card, a Seductress Crystal Lipstick in champagne, a gold Brick Phone beaded in the finest Austrian crystals; and the animals and nature: a Zebra Rocking Horse, an Embellished Rose.

Lily picks up the blue crystal Gummy Bear clutch, which she remembers Patrick giving to Hailey during the *Platinum Triangle* Christmas episode. It was the prettiest thing Lily had ever seen. That Christmas, all Lily got were some free samples that came with a cosmetics purchase her mom made at the drugstore.

As she replaces the Gummy Bear clutch, Lily accidentally knocks a Jimmy Choo shoe box in a stack at the back of the closet. It falls off the shelf and hundreds of white-chocolate pretzel balls spill out and roll across the floor.

"What the . . ."

Lily turns to face the wall of shoe boxes. She opens the lid on a Chloe box. It's packed full of Twinkies. There are rainbow sour belts in Saint Laurent and saltwater taffy in Tom Ford. She tears off more lids. Swedish fish, gummy bears, and soda-can gummies packed to the brim in Gianvito Rossi. Chocolate-dipped cake pops in Manolo Blahnik. Potato chips covered in Belgian chocolate in Stuart Weitzman. Peanut-butter-cup popcorn in Aquazzura. Dozens of boxes of shoes, all with candy inside. Except for the Charlotte Olympia box full of laxatives.

As she scrambles to put the white-chocolate pretzels back where the Jimmy Choos should be, Lily hears a car pull up outside. She puts the box back on the shelf and turns off the light. From the bedroom window, she can see Hailey stepping out of an Uber. Her sequin dress looks so distorted by the morning light. There are sequins missing, and Lily can see that Hailey's eye makeup is smudged.

Lily dashes out of the room, runs down the stairs, and swings open the front door to greet Hailey just as the Uber is driving off. Hailey trips coming up the driveway—the heel of her Louboutin rolls over a loose stone. She drops her Judith Leiber Pink Diamond clutch and the contents spill out. No cake pops or gummies this time. Just a real Black Card and some makeup.

"Where'd you run off to last night?" Lily asks. She bends over and picks up a Guerlain Météorites compact, passing it to Hailey.

"Was that Joel's Porsche my Uber passed on the street?" Hailey asks, staring intently at Lily.

"Yeah." Lily scratches her neck. "The party went kind of late."

Hailey keeps staring. "Did you two film together last night?"

Lily smiles. "There was no camera," she says.

Lily breaks eye contact first, bending down to pick up Hailey's bank card.

"I'd be careful with Joel if I were you," Hailey says, accepting the card as Lily passes it to her. "Joel may seem charming, but he's only interested in you because you're new. He has a private Instagram account full of photos of all the girls he's piped. Just ask Valeria. We *all* know what Dora was exploring . . ."

"Is that why you've been chasing him on the show?" Lily asks.

Hailey's eyes narrow. "Of course you watch the show."

Lily's spared from replying by Patrick's Aston Martin pulling through the gate. The car parks and Patrick steps out, waving over at them.

"Morning, girls."

"Hi, Daddy," Hailey says, her voice suddenly sweet. "How was set?"

Patrick bends over to pick up a tube of lipstick. Housewife by Priscilla x Rincón Cosmetics. Lily saw a "What's in Your Purse?" video on the MKTV YouTube channel where Whitney dumped the contents of her handbag and held up the same tube of lipstick, claiming all the wives of the *Platinum Triangle* wore it.

Lily notices the bag of coke on the ground at the exact same moment Patrick does.

"What the hell is this?" Patrick holds up the bag.

Lily looks over at Hailey. Her face is blanker than ever.

The front door opens and Whitney steps out in a leopard-print housecoat.

"What's going on?" she asks. "Why are we all outside?" She stops when she sees the bag of drugs Patrick is holding up between his fingers.

"I asked you a question," Patrick says, staring into Hailey's eyes.

"It's—" Hailey starts to say.

"Mine." Lily jumps in. "I must've dropped it."

"Oh, Lily." Whitney looks at her regretfully, like she's thinking: *If only there were a camera filming this.* "I'm shocked."

"I'm not," Patrick says, folding the bag of coke into the palm of his hand. "I was afraid something like this might happen. How could it not? Look at her white-trash mother."

"I'm sorry," Lily says quietly, her eyes on the driveway. "It was a stupid mistake. It won't happen again."

"Thank you for being honest with me, Lily. I'm sure you understand that, as parents, we have to protect our daughter from harmful influences. In a town like L.A., that isn't easy. We can't have you making it harder on us."

Patrick turns to Whitney. "She leaves this morning."

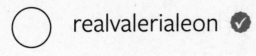

realvalerialeon ✔

3.3m followers

ilyknott You are not famous anymore

ilyknott You are not famous anymore

ilyknott You are not famous anymore

ilyknott You are not famous anymore

Valeria's phone pings on the nightstand in the Montage Beverly Hills. She snaps awake and finds herself alone in bed, her naked body tangled in the soft sheets. Patrick is gone.

She reaches for her phone and opens Instagram. She's scrolling through the comments and wondering why she tortures herself. Always first thing in the morning. Like she has to start the day off with a punch to the gut or she just doesn't feel quite right. The trolls are calling her irrelevant again. If she's so irrelevant, then stop following her!

Valeria replaces her phone on the nightstand, and that's when she notices the envelope full of cash next to a note written on hotel stationery. She picks up the note and reads it.

Order breakfast. Enjoy the suite. Have a blast. Buy a treat.
—Dr. S

◯ lily rhode

no results found

Lily stares out the passenger-side window of the moving Aston Martin. Patrick is tapping his fingers on the steering wheel. Lily wishes he would stop, or at least turn on the radio. The silence is so oppressive. Patrick's energy is almost as cold as the AC blowing on Lily's bare legs. She's covered in goose-bumps.

"Look, I don't think you're a bad kid," Patrick says finally. "I'm playing Kang the Conqueror in the new *Avengers* movie. I'm the villain on-screen, but off-screen I'm the devoted family man. Marvel is owned by Disney after all. Everyone is."

They pass a billboard for the new season of *Platinum Triangle*. It features an image of Joel surfing. Lily leans her head against the window.

She knew it wouldn't last.

Patrick glances over at her. He opens his mouth to say something but just lets out a sigh.

"Fuck it," he says.

Lily lifts her head from the window as Patrick does a sharp U-turn.

"Where are we going?" she asks. "Van Nuys is the other direction."

"I changed my mind." Patrick speeds ahead. "There's something I want you to show you."

They're stuck in traffic for what feels like forever. Patrick puts on some music and hums along. His mood has changed. He's relaxed. When he stops at a Mobil to get gas and cigarettes, Lily sits in the passenger's seat watching a StarLine bus caught in the traffic jam. Tourists sit with the sun beaming down on them through the open top, looking out at the sidewalks hoping to spot someone famous.

Lily turns up the stereo. Patrick doesn't wait to light a cigarette before they've pulled out of the gas station, like he knows he can't blow up; he's already a supernova.

When they finally reach Mulholland Drive Lookout, Lily is confused.

"Why'd you bring me here?" she asks, taking in the breathtaking sight of Los Angeles.

Patrick motions for her to follow him up the stairs that curve around the canyon.

When they reach the peak, Patrick leans against the railing, staring out at the Hollywood sign which has come into view. It almost looks close enough to touch.

"I'm going to give you a second chance, Lily."

Patrick faces her. Lily forces herself to hold eye contact with him, even though the way he's looking at her through his Ray-Bans makes her feel like she's being brought to the slaughterhouse.

"I think you have the makings of a star," Patrick says.

brandocadogan

324k followers

izabella_012 Its really a shame that certain parents feel indulging their spawn without teaching them what repeating others means, or how to conduct yourself in life and actually have a purpose. Considering the issues of certain parents who obviously are immeshed in their own issues, its not really a surprise that the results of their failures live large in their spawn. You are obviously a troubled soul, rudderless and drifting with no real sense of values or doing anything relevant and meaningful for yourself and others. Perhaps through repeated embarrassment (though that may be something you are no capable of feeling) and humiliation you might grow up one day to grasp the fact that treating people like shit, disrespecting others and acting like a punkass bitch is insufferably boring. With the opportunities you have have had (and wasted) and the people you have met (only by association, not on your own merit) does it not register that you are making a fool of yourself and your family? Likely not. Respect is earned… can't buy it or inherit it..You may think you are above others but I assure you what you think you have very meaningless in terms of what is really important in life… hopefully you won't piss away more time and effort on disgracing yourself… humble yourself and find your life., one day you may very week regret not seeking the real meaning of what a fulfilling life is about.

bing_lyon People that talk shit are just jelly 👊

"You're all peasants!" Brandon screams at the other passengers on his United Airlines flight home from Hong Kong. They're boring him. They're booing him. "My father could buy and sell you all!"

It's been a terrible, horrible, no-good, very bad flight.

He blames his dad for refusing to let him use their jet because he needed it to take his mom to Switzerland for her experimental cancer treatments. Or so he claimed. Brandon saw on IG that they were on a boat off Geneva.

Brandon's life is unbearable. The peasant flight attendant got mad at him for smoking a joint in the bathroom. First class isn't what it used to be.

Then they wouldn't give him a drink because he's underage.

"It's a thirteen-hour flight!" he yelled in the flight attendant's face. "What the fuck, man?"

She kept saying, "I'm going to have to ask you to lower your voice, sir," which Brandon really hates.

He watched as the flight attendant made a call, and then another flight attendant came up to him and was all sycophantic and shit because he's a follower or he wants to suck Brandon's dick or whatever.

And. Then. The. WiFi. Stopped. Working.

He had to take six Xanax to not totally lose his shit.

Then he fell asleep for a couple hours.

When he woke up, he was feeling refreshed and gentlemanly and the WiFi was back on so he apologized to the first flight attendant and asked her if she wanted to mile high.

She got really offended. Probably one of those #MeToo types. Shit.

Then he Skyped in with Bea and it started getting kind of hot. Bea took off her top, and then the second flight attendant stopped being all obsequious and got really huffy and told him he couldn't jerk it on the plane, and Brandon's like, first class, man! What happened? It's private or bust. Or in his case, private or *not* bust.

"If you wanna start shit, then I will fucking fight you," Brandon shouted. "I'm Brandon Cadogan and don't you fucking forget it!"

The passengers started booing him so he pissed in the middle of the aisle and all over some peasants, and one of the flight attendants, the first one, started crying. And now they're landing at LAX and there are police waiting for him on the tarmac.

paleyhailey ✓

1m followers

Hailey's head is bowed in the toilet of her en suite bathroom. She was particularly ravenous after her dad got back from dropping Lily off in the gutter where she belongs—and then Hailey saw that the basic bitch was still with him.

Hailey's extreme patterns with food started in junior high in preparation for her first Coachella. Three weeks before the festival she stopped eating, and by freshman year she'd decided that bulimia was in again.

When she binges, it's pretty much anarchy. She chokes the food down, unwrapping a chocolate bar and shoving it in her mouth while she's still chewing a handful of jelly beans, washing it all down with a can of whipped cream, and so on and on until she feels like she's about to burst. Each lick of icing off her lips is another tick of the time bomb. She loves feeling like she's about to blow. When she's totally consumed by all that she has consumed, she feels electricity in her veins. She is dangerously wired.

Her favorite part is the release. It's better than sex. It leaves her so raw and euphoric. She feels a supernatural calm and composure afterward. She always takes the best selfies right after a good purge. There are no bad angles when she has deflated, and the lighting doesn't matter—her face is flushed from her neon insides.

Whitney knocks on the bathroom door and steps inside, passing Hailey a tissue to wipe the vom off her lips as Hailey stands up and flushes the toilet.

"Why did she come back?" Hailey adjusts her Chanel red silk bow headband. "More importantly, when is she leaving?"

"If we're going to do this, we have to commit, Hails," Whitney says. "Let's shoot some scenes with Lily today and see how it goes. . . . The premiere is right around the corner. We'll need Lily front and center."

"I don't know what's worse." Hailey leans against the sink. "Lily taking over my life or my show." But Hailey knows there isn't a difference.

She catches her mother's reflection in the bathroom mirror. "What are you smiling about?" she asks.

Whitney's eyes shine. "Look what I found in your father's suit pocket!" She opens a Cartier box with a pair of Panthère de Cartier white gold, diamond, and onyx earrings inside. "Our anniversary is coming up!"

Last year Whitney bought her own anniversary present and gave it to Patrick before they shot a scene for *Platinum Triangle*, where he gave it to her. Whitney was so surprised.

"Make sure you hide them from Lily," Hailey says sarcastically.

"I'm going to put them back where I found them." Whitney allows herself one last admiring look before snapping the lid of the box closed.

Such a small box, Hailey thinks. She'd have to open a million to feel full.

Lily lies on her back on the white duvet in the bedroom of the Paleys' pool house, next to an imprint of Joel's body.

She doesn't know what part is the craziest, that she's here at all or that she spent the night in bed with Joel. It's not like anything happened, but Lily still feels different. She hasn't felt that safe at night since her mom left. Lily's been sleeping with the lights on.

Joel is nothing like how he appears on the show. On the show he seems so chill and happy. He's always goofing around with Sean Johnson, who he used to make YouTube videos with, and there's at least one scene featuring him shirtless every episode. He's portrayed as a heartthrob and a good guy—certainly compared to Idris Morcos and Brandon Cadogan. In real life, there's a quiet intensity about Joel, a melancholy Lily wasn't expecting.

Lily picks up her phone, shooting Mia a text to tell her that she's just finding her bearings, promising that they'll talk soon, and denying her request for a "close-up photo of Bea Getty's ass"—Bea is Mia's crush; she has a collage of Bea's modeling photos hanging on her locker door at school.

The truth is, Lily doesn't know how to talk to Mia or any of her other friends who want to know what's happening. She doesn't know how to explain it because she doesn't quite understand it herself. It's all happened so fast Lily hasn't processed it.

She stares back up at the ceiling. Beverly Hills feels like another planet . . .

Outside the glass doors she can hear workers cleaning up after the party in the Paleys' backyard.

The lights aren't the only thing Lily kept on after her mom left. Lily had to keep the TV in the trailer on all the time because she thought the silence would kill her. She was so lonely but had too much pride to admit it. She escaped to Zuma whenever she could.

"It's the only place where I can truly be free," Joel said one episode. It resonated with Lily so much and prompted her to request Zuma, despite having to take the bus to get there.

Lily googles Joel's Instagram on her phone. Almost every photo is of him at the beach. Lily doesn't have an account because she's never had anything she's wanted to share before, just things she's wanted to hide. Before recent events, it felt like nothing exciting had ever happened to her.

You have the makings of a star.

Something possesses Lily to pull the trigger: she creates an account. When Instagram asks her to select a username, she tries @lilyrhode but it's already taken so she uses her full name: @lillianrhode.

She follows Hailey but isn't sure if Hailey will follow her back. Hailey didn't exactly run out to greet her when Lily came back with Patrick. Lily's been hiding out in the pool house ever since, but Sam texted to tell her to keep her schedule open today—she's shooting a "girls' day" with Whitney and Hailey . . .

Hailey's feed is curated with glamorous photos, most of them starring Hailey and her superhuman tan. She uses captions like

"Don't be a Queen waiting for her King. Be a Queen ruling her Kingdom until her King joins her."

The posts are a mix of clothes and jewelry and her shoe collection and her Judith Leiber collection and modeling shots and ads and parties and private jets, and then there are the highlights, which suck you in, one after the other—behind the scenes on *Platinum Triangle*, her *Paper* magazine shoot, photos from earlier this summer in the south of France. There's a photo of her and Joel on the rooftop of Catch that Lily finds herself staring at until she loses all sense of time.

Lily climbs off the bed and walks into the en suite bathroom. Even her reflection looks different in Beverly Hills. It's like the mirror should come with a warning: *Objects may appear more beautiful than they are.*

She takes a photo and makes it her first post.

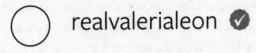

realvalerialeon ✓

3.3m followers

emmaslaays We share the same soul

emmaslaays Like you are my soulmate

emmaslaays But you have no clue

emmaslaays In another universe were probabbly married

emmaslaays Oops i spelled probably wrong .. Fuck it

emmaslaays But ily

Valeria didn't read picture books growing up; she read scripts and Old Hollywood star biographies. Her mother used to read the bios aloud to her as they sat in her trailer during long shooting days. Gloria said it was important Valeria learn from those who had gone before her. That she always remember she was born to be a myth.

In a Marilyn Monroe biography it was written that after "auditions," Marilyn would spend hours in a hot shower, washing it all away.

Valeria doesn't feel like taking a shower. The only shame she feels is over not feeling shame. This is what must be done. And only she can do it. Her whole life Valeria has taken care of her family. Her father could never hold down a job, and before her mother was a reality housewife, she was just a plain old housewife. Gloria's own dreams for stardom were placed on hold for her kids. She put all of her ambition into making Valeria a success. Since her first Welch's grape juice commercial at the tender age of two, Valeria has been her family's main breadwinner.

But it's all falling apart.

Sophia had to drop out of her private elementary school and Leo may never attend one. Both of their college funds have long since been drained. Then there's the house. They're going to lose the house.

The house was bought with Valeria's movie earnings. It's all she has left to remember that she was, at one time, wanted. Her mom and dad narrowed it down to a few different properties and they let Valeria choose. She was only ten years old, but it was her money paying the mortgage. She chose the 1930s Spanish-style house on North Bedford Drive in Beverly Hills because of its Old Hollywood history. It was once owned by Marlene Dietrich, one of the myths her mother read to her. The house had lasted, and it gave Valeria hope that she could last, too. She was ten years old and already worried about becoming a has-been. They only want you when you're seven. Valeria's sixteen and the industry doesn't know what to do with her. Every day she panics. Shouldn't there be more scripts coming in? *Better* scripts?

The house became her anchor—it's everyone's anchor, and without it, they'll all drift away.

When Valeria arrives home from her night with Patrick at the Montage, Gloria is up in her room with her glam squad getting her hair and makeup done. She has *Platinum Triangle* press with Shondra Johnson. In the trailer for season 2, Gloria accuses

Shondra of having been a prostitute in Vegas, which is how she supposedly met Sean's dad, Christoph. Shondra's the queen of drama on the show. Last season, the other wives, led by Whitney, tried to get her fired because she's too "ghetto."

As soon as she's home, Valeria forgets it all and plays her favorite role: sister. She feeds Leo breakfast and helps Sophia get ready for her summer day camp.

Sophia wants to wear a crystal choker that says "BIMBO" and when Valeria tells her it's inappropriate, Sophia shoots back, "Why did Mommy buy it for me, then?"

Valeria remembers watching an old Shirley Temple movie with her mom when Valeria was a kid. "Notice how her dress is cut shorter at the back," Gloria said. In the scene, Shirley was dancing on a tabletop. It was true. As Shirley spun around, you could see her panties. In another scene, Shirley was milking a cow and squirted milk all over her mouth. Gloria put her hand on Valeria's knee. "*You* could be an icon like Shirley Temple."

Valeria finally gets a squeamish Leo to eat some applesauce and puts him down on the floor to play. She'll leave a note for his nanny that he still needs a proper breakfast. And that the check is coming. They're a month behind. Her mom's glam squad has been paid, though. Priorities.

"Where's my My Little Pony lunch box?" Sophia is screaming. "Valeria, where is my My Little Pony lunch box?"

The kids of the Platinum Triangle are born with a silver-spoon emoji on their feed. When they throw tantrums, they aren't sent to their room, they're sent to find their light.

Valeria doesn't know how to tell Sophia that Gloria had her bring the Moschino lunch box handbag, along with a trunk full of Valeria's old clothes, to sell off at Wasteland on Melrose.

Sophia is having a total meltdown. "Where is my lunch box, bitch?"

"What did I tell you about talking like that?" Valeria snaps.

"I want my lunch box!" Sophia starts crying.

How did she become so spoiled? Valeria can't remember ever being like Sophia. She was never entitled. She was too busy to be entitled. She still is.

Leo is choking on a broken-off helmet of a G.I. Joe and Valeria is about to lose it when Gloria's voice comes through the in-home speaker system.

"Valeria, honey, are you in? Come upstairs."

Leo spits out the helmet and his face stops turning purple. Valeria sighs. *Honey* means Gloria is about to degrade her.

"Can you watch Leo for a minute, Soph?" Valeria asks, heading toward the stairs. Sophia has decided that since she can't find her lunch box, she's going to put her lunch in Gloria's Valextra tote. *It* wasn't one of the items Valeria was sent to hawk.

The glam squad is packing up when Valeria enters the master suite. She finds her mother in her closet wearing a Dolce & Gabbana LBD.

"We need a tiebreaker," Gloria says. "The Laurence Dacade sandals or the Louboutin pumps?"

"Louboutins."

Valeria doesn't have to try and make herself sound perky and genuine. It's like she's programmed.

"Anything else?" she asks.

"Patrick called." Gloria lowers her voice. "He wants to see you again tonight."

◯ lillianrhode

3,027 followers

Lily feels like she's being moved from place to place. The constant presence of the camera is hard to get used to. She feels like she doesn't have enough skin to cover her body.

They hit Rodeo Drive and are trailed by paparazzi as well as two *Platinum Triangle* cameras. The operators behind them are named James and Stefan. Lily knows that only because she went up to them both and introduced herself before they piled into the black SUV taking them shopping. Whitney and Hailey act like not only are the cameras not there, but the people behind them aren't either. And that extends to the three paparazzi on the street. Before they left, Lily overheard Sam telling James and Stefan that she tipped off a few celebrity photo agencies.

"Lily, look over here!" one of the photographers calls out to Lily as she steps out of the SUV. "Anything you want to say about your arrest?"

Hailey takes Lily's hand before Lily can think of an answer. Lily looks into the lens like a deer caught in the headlights. Hailey gives her hand a squeeze and smiles at her. It's a big change from the car ride, during which Hailey ghosted Lily and stared down at her phone the entire time.

"Balenciaga?" Hailey asks.

Lily doesn't know if Hailey's faking it for the cameras or if it's real, but Lily's grateful. She isn't sure how to answer the questions about her arrest and she wants to get away from the photographers as quickly as possible. Lily and Hailey head into the store.

"Best auntie ever," one of the paps says to Whitney as she follows behind Lily and Hailey. "You takin' care of your niece shows what a big heart you have, Whitney. What made you bring Lily to the crib?"

"Family is everything," Whitney says, smiling into the camera.

Hailey and Lily hold the door open for her. Before it closes behind them, Lily can hear one of the paparazzi call them the "new *tres amigas*," which is the nickname that Whitney, Hailey, and Greta have on *Platinum Triangle* because Whitney's always hanging out with them like a friend and not a mother.

"Your Insta stats are about to skyrocket," Hailey tells Lily, motioning through the storefront window to the paparazzi outside. "I saw that you created an account . . ." She stares at Lily and Lily isn't quite sure what it means. There's something about Hailey's attitude that feels competitive, but her face is always blank and she keeps her voice monotone so you never really know what's going on in her head.

Lily knows Hailey is right. The more she appears in the media the more followers she'll get. She already has a couple thousand, and she created the account only this morning. She doesn't even know that many people! It's all because of the *Hollywood Life* article about her arrest.

After some shopping, they head to Beauty Park Spa for an appointment with "skin care expert to the stars" Nurse Jamie. Whitney shows Lily Nurse Jamie's Instagram, @nursejamiela. It's full of celebrities getting treatments and captions that say things like "Don't treat your face like a pair of flip-flops and expect it to look like Louboutins!" Whitney and Hailey get facials every week. *Every single week.*

While they're getting IV vitamin injections and facials (Whitney gets a customized antiaging treatment and Lily and Hailey get the "young adults" treatment), Whitney tells Lily that she's scheduled a meeting with the Paleys' lawyer, Ira Shapiro, to talk over Lily's case. "He's gotten Patrick out of a few jams," Whitney says, "so I'm sure he can handle your little break-and-enter."

Lily's about to proclaim her innocence but stops herself. She's self-conscious on camera and she doesn't know what to say. How will it be edited? What will people think if they learn the truth? That she was lonely and desperate and wanted to know what it felt like, if only for one night, to be young and glamorous at a party in Malibu without a care in the world. That she wanted to be Hailey.

With fresh faces (Lily has to admit she's glowing), they go to Whitney's favorite boutique in Beverly Hills, Boulmiche, which Hailey mentions is where they filmed the scene in *Pretty Woman* when Julia Roberts gets turned away. Lily wonders if she's trying to tell her something.

Suddenly, Lily sees it clearly. She's been cast. She's the cousin from the wrong side of the tracks and Whitney and Hailey are here to save her. She may not know much about reality TV but all you have to do is watch a few episodes to see that there is always a villain, a hero, a victim . . . including the fashion victim.

"Daisy Dukes are timeless, but don't be afraid to diversify," Hailey says, looking Lily up and down. She pulls clothes for Lily and insists she try on each outfit and model for them, despite Lily's hesitation.

Lily steps out of the dressing room and the camera pans from her feet up the vintage flower-print Natalie Martin maxi dress Hailey has styled her in.

"I have the perfect belt for it," Hailey says. "We'll have to go through my closet when we get home. I have so much stuff that still has tags!"

Lily just smiles. She feels like that's all she's been doing all day with Whitney and Hailey. Maybe they're more alike than Lily initially thought. They all seem to be smiling a lot. And none of them are saying how they really feel. The chatter is surface level—a bit of gossip about some of the *Platinum Triangle* cast members, a lengthy debate about whether Lily needs filler (Whitney says no because she still has "baby cheeks" and Hailey says yes for the same reason—"Jamie will help give you some definition"). And that's about the extent of it. They rehash the party last night and Hailey details her "car ride from hell" with Greta, making it sound like she was forced into it and was scared for her life. She shows them the viral video of Greta driving a Lamborghini into the Stroms' pool. Lily mostly listens, not sure how to say what she's thinking and worried the fake talk will sound, well, fake coming out of her mouth.

She tries to protest when she sees how much money her aunt is spending on her—the camera does a close-up shot of the register as each item is ringed in—but Whitney waves her away. "How about Craig's for lunch?" she asks.

"It's like the Olive Garden for celebrities," Hailey says.

Just then, a ping comes into Lily's phone and she almost drops her shopping bags.

thejoelstrom followed you

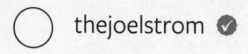

thejoelstrom ✓

1.8m followers

phlp328 @equalityforlgbtmz He's a he and that will never change no matter how many surgeries he has! @itsjessicastrom @thejoelstrom

equalityforlgbtmz @phlp328 She's a Trans woman and goes by she/her. Educate yourself, it's not rocket science!

phlp328 @equalityforlgbtmz Say what you want, he's a he will never change!! Educate yourself by reading the Bible!! Born a man, always a man!

equalityforlgbtmz @php328 The Bible? I'm sorry I'm not into that fairytale.

php328 @equalityforlgbtmz I'll pray for you then

equalityforlgbtmz @php328 Please don't

On the new season of *Platinum Triangle,* one of the most hotly anticipated storylines is Joel's dad's transition. Near the end of the first season Jessica came out, and moved out of the Stroms' family home in Beverly Park.

Jessica's big post-surgery reveal is on the current cover of *US Weekly.* Viewers are going to get to see everything that led up to it. Everything that happened after Jessica moved to Malibu.

Everything Greta has missed and that Joel has tried to be there for, when his dad has let him. Jessica has had to do things on her own time, and she's needed space . . . Joel gets it, even if it does hurt sometimes. Like, he learned that his dad was transitioning on Twitter. That was a surprise. But sometimes it's easier to tell the whole world something than it is to tell the people you love.

Joel stares at the *US Weekly* cover. Jessica looks like Greta. The same big green eyes that always look like they're seeing things outside of this dimension and are both haunted and amazed.

The nose was the first thing that changed. It kept getting smaller. Joel's dad ran a hedge fund. Joel always saw him as being on top of the world. His dad built them the biggest house in the most exclusive and private enclave in Beverly Hills. He had a closet full of bespoke suits, designer watches, and a wine cellar that he was freakishly protective of. Lucas Strom had the look, but inside, apparently, he was hollow.

When his dad got his first rhinoplasty, Joel didn't think it was that weird. A new nose is a rite of passage in L.A. He assumed his dad was just chasing perfection, like everyone else. He thought it was unnecessary, but not a big deal. Joel is used to his mom getting "touch-ups" biannually. He thought his mom's labiaplasty was the extreme.

But by the third nose job, Joel knew it was about more than perfection. He didn't say anything, but Greta couldn't keep her mouth shut. She told their dad he looked like he had septum perforation.

Joel wants to show Greta the *US Weekly* cover but he doesn't want to upset her. After their dad left, it's like Greta feels disowned, and like she might disown you.

Down in the kitchen Joel makes himself a sandwich, trying to think about the best way to approach Greta with the magazine. She wouldn't be so angry if she was willing to at least *look*.

While he's eating, he sits at the kitchen island and opens Instagram. Lillian Rhode is recommended for him. Lily. Joel clicks her profile and Likes the selfie she posted. Lily isn't anything like what he expected. He doesn't know exactly what he was expecting . . . an off-the-rack version of Hailey Paley? But Lily's obviously cut from her own cloth.

The magazine is on the counter when Greta comes downstairs after sleeping all day. She opens the fridge, pulling out a bottle of Perrier. She doesn't let herself glance down at the cover but he knows she knows it's there.

"Hailey's cousin?" Greta asks, looking over Joel's shoulder at his phone.

"Did you meet?" Joel asks.

"Not yet," Greta says. "But she's pretty." She looks at Joel like she's waiting for him to confirm that he's attracted to Lily, but he does his best to hide what he's feeling. The last thing he needs is Greta running to Hailey and creating drama over this. He'd like to get to know Lily better. Without any pressure.

Greta manages to avoid looking at the magazine on the counter as she turns it over to conceal Jessica's face.

"Nice try," she says, starting to walk away. "Tell Mom I went over to Idris's house," she calls back over her shoulder.

"Hey, Greta," Joel yells after her. "There's a Lambo in the pool. Know anything about that?"

"You, Joel Strom, are a reminder why it's not always such a tragedy when the second embryo doesn't take."

The front door clicks closed behind her.

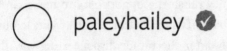

paleyhailey ✔

1m followers

malik.3sk He will never love you

tkgmball The veil is slowly uncovering on you demons!! @paleyhailey

xx_abira_xx What happened to u and Greta? U guys were like powerbffs. Sry for being nosey , jus wonderin

"Greta's totally crazy!" Fortune says.

Hailey told him to meet her at her house after shooting with her mom and Lily. They're sitting on Hailey's bed as Fortune talks to his connection at the gossip blog Nicki Swift. He's wearing a Wildfox Couture crewneck sweater that says "Blasé" on the front and Y.R.U. Partii Glitter Dimension Platforms.

"Everyone's worried Greta's gone off the deep end," Fortune says. "She was definitely driving under the influence and that's how the Lambo ended up in the pool. Did you see the video? It was the scariest ride of Hailey's life! She only got into the car because Greta, like . . ." Fortune looks over at Hailey for help.

"Held me at gunpoint," Hailey whispers.

"Held her at gunpoint," Fortune repeats. "All I can say is just wait for season 2. Everyone's going to see Greta Strom for who she truly is."

Fortune hangs up.

"So evil!" He laughs.

Not only does Hailey relish the opportunity to make Greta look bad while she comes off as the victim, but she wants to bury Lily's press. Especially after the rather disconcerting way the paparazzi on Rodeo today seemed to be snapping more photos of Lily than of her. Sam probably leaked that Lily is joining the show, and there has been new press popping up about Lily all day.

Hailey pulls a lipstick out of her metallic Diane Von Furstenberg clutch, Beach Peach by Too Faced. She applies it and smacks her lips together.

Lily has no idea who she's messing with.

Fortune is the only person Hailey can reveal herself to. She, like, *made* him. He's loyal. He'd be blocked by this whole town if he weren't. Fortune is Hailey's best friend. Sometimes she just passes him her phone and he takes photos of her for hours.

They got coked out at a party in the Hills one night and realized they're both beautiful and soulless. Literally.

At the party, Fortune confessed that he'd been living on Venice Beach. He came to L.A. from the middle of nowhere, changed his name, and reinvented himself. He doesn't like to talk about his past. Hailey sometimes hears a North Dakota accent creeping in. Like *Fargo*. But Fortune has the gayest voice in the world and he exaggerates it all the time, wearing his camp like a mask. Hailey wanted to adopt him. He was just so cute and hopeless. Broke and on the street but stylish AF. Hailey found out he shoplifted and she started going with him. It was fun. They'd go to all the stores where Hailey could charge it to her mom's account and steal as much as they were buying. It was so easy and such a rush. They got caught once but Karl Lagerfeld loved her and was totally going to put her in a *Mademoiselle* ad before he died. Hailey and Fortune outgrew their kleptomania, but they've remained the best of friends.

Fortune appears on *Platinum Triangle* because he's Hailey's sidekick and he knows how to get on the guest list for every party. Hailey sometimes thinks he sleeps at the club. Fortune doesn't have a fixed address. He hops from one guesthouse to the next. Whitney loves him and the three of them have sleepovers in the pool house all the time. It's Fortune's sole purpose in life to become a permanent cast member on *Platinum Triangle*.

The difference between a recurring and permanent role on the show is a bigger paycheck and more airtime. You get to film confessionals and be an actual part of the storylines and not just a glorified dinner guest. Hailey knows Fortune is a social climber, but his tan matches her favorite vintage Courchevel leather Kelly bag.

Hailey looks down at her phone disdainfully. "Lily shows up on my doorstep and five minutes later she's on Instagram? What's next, a modeling contract? Like, her first post is from the inside of *my* pool house."

"She's such an opportunist," Fortune says.

Lily is inching toward 10k followers. Today's press has given her a big bump.

Hailey gasps. "And *Joel* follows her!"

"I've always found Mr. ABC Family rather generic and predictable, personally." Fortune looks at his nails.

Hailey is apoplectic. "All season it looks like something is developing between me and Joel. But it was never fully realized. Sure, he'd flirt back every now and then, but that's it. The optics are terrible. It looks like I've been *rejected*."

Hailey Likes the photo Lily posted of Lily, Hailey, and Whitney having lunch at Craig's. Lily asked the waiter to take the photo and Hailey was mortified.

"You want to be made a permanent cast member on the show, right?" Hailey asks Fortune as she lowers her phone. "Get Joel to agree to be my date for the season 2 premiere. I want pictures of us walking down the red carpet arm in arm."

She can't reveal herself *completely* to Fortune. It wouldn't do for him to know that she falls asleep at night dreaming of Joel holding her. She's the loneliest girl in the world. It's easier to turn him into an object. A co-star. Hailey's designated leading man.

"The premiere?" Fortune asks. "But that's, like, less than a month away! And no offense, Hails, but Joel doesn't exactly seem interested . . ."

Hailey goes cold. "Do you want to be a part of the cast or not?"

"You know I'd give *anything* to be on the show," Fortune says. "I came to L.A. for one reason: that money and that fame, henny."

"I'll use the Paley power," Hailey says. "Everyone knows the producers will do anything to keep my dad on the show." Her eyes glimmer as she looks at Fortune. "I'll get you a full-time contract if *you* help me keep Joel Strom the hell away from Lily Rhode!"

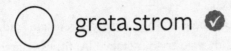

greta.strom ✓

721k followers

Yasmin Morcos lets Greta through the gate of the Morcos family's $88-million modern Bel-Air mansion, complete with a helipad on top that the city won't give Ghalib Morcos a permit to use—not that it stops him. Idris once went down on Greta on that helicopter. Ghalib, a real estate developer, builds giga-mansions, and his own is the giga-est. He just remarried. The second wife, Yasmin, is, like, twelve years old and literally so cute. Greta was Idris's date to the ceremony, which took place on The Enchanted Hill, more than a hundred acres of land that sits perched on the top of Beverly Hills, currently for sale for a billion dollars. There's a rumor that Ghalib is going to buy it. The opulent wedding footage will air this season.

Yasmin has replaced Idris's mom, Nadia Morcos, on *Platinum Triangle*. Nadia wasn't asked back by producers, but she didn't seem to mind—she'd gotten what she wanted out of the show: a divorce from Ghalib. She only had the confidence to leave him on TV. It was so performative that Idris didn't fully believe his mom was leaving until she was gone. Greta fell in love with him the moment he realized.

Nadia bought a penthouse at The Century. Greta and Nadia are close. Sometimes they go try out crazy L.A. fitness classes together, like yoga with goats jumping on your back as you pose.

Idris hasn't been answering Greta's calls. She hates that it drives her crazy. It's not like Idris has ever been monogamous. He's all about that freshman pussy (follow him on Snap). But they have fun together. He makes her laugh. Like, so hard. When Greta is with him, she forgets about everything else, and that's enough.

Yasmin tells her that Idris is in his room and Greta goes up. She finds him on the couch in front of his TV, playing *Fortnite*. She stands at the doorway and opens her Stalvey top-handle handbag, pulling out Idris's keys. The jingling sound makes Idris glance over, but he looks right back at the TV.

"I brought your keys," Greta says.

"What about the car?" Idris asks. He pauses the game and goes over to his pet albino Burmese python. He lifts the lid and feeds it a live mouse.

"Did you see how many views the video got?" she asks.

"You're some extra shit, you know that?" Idris turns around to face her.

"I'm sure I can make it up to you somehow . . ."

Greta walks up to Idris and kisses him, pushing him against the snake tank, which rattles. She playfully shoves Idris onto his bed and pulls her Givenchy Paris tee over her head, tossing it at his face. Greta lifts the lid off the snake tank and coils the snake around her neck before climbing onto Idris's lap. She can feel him getting hard when they hear a ping. Greta reaches into her back pocket and pulls out her phone.

"That *bitch!*"

"What is it?" Idris asks.

Bea just sent Greta a link. "An *anonymous* source told Nicki Swift I forced Hailey into your car at gunpoint." Greta shakes her head. Hailey's more of a snake than the python around Greta's neck, which hisses as she jumps off Idris's lap and replaces it in the tank. It can finally swallow the mouse whole.

"That's it," Greta says. "If she wants war, I'll give her war."

Greta calls her source at Radar Online. Hailey introduced her to the writer when they ran into him one night at TomTom. Hailey has a direct line to practically every gossip reporter in town. Greta was wasted and told the writer how much wine her mom drinks, and it was headline news the next morning.

"I thought you were about to apologize to me?" Idris asks.

Greta holds up a finger.

"Hi, Justin? It's Greta Strom. Boy, do I have an exclusive for you . . ."

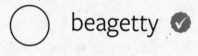

beagetty ✓

11m followers

beagetty So happy and excited to share my new @voguejapan shoot !!!! Thank you so much my friends @luigiandiango @yumilee_mua @juliavonboehm for another favorite xxxx Check out my insta story (highlights) to see the video !

B ea's mother, Olympia Miller, was the muse of Jean-Paul Gaultier in the '90s and the mistress of Bea's father, a Getty oil heir. Bea's last name was Miller until two years ago when her mom decided to change it so that Bea can claim a share in the Getty family fortune. It caused quite the scandal in the press, considering her dad's other family and everything . . . Bea opened up about it in "73 Questions with Bea Getty" for *Vogue*.

The press propelled Bea's modeling career and got Olympia cast on *Platinum Triangle*. Bea shot to fame and was suddenly all over the internet, and then she was all over Tom Ford, and it just keeps getting bigger. She's everywhere.

Bea's the waif version of her amazon mother. Olympia quit *Platinum Triangle* before the second season started shooting. She had a rough first season (Shondra Johnson accused her of sleeping with Sean's dad, Christoph, and literally almost drowned her in the Johnsons' pool—it's MKTV's most viewed

YouTube video). Olympia sold their apartment in the Sierra Towers and moved to Europe. She's still modeling, and lives in Paris with her boy toy. Bea now lives in a bungalow at the Chateau Marmont.

It can get kind of lonely on her own. Lately, Bea's been spending a lot of time at the Cadogans' estate in East Gate Old Bel-Air. Bea likes being around a family, and the Cadogans are a larger-than-life American dynasty. It makes Bea think of what her life might've been like if she'd grown up with her dad. She used to see him when she was little, but she didn't know he was her dad then. He'd come to take her mom out and would bring Bea flowers. He traded Olympia in for a younger model when Bea was six, and Bea hasn't seen him since.

Brandon's dad, L.Y., is a banker who runs the West Coast's largest steel company and, like, owned 20th Century Fox at one point. Bea is scared to death of him. Brandon's mom, Morgan, basically runs Los Angeles society, and all the *Platinum Triangle* wives are jealous because she's such a rich bitch.

Bea is hanging out with Brandon in his room when L.Y. FaceTimes Brandon from Switzerland. He doesn't even say hello; he just starts screaming at Brandon about his behavior on the United Airlines flight from Hong Kong. There are *several* passenger videos floating around the internet.

"If I had my way, I'd ship you off to military school!" L.Y. screams. "But your mother is against it. Lucky for you, I'm prone to making her happy at this time. I'm sure even you can understand."

Brandon doesn't say anything.

"You're a disgrace, Brandon. I'll have my secretary issue a public apology on your behalf. You're to lie low. I'm taking away your toys. No cars, no allowance, no more little parties while we're away. No more bastard heiress Instamodels holed up in your bedroom."

Brandon looks at Bea over his phone like he thinks it's a big joke, but Bea knows it's a defense mechanism. Brandon would give anything to make his dad proud, but he never seems to manage it, which is why he's so self-destructive.

"Do you know why your grandfather left most of his estate to charity and nothing to you?" L.Y. asks. "Do you think it's because he suddenly felt *pious* on his deathbed? You think *I'm* bad? You should've been raised by my old man. *Ruthless* doesn't begin to describe him!"

Sometimes, after the glow of the party has faded and she and Brandon are cuddling in bed together, Brandon opens up to Bea. He has told her that L.Y. was so remote during his childhood that Brandon turned to his grandfather for affection and absolutely idolized him. So much so that he used to mimic his granddad's mannerisms—walking with one arm behind his back, gesturing with his right forefinger, clasping his hands for emphasis, and pushing up the sleeve on his left arm. He was so hungry for approval.

Brandon's grandfather returned little of Brandon's affection, but then Brandon started posting all these #richkid photos on Instagram. Like, on the first day of school he'd take a photo of a stack of money and a Rolex and caption it, "School supplies," or he'd pose doing a handstand on the wing of the family jet, and his grandfather thought it was vulgar. He came from the generation that believed your name should appear in the newspaper only three times: when you're born, when you marry, and when you die. The fact that Brandon was getting so much attention for his wild antics and lavish displays of wealth led to them falling out.

Brandon speaks quietly on the phone. "He left Conrad a trust." The way he says it makes Bea feel so guilty. She's not going to answer the DMs Brandon's older brother sends her late at night ever again!

"And not you," L.Y. says. "Because he thought it would be put to *better use* elsewhere. He even had it put in writing! Your grandfather saw you for what you are."

Brandon is always being compared to Conrad, the golden son who is currently in Chile working for Raleigh International. L.Y. has plans to make Conrad the next JFK.

"Your mother is fighting to cure her cancer and *this* is what she has to deal with?" Once L.Y. starts going he can't stop. There's an epic scene on *Platinum Triangle* where he lost his temper when Brandon accidentally spilled soda on L.Y.'s stamp collection. "If this stress in any way sets back her recovery, so help me, Brandon . . ."

L.Y. loses his shit for a while longer and then finally lets Brandon go.

"I don't see why he's so upset," Bea says. "Isn't your mom faking cancer for the show?"

She regrets it as soon as it comes out of her mouth. Brandon flinches like Bea just slapped him.

"That's a fucking lie!" He jumps up from the bed, his face instantly red, the vein throbbing on his forehead. "That's just Whitney Paley and Kathy Strom's way of creating a storyline!"

Bea quickly nods and doesn't press the issue. Brandon can be as explosive as his father. But Bea is pretty sure the gossip is true. The other day Bea saw Morgan swimming laps in the

Cadogans' seventy-five-foot swimming pool. She looked the picture of health. Then, later that same day, Bea heard her with her stylist getting a gown fitting for some charity gala. But when L.Y. got home from work, Morgan was suddenly too weak to even come downstairs, so L.Y. brought her dinner in bed.

Brandon paces beside his bed, his fists clenched. Bea's worried he's about to blow. But then he suddenly stops, facing her, and takes a deep breath.

"Well, you heard the man. No more little parties while he's away . . ." Brandon smirks. "But he didn't say anything about a big one!"

paleyhailey ✔

1m followers

loivaire_pst You and Lily are literally twins 👯

Hailey's up in her room when she receives a Google Alert. A new story on Radar Online. Greta wasting no time with a counterattack?

Hailey holds her phone so tight the screen almost cracks. The story is all about Lily's arrival in the Platinum Triangle and how she's already caught the attention of Joel Strom. The article makes Hailey sound like a loser who hasn't gotten the guy all season. Again!

Greta's out for revenge because of the whole "held at gunpoint" thing. And Greta knows the best way to get to Hailey is through Joel.

If it wasn't Greta who planted the story on Radar, then it was *Platinum Triangle* production. It's almost hard to believe because it's happened so fast. Lily has landed in Hailey's pool house and already gotten herself a storyline. . . . Everyone loves a classic love triangle.

This is all Sam's fault! Whitney's elaborate plan for sympathy Likes should've never been indulged. It's gone too far. But Sam has wanted to spice up the teen storylines all season. Valeria and

Sean have been playing it safe. Sometimes when they're all film-ing together, they fall into the trap of never saying what's *really* happening. Hailey knows that Sam is playing her mom just as much as Whitney is trying to play Lily. Sam didn't bring Lily in to make the Paleys look good. She brought her in to cast a new nemesis for Hailey.

Hailey's connection at Radar answers on the first ring.

"I hope you're not calling to try and get me to reveal my source," he says.

"Actually"—Hailey twirls a strand of hair around her finger—"I have another story I think you'll be interested in . . ."

Just wait until Lily sees what kind of headlines she makes next!

After planting the hit on Lily, Hailey grabs a Tiffany's shop-ping bag off her dresser and goes down to the pool house.

She finds Lily sitting on the couch in the dark. She's on her phone, and the glow of the screen lights up her face. She looks so lost. Hailey almost feels sorry for the girl. She has no one. Hailey's Aunt Erin is the worst mom ever. How could she just abandon her own daughter? Hailey would be so devastated. Hailey and Whitney are best friends. They went to Burning Man together last summer.

"I snuck off today while we were shopping," Hailey says, turning on the light and passing Lily the Tiffany's shopping bag. She sits next to her on the couch. "It's my way of saying thanks for taking the fall for me this morning with my dad. It was really cool of you."

Lily pulls out a small box. "You really didn't have to do this," she says, genuinely touched. Inside is a charm for the bracelet Hailey gave her for her tenth birthday, a Tiffany-Blue-and-white enamel Bon Bon Candy Charm. "Oh, wow." Lily holds it up. "It's . . ." She puts the charm back in its box. "I love it."

"I'm so glad. And I'm so glad you're here, Lily. L.A. is a cutthroat town and it can get so lonely. I could really use a friend."

A few months back, Hailey gave an interview to *Paper* magazine where she said she wanted to escape it all and live on a horse ranch in the Pacific Palisades one day. No more social media. But it was a lie. Hailey could never leave it.

"You have no idea how much it means to me to hear you say that." Lily gives Hailey a hug. "I always thought we would've gotten along if we'd known each other better growing up. If our moms weren't such adversaries, I mean," she says as she pulls away. "My mom was just so *jealous*."

"And you?" Hailey asks.

"I never thought you were happier than me just because you had more," Lily says. "I was never that naive."

"Money and fame aren't everything." Hailey struggles to keep a straight face. "I'm glad you know that. I'm glad you know what's really important." Hailey touches Lily's hand. "Family."

Lily looks embarrassed, but she's buying it—Hailey didn't bring a camera crew into the pool house with her for a reason.

"We're going to have the best end of summer ever!" Hailey gushes. "I hope you'll be here for the premiere! And how do you feel about being on the show?" she asks. "I feel like we haven't had a moment alone to really talk, you know? It's just been, like, one giant shoot since you got here."

"Apparently it's going to be like that all week," Lily says. "Sam cornered me when we got back from shopping. They're going to film me lifeguarding at Zuma, and I guess some scenes with your dad's fancy lawyer . . ."

"Shapiro," Hailey says. "He's a total psychopath; you'll be fine. The question is, are you willing to air it all on television?"

"I'm still getting used to the idea," Lily admits. "Any advice?"

"Just be yourself. The audience can always spot a fake. And no matter what—never believe the press."

"I take it you read that Radar article?" Lily asks. "Where are they getting this stuff?"

"There are always going to be leaks," Hailey says, rolling her eyes. "Some people have no morals."

"Well, for the record, there's nothing going on between me and Joel. I just met him last night. If you two are . . . I mean, I know you have history. I've seen the show and—"

"Girl, stop!" Hailey laughs, cutting Lily off. "If I wanted Joel, I'd have him." Hailey hides behind her phone. "Do you want to come to a party with me tonight?" she asks. "Brandon Cadogan has a Gatsby complex."

"Sure." Lily smiles. "Sounds fun."

"You should wear your new Hervé Léger bandage dress!" Hailey looks up at Lily over her phone. "It's *so* slimming."

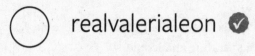
instavon237 @andcrmarvel basically in the comics Kang doesn't
have any superhuman powers but he's 'the master of time' and
has armor that gives him advanced strength and the ability to fire
lasers from his hands and chest

"*Kang does not give up, primitive,*" Patrick says. He's determined to make Valeria come.

Patrick is covered in blue makeup and wearing his purple-
and-green costume after a day of filming. Some of the makeup
is rubbing off on Valeria's skin.

Kang is ruthless and egotistical. His ship alone could destroy
the moon. Not to mention he can time travel. Although Valeria
doubts there's anywhere he'd rather be than between her legs.

Valeria's face turns red and her breathing becomes jagged.
She tightens her thighs around Patrick's head and her body
shudders. She's legit going to win an Oscar tonight.

Patrick sent a car to her house to bring her to the *Avengers*
set. She had to get in the trunk. No one can know. It's obvious
to Valeria that a part of the turn-on for Patrick is the thrill of
how dangerous she is.

"I have something for you." Patrick gets off his knees as
Valeria hikes down her skirt. He reaches into his jacket pocket

and pulls out a Cartier box. Valeria has already evened her breathing. Already forgotten.

"What's this for?"

She opens the box to reveal a pair of Panthère de Cartier earrings. They're sparkling and iconic.

"I wanted you to have something just for you," Patrick says. He must know that her mother is taking all of the money.

"Something special."

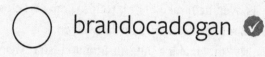

brandocadogan ✓

325k followers

staciekiimmills Wavy 👅

theefrankee_ "LOVE HUMILIATES YOU... HATRED CRADLES YOU." 🖤

samanthaberns Oh my god, Brandon, I LOVE your shirt! Is that new? 😏

margarita_i_am Russia loves you 🖤

k.smanos @ryancarr3 Gucci

timlana2231 Desperate for attention is what you are...

guesstancrel We all are

Brandon uploads a photo of his shirt to IG. It has "Blind For Love" written on the back. But actually, he's blind drunk.

He's bored at his own party, which always happens. Brandon has to liven this shit up. Everyone else thinks his parties are so legendary, but within an hour Brandon wants to unfollow the DJ and kick everyone out. He's seen it all before.

Two topless girls drag him into the hot tub and he's entertained for a fleeting moment. It never lasts. He sees Bea through the crowd, rocking a bright yellow Giambattista Valli tulle dress.

Bea doesn't hold him down. He hasn't talked to her all night, and he's currently in a hot tub with two half-naked girls, but when the party is over, he'll take her up to his room and close the door and she'll rub his head until he falls asleep.

The topless girls start making out but Brandon isn't paying attention; he's on his phone, going through DMs from more girls. He sends the location. He isn't even sure who he's contacting. His vision is too blurry to focus on the nudes they're sending him. Followers all look the same after a while.

A new photo appears at the top of his feed. It's of his mom with IVs in her arms, dark circles under her eyes. She captioned the photo "Keeping the faith! Finding a cure! Believing in the healing power of love! #holistictreatment #nottodaycancer." Brandon tries to focus on the picture but his mother is so distorted it's like she took the photo with a really old iPhone. Her low-res smile hides her pain.

He keeps scrolling and stops at a photo someone posted from the party, which is of this blond girl who doesn't notice that her photo is being taken. Brandon realizes it's Hailey's cousin Lily, who everyone has been buzzing about. One of the comments is a link to an article on Radar Online. Brandon opens it.

Finally, some excitement! Hailey's cousin is getting dragged *hard*.

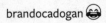

brandocadogan

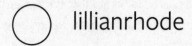

lillianrhode

11k followers

christinanatalia_v How r u so white trash yet so high fashion at the same time....

It feels like the entire party is looking at her as Lily steps through the open back doors of the Cadogans' house to where the party is spread across the sprawling grounds. You could host a festival here. The yard slants down a hill leading to a fountain spouting water. A bunch of kids are sitting around it. Some people are in the pool, and others are getting naked in the hot tub. A DJ booth is set up in front of the pool house. Lily goes up to someone pouring beers from a keg and gets a drink in a red Solo cup. She sips from it as she looks out at the party.

Lily's on her own—Hailey split from her practically as soon as they walked through the front doors. Lily doesn't get it. They drove over together in Hailey's Mercedes and it was a continuation of the conversation in the pool house. Hailey was mapping out what they should do together for the rest of the summer. She was even saying they should go up to Ojai for a weekend. Lily thought she and Hailey were finally breaking ground and starting to build a relationship.

Two guys bump into Lily on their way into the house, spilling beer on her new Aquazzura sandals.

"Dude!" one of the guys says as he looks at Lily. "It's that girl!"

"Is it true that your mom started doing porn when she got out of jail?" the second guy asks.

They stumble off laughing, leaving Lily standing alone. She looks around the party. People keep looking over at her. She feels instant dread and pulls out her phone to check her notifications. It's like she hasn't just physically arrived in the Platinum Triangle; her digital self has arrived with her. And it has a life of its own. Another story about her has leaked on Radar Online.

The headline: "Whitney Paley's Niece Lily Rhode: From Trailer Park to Trousdale!"

Accompanying the article is an image of the trailer where Lily grew up *and* a photo of her mom's mugshot for writing bad checks. It was before Lily was born, but still embarrassing. There's a photo of Whitney and Hailey posing on a red carpet, looking the picture of glamour and perfection, and then below it, Lily and Erin's mugshots are side by side. Erin's dark roots are showing in her bottle-blond hair. Lily feels her face burning. Has everyone at the party seen this? The comments at the bottom of the article are full of shade like what that drunk guy said, gossip about her mom and Lily's past in the Valley.

"Hey, Lily!" Lily looks up from her phone and sees Idris coming toward her. "How's that pool house life?"

"What do you want?" Lily asks coldly.

"Aw, come on! Don't be like that. I'm sorry, okay?" Idris gives her these big puppy-dog eyes, an expression Lily's seen him make on the show. His forehead wrinkles like a shar-pei. "I wasn't going to try anything, I swear! It was Hailey's idea to haze you. She gave me the drugs."

"Hailey?" Lily's phone pings and she looks down at it. Instagram is blowing up with notifications.

"But you probably don't need to get high." Idris smirks. "Aren't Valley girls always down to fuck?"

Lily's eyes flash up from her phone.

"Since you so generously got me a drink last night, allow me to offer you one." She throws her beer in Idris's face and storms off. Lily enters the house, quickly ducking down a long hallway and into one of the mansion's bathrooms. She locks the door and leans against it, closing her eyes.

A ping comes in to Lily's phone. A DM from Joel. He's at the party and wondering if Lily's here. Lily holds her phone to her chest and takes a deep breath. She isn't sure if she can face him—or anyone. She once again feels like her identity is being defined for her. Lily is being reduced to sound bites and head-lines, and that seems to be all anyone cares about, all they believe.

Lily reads the Radar article more carefully. It's written in a way that makes it look like it was Hailey's idea to bring Lily to Beverly Hills. An inside source claims that Hailey heard about Lily's arrest and about how she'd been abandoned by her mom, and she felt guilty for being so privileged and knew she had to help "pull her cousin out of the gutter."

"'Hailey and Whitney are super close,' the source reveals." Lily reads aloud to herself, performing it like she imagines Hailey telling the reporter. "'She feels so guilty that Lily's mom abandoned her! Lily comes from a different world than Hailey, but Hailey doesn't judge, and she's the one who insisted they move Lily into the pool house. Lily's going to be on *Platinum Triangle* because of Hailey . . .'"

Lily stops reading, circling the Tiffany charm bracelet with the new Bon Bon pendant around her wrist.

"The question is, Who benefits?" a voice says from behind the shower curtain.

Lily almost drops her phone in surprise. Valeria Leon pulls back the curtain. She's lying in the tub, holding a red plastic cup.

"I didn't realize anyone was in here!" Lily's embarrassed. She got way too into that.

"Sorry," Valeria says. "I didn't mean to scare you." She climbs out of the tub and goes over to the mirror. "Good read, by the way." Lily can't pick up any emotion as she watches Valeria staring at herself. "There are fourteen bathrooms in this place. I thought I could hide out for a while. Then you came in and I held my breath without even realizing it. Do you ever do that?" Valeria looks at Lily through the reflection.

"What are *you* hiding from?" Lily asks. She's starstruck. Valeria is her favorite on *Platinum Triangle*. She seems the most down-to-earth, and she's always helping her mom with her younger siblings.

"Same thing as you," Valeria says, opening her black leather envelope clutch and touching up her eyeliner. "Escaping the groupthink."

There's something mysterious about Valeria. Even on the show, which is all about projecting your life, there's the feeling that Valeria is holding something back.

"So?" she asks. "Who benefits?"

Valeria drops her eyeliner pencil in her clutch.

"It's possible someone from production called Radar," she

says. "Trust no one. The producers play dirty. But not quite as dirty as the cast . . ."

"You think someone is purposely trying to embarrass me?" Lily asks.

"While making themselves look good." Valeria turns to face her, leaning against the bathroom counter. "Any idea who might do something like that?"

Lily looks back down at her bracelet. Was Hailey just trying to disarm her?

"Be careful with Hailey," Valeria says, as if reading Lily's mind. "She only looks out for herself."

Valeria sees the look on Lily's face and smiles.

"So you're trending," Valeria says, turning back to the mirror and fussing with her hair. "You can either enjoy it or ignore it. No point it letting it have any other effect on you. Certainly no point in letting it hurt you. Reputations are constantly changing from moment to moment. One minute you're a joke, then you're a hero, then a villain. . . . It's exhausting, really. There's no such thing as permanence, which is kind of fucked up because nothing lasts and so maybe nothing really matters. But it also means you're never stuck with a single label."

Valeria meets Lily's eyes in the mirror.

"Take it from me: it's better to have a label, even one that makes you cringe, than to have none at all. In this town there's only one thing worth being ashamed of."

She looks back at herself.

"Anonymity."

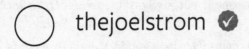

thejoelstrom ✓

1.8m followers

The Jen Stark graphics being projected on the back of the Cadogans' neoclassical house are colorful cloud-like patterns that dissociate you from reality.

Joel stares at the graphics, unblinking, until they suddenly cut out. His eyelids close like the shutter of a camera and he slides back into himself, literally gasping for breath.

"Time to get this party started!" Brandon's voice booms into the mic. He's standing on the DJ booth. "Presenting a Brando Cadogan Original!" He hooks up his phone and projects a video onto the side of the house. Everyone outside turns to watch, and more people inside the house come out to see Brandon's latest stunt.

In the video, Greta is passed out on a bed, wearing nothing but an oversize Yeezus tee-shirt with a graphic of the grim reaper on it. Brandon is recording, but the video is bouncy AF because he's laughing so hard as Idris takes a selfie stick and prods Greta with it. . . . She's unconscious. She looks dead.

"Let me try, man!" Brandon takes the selfie stick and trails it down Greta's body, hitting her boobs with the end before taking it lower.

There are other voices and laughter off-screen. They had an audience.

"What the fuck, Idris!" The sound of Greta's screaming pulls Joel away from the projection. Greta is repeatedly hitting Idris, who laughs as he ducks her blows. "When did this happen? And you *filmed* it?"

Hailey is looking over at Joel, and, never missing an opportunity to be the hero in his eyes, she starts yelling for Brandon to cut the video. But Brandon's relishing this, gazing up at the projection like it's a masterpiece.

All the sound drains out of the party. Joel can't hear the gasps or the laughter or the comments from everyone around him. He just hears his heartbeat pounding in his ears.

Joel charges at Brandon, pushes him off the DJ booth, and grabs the mic out of his hand. He uses it to bash Brandon's smug face before throwing the mic to the side and punching Brandon with his bare fist. Brandon goes down and Joel jumps on top of him, wrapping his hands around his neck and squeezing. Someone pulls him off. The sound turns back on.

"Chill, man! Chill." It's Sean. He actually looks scared.

Brandon's nose is bleeding. Bea dramatically flings herself on top of him, screaming and crying for help. The party around Joel begins to swirl. He's a part of the hypnotic pattern, and all he can do is go around and around in this cloud. Everyone's staring. Even Hailey takes a step back.

Then he feels someone reaching for his hand.

lillianrhode

13k followers

Lily takes the keys to Joel's Porsche Targa from Joel and drives them through the Bel-Air East Gate to the beach. It's the only place she can think of going; it's where she goes when she needs to get out of her head. Joel sits in the passenger seat, his long eyelashes batting under the rim of his HUF hat.

When they pull up to the beach, Joel leaps out of the Targa, walks onto the sand, and throws himself down. He sits and stares out at the water. They can hear the sound of the waves breaking. He covers his face with his hands; his knuckles are bleeding. Lily comes up behind him, leaning down and rubbing his back. It starts shaking. Lily rests her head on Joel's shoulder and the physical contact seems to calm him. She can feel him collecting his breath, and she feels so close to him it's like he's breathing into her.

Lily suddenly jumps up and kicks off her Aquazzura sandals. Joel looks up at her in surprise. Lily smiles at him before she starts running toward the water. She looks back and sees Joel watching as she tears off her bandage dress. She lets it fly in the wind behind her as she runs, the dress landing on the sand.

Joel wipes the last tear from his cheek and leaps up, kicking off his shoes and chasing after her. He takes off his jeans and his shirt, reaching for Lily's hand as they walk into the ocean. They let the pull of the waves take them deeper. Lily slips off her Tiffany charm bracelet and throws it into the water. She feels Joel's arms around her body. They kiss and go under.

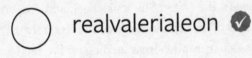

realvalerialeon ✔

3.3m followers

mariachantal.lmfao 1 Timothy 4:12 Don't let anyone look down on you because you are young, but set an example for the believers in speech, in conduct, in love, in faith and in purity.

erikabeloved0403 how do people not believe in God after laying eyes on her?

jaclyntatramaine B your own leader don't follow crowd into hell

The Leons go to Hillsborough Church every Sunday, even when they're not filming. When they are filming, the pastor allows the cameras into the service because having the self-professed megachurch packed with young Hollywood types and featured on TV brings in more members to the congregation. Everything comes down to followers.

For as long as Valeria can remember, Sundays have meant church with her family and then Sunday brunch at home. Valeria's dad cooked eggs and sausages and pancakes, and it was the one day a week when Valeria was allowed to indulge. Her cheat day. She always associated church and God with cheating, and eventually betrayal became a form of worship.

Her dad hasn't been around to cook breakfast for a long time now. He's still in Vegas. He left right after filming for season 2 wrapped. Valeria doubts he'll be back before the premiere party at the Sofitel Los Angeles at Beverly Hills, at the end of the month. Valeria can't wait for *Platinum Triangle* to start airing again. It's good for her brand to get herself out there. And she wants her dad home. He'll be back for the red carpet, no doubt. It's where they rapture.

The Hillsborough congregation stands to sing a hymn. Valeria holds Leo in her arms. The Leons are a faithful, loving family. They fear God.

Valeria just lip-synchs because what's the difference?

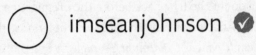

imseanjohnson ✔️

1.5m followers

sayadameer @imseanjohnson I know what chemicals you've done

laticiajenner_ Bring back the dreads 😭 🤩

amina_beca I loved you now you are ugly you was beautiful and cute when you was child

pablobonieten Yo huge fan of you since day one cuh. It'd be sweet af if we could meet up and skate sometime man. Know it's a stretch bc you're famous and all but it'd be cool if I could get a reply or follow back or something man. Lmk

erycsum I miss the old version of you this version...

Growing up, Sean thought his dad walked on air. He jumped like he could fly, as if he had wings. Christoph was like a Nephilim. He was this giant superhuman in Sean's eyes and in the world's. On the basketball court, Christoph was all focus, and Sean would sit courtside filled with pride that he was the son of a legend.

Now Sean doesn't know what his dad is. Christoph and his squad are in Miami for the weekend. Shondra's with them. Sean has the house to himself for a change—his dad's friends unofficially live in their Tudor-style Holmby Hills house. It's usually a nonstop party.

Sean's out back grilling steaks on the barbecue for the pit bulls his dad keeps chained up down in the basement.

After Christoph retired from the NBA, he started partying and traveling a lot. Sean's mom, Robyn, died when he was a baby. He doesn't remember her. She was an aspiring singer when she met Sean's dad. She died of breast cancer, which is why Sean's trying not to be too hard on Brandon Cadogan, even if he is indefensible sometimes.

During filming of the first season of *Platinum Triangle* Sean was spending so much time with the Stroms in Beverly Park that Kathy joked he was her second son. "She just wants a black baby because she thinks she's Angelina Jolie," Greta once told him, rolling her eyes. But Sean liked the sound of it. The Stroms have their issues, but their bond is unbreakable.

TMZ streamed Christoph's Little White Chapel wedding to Shondra, a Vegas stripper he'd met the night before. Sean watched with the rest of the world. Shondra's happy to leave Christoph to his vices as long as she's his number one and she gets the perks that come with that position—her credit card paid off and a gig on *Platinum Triangle*. Shondra's willing to keep Christoph's secrets, including the dogfights Christoph hosts in the basement, as long as he keeps her a star. Sean wishes he could resent Shondra more, but he keeps his dad's secrets, too. And when it comes down to it, he keeps them for the same reason.

When Shondra's lit, she pulls Sean into a hug and calls him her baby. She wants a baby of her own one day soon. Her challenge getting pregnant is her storyline on the new season of the show. Maybe it's because Christoph is drunk and stoned 24/7.

Sean turns off the barbecue and goes down to the basement with a plate of steaks. He opens the cages and holds out the plate with the meat but the dogs just tremble and refuse to come out.

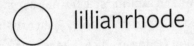

lillianrhode

27.5k followers

tashaa_eve @sofia_prophet she's my new goals

sofia_prophet @tashaa_eve Her hair is kinda bad tho

tashaa_eve @sofia_prophet needs to b me

asya_itatli No puedes ser tan perfecto, estoy casi segura que te crearon en un laboratorio.

imogenrosecord My heart is broken what does Joel see in her? @thejoelstrom @lillianrhode

janetsocvuet Did you stan hailey growing up? That's what I heard

L ily's been shooting scenes for *Platinum Triangle* all week and hasn't had a minute to herself. There's a camera on her every time she goes for a swim in the pool or makes herself a sandwich. (She did that only once, because the Paleys' housekeeper, Ana, was offended and insisted she finish making it for her. Lily is too shy to ask, so most of the time she just starves—on camera.)

Sam explained to Lily that they need as much "Real Home" footage of her as possible to edit into the final episodes of season 2. They shoot Lily swimming in the pool, sunbathing, hanging out in the pool house. At first she felt pressure to perform for the cameras, but the more she shoots the more she realizes that they're just waiting for that one natural moment to happen, like Patrick running out of the house in his Kang makeup and doing a cannonball into the pool to wash it off, splashing an unsuspecting Lily as she sits on a chaise lounge flipping through a magazine.

As horrible as it sounds, Lily's getting used to ghosting the cameras. The more you think about the presence of the cameras the crazier you start to feel. But sometimes they're unavoidable.

When Lily steps out of the shower that morning, she's greeted by a *Platinum Triangle* camera. Sam is standing off to the side and gives Lily a wink. Evidently they want to get Lily changing into her Los Angeles County lifeguard uniform.

Lily tightens the towel around her body and changes in the privacy of the bathroom. She can tell Sam is disappointed she's not wearing a *Baywatch*-style swimsuit. Lily zips up her bright orange jacket and pulls her baseball cap low to cover her eyes.

"We're going to join you at Zuma," Sam says as Lily's getting mic'd for a breakfast scene in the kitchen with the Paleys. "I can't wait to see you in action!"

Lily previously agreed to letting production film her at work, but she's regretting it. There's a look in Sam's eyes that Lily distrusts, like she has something planned for Lily during her lifeguarding shift. Lily wouldn't put it past Sam to orchestrate a drowning scene to film Lily running into the water and "saving" someone. An extra hired by the *Platinum Triangle* production. It's obvious that things are fake AF in the reality TV world. Hailey has been ghosting Lily around the house ever since Brandon's party, but when they're on camera, it's like she's pretending to be Lily's mentor.

Lily's about to tell Sam that, on second thought, she can't be filmed at the beach while she's working. But she doesn't want to be ungrateful to the Paleys. They've brought her into their home, and being on camera is a part of the deal. Maybe they won't film her entire shift.

"Just please stay out of my way," Lily says. "I have to do my job."

It only gets worse when the camera follows Lily into the main house. There's a second camera already filming the Paleys.

Patrick is on the phone with his agent, Ana is blending celery juice (which is all Lily's seen Whitney eat, and which Whitney swears is the reason for her dewy skin), and Hailey is leaning against the kitchen island scrolling through her phone as she talks about the Dress for Success charity fashion show she's hosting next week.

Hailey always has a project. It was her idea on the first season of *Platinum Triangle* to get Greta, Valeria, Bea, and their moms to all come over to the Paleys' house for a tea party and bring old dresses to donate to underprivileged girls in need of something to wear to prom. In another episode Hailey volunteered at an animal shelter—and showed up wearing an alligator-skin backpack.

Lily is trying not to be cynical as Ana passes her a glass of celery juice. Lily's stomach grumbles for real food. She just wants to get to the beach. Maybe hit a hot dog stand?

Whitney is in a somber mood. Lily saw on Instagram that it was her and Patrick's wedding anniversary last night. Patrick was on set all night, and when he got home, he totally forgot what day it was. Whitney wrote a cryptic tweet about it that's getting picked up on all the gossip blogs.

Lily downs her juice, jumping as Patrick snaps at his agent. He's not happy with the latest rewrite of the *Avengers* script.

"I have to go," Lily says, checking the time on her phone as she brings her glass over to the dishwasher. Ana takes it from her before she can load it herself. "My Uber's pulling up." She's lying. She's not checking the Uber app on her phone. She's hitching a ride with Sam and the crew. She just wants to get out of the kitchen, out of this scene.

"I was thinking maybe we can find a time to all have dinner together?" she asks before she goes, looking from Hailey to Whitney. "I'm no chef but I learned how to make a mean risotto while I was on my own. I'd like to cook a meal to show my appreciation for letting me stay here. It'd be good to spend some real time together without the . . ." Lily glances at the prying cameras. "Just as a family," she says.

"That's a terrific idea," Whitney says. "How about this weekend? Patrick won't have to be on set."

Lily smiles. Maybe she's being too hard on the Paleys. Maybe they aren't completely fake and just need to spend some genuine time together.

"I love the orange," Hailey says, looking Lily over in her lifeguard uniform. "It matches your bleach-out."

And there it is. Hailey just can't help but blow her own cover and show the viewers who she truly is. No amount of charity projects can conceal it. Hailey is a bitch. Lily hasn't said anything about the story on Radar. She knows Hailey will deny being behind it and find a way to make Lily look hysterical and insecure on camera. Hailey has Lily exactly where she wants her—trapped behind the lens.

"Before you go, Lily," Whitney says, "I talked to Shapiro this morning."

The Paleys' lawyer had better come through for her.

"He had good and bad news," Whitney goes on. "The good news is that he got the charge dropped to a misdemeanor. The bad news is that Chris Taber is refusing to budge. He's standing behind his statement that you were in on the break-in. He's even been telling the press it was your idea."

"That liar!" Lily snaps. She's furious. "He dragged me into it and he knows it!"

Hailey looks up Chris on Instagram. Lily sees the camera zoom in on his photos.

"Dude does more steroids than Zac Efron!" Hailey laughs at a photo of Chris showing off his guns.

"I bet he heard that you're staying with us." Whitney shakes her head as she sips her celery juice. "And now he thinks he can get money out of you."

Lily wants to track Chris down, even if only through DM, and convince him to stop running with this Bonnie and Clyde story and admit that it was all his stupid idea! But she's under strict legal advice to avoid all contact with Chris or risk it being used against her in court.

"Well, Lil," Hailey says, all smiles as she hoists herself up and sits cross-legged on the kitchen island. "The way I see it, you only have one option. You have to rise above! Show Chris and the world that you are not defined by your arrest. Do something that gives back. Maybe by being in my fashion show?"

"Oh, that's a wonderful idea!" Whitney exclaims.

"As a model?" Lily asks.

"Not *just* a model," Hailey says, raising her glass of celery juice. "The showstopper."

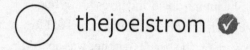

thejoelstrom ✓

1.8m followers

thejoelstrom I was catching some waves and I had some time to reflect… I was thinking a lot about "value". What has value in my life? What is my value? Being unable to find an answer was kind of an answer of its own. I could spend the rest of my life trying to figure out the value of things, constantly trying to figure out how much time or energy something would take, if I'd enjoy it or not, if it really adds value to my life. But the truth is we never really know if something is going to be of value until we've experienced it. And how can you even begin to figure out your own value? You are INFINITE because you are LIVING and an embodiment of ENDLESS POSSIBILITY. The happiest moments of my life have been the moments where I've just dived in, no fear…. Those have been the moments where I've experienced real beauty and growth. There is no such thing as failure if you learn from all of your PERCEIVED failures and mistakes. That's how I want to live… free of any kind of restraint or limitation. Just free to be who I am, who I'm becoming, who I'm meant to be. I'm not going to try and assess the value of each and every moment, I'm just going to live it.

Joel can see Lily sitting at the top of the lifeguard tower at Zuma as he rides to shore and tucks his surfboard under the arm of his wet suit. There's a *Platinum Triangle* crew on the beach—two cameras and Sam up the beach taking calls.

Lily smiles down at Joel as he walks up to the lifeguard post, her blond ponytail blowing in the wind. "I didn't know you were going to be here!" She jumps down and gives him a hug.

Joel's cheeks are red from the sun and the smell of Lily's hair. The last time they were on the beach together was amazing.

Sam was the one who told Joel to be at Zuma for the shoot. She said she wanted footage of him and Lily together, and at first Joel said no, but then the more he thought about it . . . Joel trusts Lily. She dodged the cameras with him at Hailey's milli party, so maybe she's not like all the other girls hoping to get close to him to be on the show. And maybe it's not a bad idea for them to have a scene together this season. Joel's a moth to the flame. All he knows is how to catch fire and burn. A scene with Lily is the exact right play after Hailey kissed him at her party. Joel's sick of letting Hailey call the shots and catch him in her web of storylines.

"Funny you're here," Joel says. "I was thinking of you today." It's one of the rules of the show. Never break the fourth wall. Don't look at the cameras and don't reference anything related to the production. Pretend you just bumped into each other and cameras happened to be there to capture it all.

"I actually have a break right now," Lily says. Another lifeguard is coming over to take her post. "You wanna walk?" she asks Joel.

They walk along the shoreline with the cameras, one walking backward in front of them and the other filming them from the side, framed against the ocean.

"It's official," Joel says. "I'm not leaving the beach for the rest of summer. It goes so fast." Just under a month until the new school year starts. But Joel knows the real end of summer will be the premiere of *Platinum Triangle*. It'll be a circus, and Joel will have to do the red carpet and interviews; he'll have to be "on" and pretend.

"When did you start lifeguarding?" Joel asks.

"This is my first summer," Lily says. "But I've always been drawn to the water. I taught beginner swimming lessons last summer, and I'm on my school's swim team."

"Maybe you'll try out for New Beverly's team in the fall," Joel says. New Beverly High School might actually be bearable if Lily is around for junior year. School is like everything else in Beverly Hills: just another playground full of drama . . .

"If I'm still here," Lily says. "The Paleys may not be a permanent state of surreality."

"How's it going so far?" Joel asks.

Lily stops and stares out at the water, considering how to answer. Joel can tell she's self-conscious on camera. It's the beginning of the end when you realize that people are watching you and that your thoughts are immortalized and so it's dangerous having them. You can lose everything because of a single thought, and so you have to measure them. Thoughts become lies.

"I just don't know if I can trust it," Lily finally says. "I don't know if it's real . . ."

Lily starts to pace up the beach, as if to get some distance from the cameras that follow anyway, and Joel is right with her.

"This morning at breakfast I felt like I couldn't speak. My Aunt Whitney brought up my court case and I just don't feel like I can explain myself at all. Like it has already been explained for me. Do you ever feel like you've been cast and are just playing a part instead of living real life?"

"All the time," Joel says. Joel is on a billboard advertising the new season of *Platinum Triangle* near the Chateau Marmont. He wants to blow himself up.

"It's not that I won't talk about my arrest," Lily continues as they keep walking along the beach. "I *want* to talk about it. I want people to know the truth. But it's like there's no room for the truth in the narrative. . . . If I'm not the bad cousin from the wrong side of the tracks, then I'm the victim abandoned by her mom and falling in with a wild crowd. No matter how it's written, every time we're in a room together it ends up the same. With Hailey and Whitney acting like only they can save me."

Joel knows that by "in a room together" Lily means "filming together" because that's what it starts to feel like for every family on the show. At a certain point you realize that you're never together as a family unless there's a camera on you.

"I don't want to sound ungrateful," Lily says. "But it wasn't terrible on my own, you know? I wasn't scared. I realized I could do it. That said, it's kind of nice to not *have* to do it. To have people who want to take care of you . . . or at least pretend to."

It's like once Lily starts opening up she can't stop. Joel knows how dangerous that can be. If being on camera doesn't make you censor yourself, then it has the opposite effect—it makes you think there are no consequences, that you can say and do anything because you really are just a character playing a part.

"There's a part of me that thinks I'd be better off if I were still in the Valley," Lily says. "I don't think Hailey really wants me around. It's like I'm the equivalent of the fashion show she's planning, like I'm her new project or something."

"Hailey's a puppet master," Joel says. He knows it'll be a line that goes viral when the episode airs, but Joel doesn't care. He doesn't owe Hailey his loyalty. Joel heard Hailey laughing in the background of Brandon's video. He knows what's up. Hailey isn't there for Greta when it counts. She's more interested in the drama of the moment than in a real friendship with his sister. It's taken Greta so long to learn that. He doesn't want Lily to fall into the same trap.

Joel reaches for Lily's hand. He feels her thumb delicately tracing over the scab on his knuckle from the fight.

"You should stick around," Joel says. He remembers the first night they talked in the pool house. "You *can* survive here. You can make yourself."

realvalerialeon

3.3m followers

robertaalistair @RealValeriaLeon Are you even real?!

amyhayyter U so perf

amyhayyter Like wtf

amyhayyter How can anyone be that much perf

jillsami_ Your dad is crazy @realvalerialeon

krista_kahn_ Has been ! No one will ever care again

ellelkools Beta kitten programming 🐺

Valeria lets herself into Patrick's suite at the Montage Beverly Hills. Patrick gave her a key in his trailer on the *Avengers* set after he gave her the Cartier earrings. She took precautions, including oversize sunglasses and a blond wig her mom once forced her to wear for an audition.

She didn't get the part.

Maybe she should keep the wig on. Patrick might like it. But no, he has enough blonds in his life. Isn't he meeting her because she's different? Or is it just because she's young? That's why she agreed to this arrangement with Patrick: because if she didn't, there might be another man willing to help, a man who likes them even younger. Valeria has to protect Sophia. As long as her mother's claws are sunk into Valeria, her little sister is safe.

Valeria will meet Patrick, but she draws the line at the hotel room auditions her mother has tried to set up for her. Her talent is the one thing Valeria still has. She won't meet a producer in private, no matter how powerful.

Her phone rings. "Dr. Seuss" appears on the caller ID.

"You in the suite?" Patrick asks as soon as she answers.

"I'm here," Valeria says.

"Good girl. Wearing the earrings?"

"Yes. Where are you?"

"I'm still on set. Get naked. Leave the earrings on."

"When will you be here?"

"Get naked," Patrick repeats. "Lay down on the bed and wait for me."

He hangs up.

Valeria isn't going to strip right away. The air in the suite is kind of cold. How long does he expect her to wait?

A text comes into her phone. *Naked?*

She lies and says yes and asks for his ETA.

Send a photo, he replies.

Valeria's about to refuse, but her mother told her to take this as an acting job, and in acting, when a casting director asks you if you can do something, you always say yes. Can you horseback ride? Yes. Can you samba? Yes. Can you fly? Yes. *Of course*. You say yes, and figure out how to grow wings later.

So Valeria takes off everything but the Panthère de Cartier earrings, and once she's completely naked, she lies back down on the bed and takes a photo. She's never sent a nude before. She's always been aware of the Twitterstorm if it were to leak.

But she trusts Patrick. If she goes down, he goes down harder.

ETA? She asks again.

He doesn't respond for fifteen minutes. Valeria just lies there, naked and cold, staring up at the ceiling.

I like thinking of you lying there thinking about me, Patrick texts back. *Don't think about anything except me.*

Valeria replies with a wink emoji, but she's not into his game and doesn't think about him. She tries not to think at all, but her mind can't stop worrying about how her agent hasn't called all summer.

An hour passes and Patrick still hasn't shown up. Valeria gets bored and turns on the TV. *TMZ* is on. She half watches, simultaneously scrolling through Instagram. A story about her dad comes on the show, drawing Valeria's eyes up to the screen. Luis Leon was kicked out of the Hard Rock Cafe in Vegas for counting cards. Valeria isn't surprised. Her father is a mess. He's the reason why she's here. He took out another mortgage on their family home. Hopefully her mother manages to grow a backbone and stops giving him money. He always takes it and doesn't ask any questions. He doesn't want to know.

Valeria doesn't want to know either. She turns off the TV and stares at the blank screen.

A text comes in from Patrick. *What are you thinking about?*

You daddy.

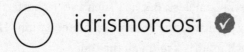

idrismorcos1 ✓

570k followers

kingchrisss U fine asff

xnmlex I just realise you where still alive lmao

b.goldden marry me

zsazayngabor What a vampire 😭

Idris goes to a *Nylon* #YoungHollywood party at Avenue, but he's bored and thinking about that time he posted how he loves making people who already hate him hate him more and how transparent that was.

Greta is ghosting Idris because of #selfiestickgate, and it's not like it's the first time she's ignored him: they've been hot and cold all year. Idris didn't think things were going to last as long as they have between him and Greta, and he's been waiting for it to all implode since they got together last summer. Idris's dad is in real estate development but Idris won't join the family empire. He's busy burning bridges.

Idris watches Fortune in his element, posing for photos and telling fans that he doesn't use a stylist. Fortune's wearing a rainbow fleece from Jaded London and the shortest shorts ever. His legs are tanned and as shiny as his silver hair, which is up in a topknot. No one really knows anything about Fortune but there are so many rumors. He slept on the beach when he first came to L.A. He's still homeless. But he's such a social butterfly that he has a way of attracting luxury accommodation. He crashes on the couch in Idris's room all the time.

What Idris likes most about Fortune is that he can always tell exactly what Idris is feeling. Like he knows Idris is literally suicidal right now and doesn't want to be at this party, he's bored and angsty AF and drinking too fast and he'll probably need to take some pills if he's going to get through the night. He's not even hitting on any of the girls. Fortune knows that Idris is just in one of his moods where nothing is good enough; too much of everything is never good enough. And Fortune doesn't make it worse by getting mad at Idris for ruining the vibes or whatever; he just adapts to Idris's mood, and it's chill. Fortune is soothing, sort of like a cat purring on Idris's lap.

They ditch the party and drive to Idris's house in Bel-Air in his classic 1956 Packard Four Hundred painted hot-pink with white and baby-blue stripes. At the house, they go up to Idris's room and flop down on the couch. They're lit up by the glow of the TV as they take bong rips and play *Fortnite* until the sun comes up and they finally fall asleep, Idris's face buried deep in Fortune's fleece.

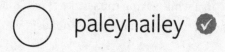

paleyhailey ✔

1m followers

princepaley Hailey you are iconic 😍

princepaley 🔥🔥🔥

princepaley 💥 🎬 ★ YOUUUU SLAYYY ME!!! 🎬😍

princepaley Epic

princepaley 🌟 🌟 🌟 🌟 🌟

princepaley Love you so much beautiful! 😘 💋

Hailey is sitting out by the pool of her house with Bea, who just came from shooting a Tommy Hilfiger campaign with Kaia Gerber on the Malibu Pier. Bea's agreed to be in Hailey's Dress for Success charity fashion show.

"I can't thank you enough for modeling," Hailey says. "I know you have legit work so it means the world. Especially since I can't depend on Greta. She's been so self-destructive lately. It'll be a miracle if she manages to walk down the runway in a straight line."

"Oh my God," Bea laughs, "selfiestickgate will not die."

On the upcoming season, Greta and Bea will fight over Hailey's friendship. Greta is the old friend and Bea is the new friend and they compete to see who knows Hailey the best and who is closest to her. Hailey just sits back and watches them duke it out, every once in a while saying things like "I don't like her more than you, I swear. Can't we all just be friends?" while secretly lapping it up.

Hailey and Greta have been friends forever. It's, like, social media platforms suggest friends, right? And maybe the universe does, too. Greta and Hailey come from similar backgrounds, both precocious Beverly Hills princesses wearing Kate Spade for kids. Their nannies liked to gossip with each other at the playground, so they followed each other. And they've never questioned it because that's the way it's always been.

Bea became Instafamous over the controversy surrounding her paternity, and Hailey collected her like a Judith Leiber.

"How's Brandon doing since the fight?" Hailey asks. "I've never seen Joel lose it like that before . . ."

"He has a black eye but the swelling's gone down. I think Brandon's depressed," Bea says. "His parents get back from Switzerland tomorrow. I know he's worried about his mom."

The teen cast tries to keep out of their parents' drama on the show. They have enough of their own. Brandon hasn't said anything to Hailey about Whitney accusing Morgan of faking cancer. Hailey goes way back with Brandon and the Cadogans. She lost her virginity to Brandon's older brother, Conrad. Unofficially. The virginity storyline is, of course, a huge arc on the first season of *Platinum Triangle*. Hailey and Patrick were filmed as a part of a ceremony at Hillsborough Church with fathers giving their daughters purity rings and the daughters taking a vow of chastity. Never mind the fact that Patrick is Jewish. Hillsborough is trendy and everyone wants to be spotted there.

"I *still* haven't heard back from Valeria." Hailey checks her phone. "I have no idea if she's modeling. Why do I feel like I'm always chasing that girl?"

"She's been so secretive all summer," Bea says.

"It's because the Leons don't have a storyline and everyone knows it," Hailey says. "Gloria refuses to air her dirty laundry. She's determined to pretend like there's no trouble in paradise, but have you seen the latest?" She shows Bea the TMZ article on her phone about Luis getting kicked out of the Hard Rock Cafe. "I'd hate to have a dad like hers," Hailey says.

They hear voices and footsteps coming from around the side of the house. Hailey goes cold when she sees that it's Lily—and that Joel is with her. She can tell Bea is looking at her to see how she'll react.

"Hey, guys!" Lily waves over at them. She's still dressed in her lifeguard uniform. "What's up?"

"Just helping Hailey with the Dress for Success show," Bea says. "What are *you* two up to?" The good thing about Bea, aside from her 11 million followers and iconic lineage, is the way she loves to stir the pot.

"Bumped into Lily on the beach today," Joel says. "So I gave her a ride home."

Hailey doesn't react but inside she's screaming. Did they spend *all day* together? And didn't Lily's shift end a couple hours ago?

"Will you volunteer for the fashion show, Joel?" Hailey asks, keeping her voice light. She's not even looking over at Lily. "I'm short male models and we were donated *the* cutest pair of Vilebrequin swim shorts with a sardine print."

"It's for a good cause," Bea adds.

"Sure." Joel shrugs. "Count me in."

lillianrhode

33k followers

officialluca Real life Cinderella xx

yann_boisjeaubault94 tu es magnifique ma princesse 🖤😍😍

levi.rambo1 Try my magical wand..

ediebliss You are like Cinderella 🖤 but you are much more beautiful than Cinderella

nicolasmorales1424 Hermosa, mi amor, amo a la Princesa Lily. 😍😘😘😘

After Joel leaves, Lily goes into the pool house through the sliding glass doors that lead to the bedroom. She leaves the door open and the lights off and falls on her back onto the bed, the *Land of Hopes & Dreams* sign above her, glowing neon blue above her head. She can't stop smiling to herself. Joel surfed until the end of Lily's shift and then they went for a drive along the coast. They drove back into L.A. and stopped for dinner at In-N-Out Burger, sitting on the same side of the booth and sharing a Neapolitan shake. Joel kissed her again before they got back in his Targa in the parking lot.

Lily sighs dreamily and rolls out of the bed. She changes out of her lifeguard uniform and into her old jean shorts and a plain white tee-shirt. It doesn't matter how many fancy clothes she has; she's still the most comfortable in her old things. Being in her lifeguard uniform reminded her of that. She didn't feel self-conscious once all day, and maybe a part of it was because she enjoyed being around Joel so much, but it's also because she was in her own element, doing her own thing, not dressing up for someone else's life.

Joel's face was sunburned as they sat in the In-N-Out booth—his HUF hat bumping into her head, they were talking so close. She could smell the mustard from his burger on his breath. He told her things she's never heard him say on camera. Like how he's worried about the new season and how the viewers are going to react to his dad's transition. Joel confessed that he thinks Greta's about to snap from the pressure.

Through her open bedroom door, Lily can hear Hailey and Bea still talking by the pool. Hailey won't shut up about the fashion show.

"With Greta out and Valeria a question mark, we may be short of female models as well as males," Lily overhears Hailey saying.

"You're opening the show, obviously," Hailey tells Bea. "But I can't model *every* other look myself! No way will the dresses I selected for Greta and Valeria fit me."

"Any idea what I'm wearing yet?" Lily asks, stepping out of the pool house and sitting on the edge of a chaise next to Hailey and Bea.

"I told you," Hailey says. "You're modeling the showstopper. It's this gorgeous Nicholas The Label. You're the guest of honor, silly! All eyes will be on you. I promise."

Hailey checks her phone and looks over at Bea. "We should get going."

Lily can tell by the blank look on Bea's face that she has no idea where to.

"Soho House?" Hailey prompts her.

"Right!" Bea jumps up from her chaise. "I almost forgot."

"Sorry, Lily," Hailey says. "We'd invite you but it's members only. Catch you later?" She flashes Lily another smile before shuffling off with Bea and leaving Lily sitting alone, staring into the pool. Lily doesn't know why she bothers. Hailey has made her position clear. Off camera, Lily is irrelevant.

Lily gets up and goes into the main house looking for Whitney and finds her up in the master bedroom. Whitney is in a "wellness bubble," which was set up by Nurse Jamie and supposedly creates an atmosphere of 99.9% pure air to help the skin fight free radicals. Whitney's been in it getting a facial and massage. It's literally a translucent bubble that takes up most of the bedroom. Lily can see Whitney's blurred image through the plastic. She's lying on a massage table wrapped in a white towel.

"Hailey, is that you?" Whitney asks. Her voice sounds muffled.

"It's Lily. Can I come in?"

"Quickly!" Whitney says. "Don't let all the good air out."

Lily unzips the entrance to the bubble and steps inside.

"I decided to pamper myself." Whitney sits up on the massage table to face Lily. "I deserve it." She touches her earlobe and stares off. "I think Patrick is having an affair . . ."

Lily doesn't know how to respond. She read in one of the tabloids her mom left lying around the trailer that Patrick didn't want to do the show. He doesn't think it's good for his acting career to do reality TV so he's featured as little as possible. He said on *ET* that agreeing to the show was his "gift" to Whitney.

At first Lily didn't know what Patrick meant by that, but then there was *that* scene in the final episode of *Platinum Triangle* season 1. It was such good reality TV because it was real. You couldn't make it up! Whitney drank too much at a party thrown by Morgan Cadogan and picked a fight with Patrick. She started crying and said she gave up her career to be his Hollywood housewife.

It was the only time all season that Whitney acted like her life was anything but perfect. Patrick lost his temper.

"What career?" he shot back. "Just because you modeled a swimsuit in *Sports Illustrated* once doesn't mean you had a career!"

Whitney's hand drops from her ear and her eyes snap back up to Lily, standing at the end of the massage table.

"But enough about that," she says. "You wanted to see me? Please, sit." She motions to a chair.

"Why are you wearing your old shorts?" Whitney asks. "Don't you like the new things we bought?"

"It's not that," Lily says. "I'm just not sure that they're me. To tell you the truth, I'm not sure that any of this is."

"I know what the problem really is. You're just feeling unworthy. I'm going to let you in on a little secret, Lily. No one believes they deserve it. We're all just pretending that we do."

Lily came up to talk to her aunt because she wants to know the truth. Is it all for show? If it is, then Lily will stop trying to make the Paleys be a real family and continue to let them be co-stars, and Lily will consider her time in the Paleys' pool house a guest spot. Nothing more.

"I talked to Sam tonight," Whitney says. "She said she got some great content of you at the beach today. Production's happy."

"What about Hailey?" Lily asks. "She only seems to want me around when there's a camera on us. What happens when we stop filming? Will I stop existing to you, too?"

"Of course not! How could you even think such a thing? Hailey hasn't been too tough on you, has she? I hoped that you taking the fall for her over the coke would've softened her up."

Whitney gives Lily a wink. "Hailey wants desperately to be the protagonist but she always falls a little short. She has *villain* written all over her. The girl used to quote Regina George as a toddler."

"She hates me," Lily says quietly.

Whitney gives Lily a little smile. "You just have to be patient with Hails," she says. "She's really gone through it this season. You'll see once the show starts airing. She finds out Greta has been selling stories about her to the press. Can you blame her for finding it hard to trust people?"

Lily holds a breath of the pure Beverly Hills *verified* air. She tries not to choke on it.

"You're exactly where you're meant to be, Lily." Whitney lies back down on the massage table. "The camera loves you. You're a natural. Maybe once you watch how right it looks on the show you'll see that you belong."

Back out in the pool house, Lily pulls out her phone and checks Instagram. She's shocked every time she opens it and sees how many followers she's getting.

Lily feels like she's on the precipice of something. She isn't exactly sure what. But she knows there will be no turning back.

She opens her DMs and replies to Mia's latest message, promising that they'll hang out soon, before the end of summer definitely, but deep down Lily knows they probably won't. She can already feel herself letting go of her past to make room for her future, like a snake shedding its skin.

Her phone pings. Someone is requesting to send her a DM. She opens it and stares down at the messages, a chill running down her spine.

princepaley Sleep with one eye open bitch

princepaley You'll NEVER be Hailey

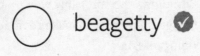

beagetty ✓

11m followers

bemyaesthetique I cut myself because I'll never be as pretty as @beagetty or have as many followers

"Sorry to disturb you so early, Miss Getty, but your . . . car has arrived."

"My car?" Bea says sleepily. She's only half-awake, curled up in bed in her bungalow at the Chateau Marmont. She and Hailey partied late at Soho House last night. "I didn't arrange for a car," she tells the concierge, rubbing her eyes. She picks up her phone from the nightstand and opens her e-mail to see if her agency booked her for a gig. "Tell them there's been a mistake." Bea yawns. "And that I'm sleeping."

She's about to hang up when the concierge's voice stops her.

"If you don't mind telling the driver yourself, miss. He doesn't seem interested in listening to any of the staff, and the vehicle needs to be moved. It's blocking the entrance."

Ugh. Life.

"I'll be right there," Bea says.

She hangs up the phone and sits up in bed, the room spinning from her hangover. Her agent always sends the tackiest cars. She doesn't need a stretch limo to take her to shoots! And why did no one tell her she's working this morning? Bea doesn't get out of bed for less than 10k new followers a day.

Bea puts on a white terrycloth housecoat and a pair of Tom Ford sunglasses and leaves her bungalow. She exits through the gate that separates the pool area and bungalows from the château and stops in her tracks when she sees what's parked at the entrance.

An RV honks. What the hell's happening? Is she doing the shoot inside that thing?

The RV door pops open.

"Hop aboard, princess." Brandon climbs down the steps and beams at her. "We're going camping!"

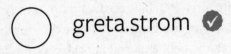

greta.strom ✓

725k followers

teapoota2 @victorianarana I personally hate when people use mental illnesses as a fashion statement

victorianarana @teapoota2 its just like no, i don't want the people to think that being sad is cute

teapoota2 @victorianarana exactly, like I am diagnosed with anxiety and fuckin hate it, makes my life hard sometimes on myself so this is just fuckin horrible.

victorianarana @teapoota2 OMG yeees THIIIIISSSSS, this is what i'm talking about. Having anxiety, depression, or any mental disorder It's not fun It's not something you want to brag about or use as an accessory to be "cute", if I could get rid of it as easy as removing a clip from my hair i will do it forever.

"Camping?" Greta asks from her bed. She's wearing a diamond-encrusted "Anxiety" hair clip. She loves making her followers lose their minds.

Joel's standing at the doorway. He just got out of a group chat, and Brandon wants the whole squad to go camping.

"Brandon's probably been smoking Spice again," Greta says.

"He texted that he deleted the video of you and that he was blackout drunk when he projected it," Joel says. "He doesn't remember any of it."

Greta rolls her eyes. "Convenient."

"Thought you might like to see this." Joel shows Greta a photo Brandon sent him of his busted face. His left eye is so bruised he can barely open it.

"You should've left him for me." Greta's thankful that Joel defended her, but she was scared, the way he lost control at Brandon's party.

"I'm not going camping," Joel says. "I'm done with Brandon *and* Idris." He gives Greta a look like he's waiting for her to confirm that she and Idris are over. He's never trusted Idris. "Wanna hang out? Maybe drive up to Malibu?"

"Who's going camping?" Greta asks.

"Everyone," Joel says.

"Including Lily?" Greta raises an eyebrow. She can tell Joel really likes Lily, and isn't that interesting . . . Hailey has been after Joel since the show started, and Greta thought that's where the storyline was heading. Lily Rhode is an unexpected revision.

"You should go," Greta insists.

She hopes Joel and Lily get closer on the camping trip. Let that be her revenge against Hailey! She's sick of their fake friendship. Hailey's there for Greta only when they're on camera. When it really comes down to it, Hailey doesn't care about her. Hailey doesn't care about anyone but herself. Greta's not hung up on the negative stories Hailey plants in the press. That's just fun, trivial shit. It's the laughter in the background of Brandon's video that Greta can never forgive.

"Not my scene," Joel says. "And by the way, when I said Malibu, I meant Zuma. Not Dad's. You up for some surf later?"

"Sure." Greta smiles. It's been a while since they've surfed together.

Joel looks surprised but happy. He heads off to his room, and Greta goes downstairs to make something to eat before they leave. She stops on the stairwell when she hears Kathy's voice coming from the living room. Greta forgot that *Platinum Triangle* is finishing up shooting her mom's confessional today. It's late because Kathy has been rescheduling the shoot. She filmed one day of confessionals but wouldn't talk about Jessica. The biggest storyline of the season! She's been putting it off, but finally the producers came down on her. She's contractually obliged to spill all the gory details of her divorce and her husband's transition, and they need to lock down the footage to fit it into this season.

Growing up, Greta was always closer to her dad than her mother. She thought it probably started when Kathy chose to use a surrogate to carry Greta and Joel. The official *Platinum Triangle* confessional story is that their mom had a potentially life-threatening condition called placenta accreta that prevented her from being able to carry her own children. According to Greta's dad off camera, Kathy just didn't want to lose her figure.

"I just feel like it was all a lie," Kathy is saying from the living room. "People ask me how I didn't know. But I really had no idea."

Greta feels her skin prickling. She strains to hear.

"And now I've been turned into this villain, this person who didn't let Lucas be the person he was always meant to be. Like I held him back for my own selfish reasons. But how was I supposed to know? I loved him. Obviously I loved him. I married him. I had children with him. And I wouldn't change that for anything in the world because the twins mean everything to me. They're my whole world."

Kathy stops and collects herself.

"I want to support Jessica. I do. I do want to support her. But it's complicated. It's torn our family apart, and our kids, they need their family to be a whole unit. They need to know they're loved. They need to feel secure. But how am I supposed to give them that love and that security when I don't have it myself? How am I supposed to keep them whole when I feel so broken?"

Greta leans against the stairwell. It's a bit of a soap opera—Kathy loves the attention. Whitney is always teasing her because Kathy can really turn on the waterworks. There are all these scenes of her just shattering into tears. Greta used to think it was phony, but watching Nadia Morcos gain the courage to end her marriage to Ghalib on camera last season made Greta realize that her mother feels comfortable releasing her emotions only when she's performing them.

"It's a hard thing when you wake up in the morning and feel like your whole life has been this giant lie."

Kathy stops. Greta imagines her drying a tear from her face. The perfect lighting. The ball gown with costume jewelry she's wearing during the day. The confessionals are extra. Kathy keeps a glass of chardonnay below the camera and sips it throughout filming.

"It's hard not to question yourself," Kathy says, quieter, a bit more real. "I understand that Jessica suffered with this identity crisis for his whole life—for *her* whole life, I mean. But now it's like it's passed on to me. I wake up in the morning and I look at myself in the mirror and I don't know who I am anymore."

Greta silently walks back up the stairs and knocks on Joel's door, poking her head inside.

"I changed my mind," she says. "Getting out of the house for the night doesn't sound like such a bad idea after all."

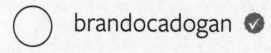

brandocadogan ✓

329k followers

brandocadogan My brother Forrest once said nothing can kill us, we can't never die.

"All right, listen up, people," Brandon says in the motor gallery of his house in Bel-Air. He's wearing Versace navigator oversize sunglasses to hide his bruised eye. "My dad cut me off and I'm banned from United Airlines, but who needs 'em?" Brandon jumps up the steps of the RV and honks its horn. "Who says I can't rough it like the peasants?" he yells down to the rest of the squad, who are exchanging looks as they stand next to their parked cars.

"Where'd you get the RV, bro?" Idris asks. He drove over to the Cadogans' estate in Bel-Air in his new Rolls with an illuminated Spirit of Ecstasy.

"This, young Morcos, is much more than an RV," Brandon says, jumping back out of the vehicle and tapping it on the side. "It's freedom!"

Idris, Bea, and Sean share another look. Fortune records video of Brandon, apparently hoping to strike viral gold with another Brando Cadogan Original. Brandon's rants are as legendary as his parties.

"If your dad cut you off, how'd you pay for it?" Sean asks.

"I sold one of my dad's Rodins." Brandon shrugs.

They all turn to look as Hailey's Mercedes pulls up. Lily is riding shotgun. Bea told Brandon that Hailey didn't want to invite Lily but her mom made her. *Platinum Triangle* isn't filming but the producers requested that they all post the trip on social media. It'll be great buzz in the lead-up to the premiere in three weeks.

Hailey steps out of her car looking like it's fashion week and not like they're about to go camping. She asked in the group text if there was room for her to bring her glam squad. She puts a hand on her hip. "Can someone help me with my bags?"

She pops the trunk and Idris and Sean go over to unload the half-dozen pieces of Louis Vuitton luggage.

Lily, on the other hand, has only a single backpack slung over her shoulder. Brandon gives mad props to the girl for still standing. Hailey likes to eat them alive.

"Welcome, Lily," Brandon says. "Glad you can join us!"

"Are you kidding?" Lily asks. "I wouldn't miss it for the world. I've seen the cast trips on TV. I have to find out for myself how things always go so sideways."

"Careful what you ask for, girl," Fortune says over his phone.

"And don't forget the blender!" Hailey calls over to Idris and Sean. She walks up to Bea and double-kisses her. "I just don't feel right if I don't have my celery juice in the morning. And is there a yoga studio nearby?" She turns to Brandon. "A massage would be fabulous."

"Yes, Queen Hailey," Brandon says. "You can get a massage under the stars." Brandon wanted to go camping, *not* glamping, to prove he's rustic AF but Bea helped pick the place. Ventura Ranch KOA. It'll be roughing it for these kids, who are used to bottle service and blow jobs from their maids.

Hailey points at the RV. "*That's* what we're riding in?"

Another car pulls into the motor gallery. It's Joel's blue Porsche Targa. Greta's with him. Brandon didn't think they'd show. Joel steps out of his car and he and Brandon lock eyes.

"Strom!" Brandon offers a fist-bump. "Glad you could make it, bro!" Brandon's being fake AF but he's spent enough time on TV to know how to keep it rolling. Never complain, never explain. Except in your confessionals.

Brandon turns to Greta. "You too, Greta," he says. "I'm honored."

Greta holds his stare. "Don't be," she says. "You're just the lesser evil." Greta heads toward the RV. "Where are we going, anyway?" she asks.

"Near Santa Paula," Idris says. Greta ghosts him.

She climbs the steps into the RV. Brandon and Idris share a look. Seems like #selfiestickgate isn't totally behind them.

"This is going to be lit!" Brandon says, clapping his hands together and trying to rouse the crowd. "We're leaving it all behind, people!"

"Including Valeria?" Bea checks the time on her phone. "She's still not here and she's not replying to my texts."

"We should wait for her," Sean says.

"I'm so sick of that girl's diva attitude." Hailey steps up into the RV. "It's not all about her!"

realvalerialeon

3.3m followers

tur_tle_time FB

irma_st24 lb

irma_st24 cb

irma_st24 fb

rocklynracho lb

rocklynracho fb

bestmusicpnp Follow back!

yolanda.maze22_ Lb

yolanda.maze22_ Fb

Valeria is up in her room packing a carry-on for the camping trip. Bea keeps sending her texts telling her they're all at the Cadogans' house and they're going to leave without her if she doesn't hurry. Valeria is running late because Sophia threw a fit this morning and was refusing to eat the pancakes Valeria made her for breakfast because they're "empty calories." Sophia kept narrowing her eyes at Valeria and saying, "Aren't you afraid of getting fat?"

Valeria picks up her phone and shoots a quick text back to Bea promising she's on her way. Valeria could really use the escape.

There's a knock on her bedroom door.

"You have a minute?" Gloria asks.

Valeria drops her bag of toiletries into the carry-on. She freezes when she sees that her mother is holding a script in her hand.

"Sheldon Bell sent this over," Gloria says.

"You mean, my agent is still alive?" Valeria asks. Her heart is racing. She's been lip-synching her prayers for this.

"It's a guest part for a new sitcom premiering mid-season on ABC," Gloria says. She passes the script to Valeria, who almost expects Gloria to yank it away from her before she can grasp it.

Valeria stares down at the title: *Almost Everything*.

"God, we need this, Valeria." Gloria gives Valeria a sheepish look. "I had to send your dad some money . . ."

Valeria's heart stops. "Mother, you didn't!"

"I had to! He said he was in trouble. That he had some people to pay off, and then everything would be all right. He'd use the rest of the money to settle his hotel bill and book a flight back to L.A."

"And you believed him? He's a pathological liar!"

"He's your father. You'll show him some respect—"

"Why should I respect him? He's off in Vegas spending money his daughter made . . ." Valeria clutches the script to her chest. "Why should I care about him? Does he care about me? All he cares about is gambling. He's abandoned us, Mom. He's left you to deal with the bills, and the banks, and the house. He's left you to become a pimp. A role that seems made for you!"

Gloria slaps Valeria across the cheek so hard that her neck cracks. It knocks the script out of Valeria's hands. The pages come loose and flutter to the floor. It would've made a beautiful shot if the cameras had been on them. It would've made all the trailers.

"I know the sacrifices you've made," Gloria says calmly. "Your whole life you've been the one making sacrifices for this family. But I've made my share, too. I know you think I've been hard on you, but it's just because I saw your beauty and your talent and I knew . . . Valeria, I just *knew* that you were special. From the moment you were born you lit up a room, you made people so happy. I committed myself to you. I stole neighbors' newspapers for the coupons, and I skipped meals when the money was tight so that I could pay for your headshots, so that I could buy you a new dress to audition in. . . . Because I knew that you were destined to be a star!"

"Stars fade, Mother. Then what?"

Gloria grabs Valeria's wrists, squeezing as tightly as Patrick does when he holds them above her head.

"Don't you dare! We've faced rejection before. All it takes is one break. Your star hasn't faded. There's just been some smog over the Leon house, but when it clears, you'll see. You'll sparkle yet."

"You mean *you* will." Valeria pulls her arms away. "Through me. Isn't that the real reason you made all those 'sacrifices'? To fulfill your own childhood fantasies? Aren't you just a fucking cliché?" Valeria braces for another slap, but it doesn't come.

Gloria deflates. That scares Valeria most of all. If even Gloria Leon can't fake it, there's no hope for the rest of them.

"Maybe you're right," she says quietly. "But you loved it.

When it was good, you were happy. And I know you will be again." She reaches for Valeria's wrist; she's gentler this time, and kisses her hand. "All I want for you is to be happy." Valeria knows she means "rich and famous."

Gloria reaches into her pocket and pulls out the Panthère de Cartier earrings Patrick gave Valeria.

"You used to hide candy in your pillowcase. Your father was always giving you sweets, even though I told him you needed to watch your figure."

Gloria tells her, "I had them appraised. It'll be enough to get the bank off our back for a while."

"No!" Valeria tears the earrings out of her mother's hands. "They're mine."

Valeria's face burns, from the slap and from shame. She knows it's stupid, but the earrings mean something to her. When she wears them, she feels different. It's like when she used to put on a costume for a role. When she wears the earrings, she feels transformed.

"We can't lose the house, Valeria."

"We won't lose the house!" Valeria refuses to be a part of Hollywood's ritual sacrifice. "I'll book the role. And there will be other offers. Or I'll work the damn yacht circuit during the Cannes Film Festival if I have to . . . but we will *not* lose the house!"

fortunefitzroy ✓

143k followers

oliviawgeorgio fuck it up babe

oliviawgeorgio FUCK

oliviawgeorgio IT

oliviawgeorgio UP

The only person who packed more for this trip than Hailey is Fortune. He doesn't do camping. But he also doesn't do recurring. It's not fair that Fortune hasn't been promoted on *Platinum Triangle*! He's basically just "one of Hailey's gays" on the show, just part of her glam squad. Fortune knows he can be so much more. He's destined to be a star . . . That's why he ran away from those crazy fucking Jehovah's Witnesses and came to La-La Land. He's always lived in a la-la land in his head.

Meeting Hailey has been Fortune's big break. He's become her favorite pawn, and he likes being used by her if it means more camera time. Fortune feels like he's proven his ability to entertain the masses. He's tried to sell Sam on ways to expand his storyline, but she wants to focus on the "families" of the Platinum Triangle, and Fortune doesn't have one.

Fortune depends on the show to make a living. Right now he's surviving on the kindness of strangers and the ads he promotes on Instagram. But it's not like he has a platform like Hailey's milli . . . Fortune needs to take his brand to the next level. The problem, is he's not exactly the most likable character. Unlike Hailey, Fortune is more than willing to show his claws. He loves being a bitch!

"Can you please get it through your thick skull that I don't want you anywhere near me?" Greta screams from the back of the RV. And there's nothing Fortune loves more than when someone is being an even bigger bitch than he is.

There's a bedroom with a king-size bed at the back, where Greta went to read her *Glamour* magazine—she's ghosting Hailey and Hailey's ghosting her and Fortune is living for it all. Idris followed Greta to the back room, predictably, and now Greta is making a scene. Predictably.

"This is an RV," Idris says. "Limited space. And you have to talk to me sometime!"

It's going to be a *long* two-hour ride to the Ventura Ranch KOA campground. Fortune's sitting next to a window near the back. Brandon's driving and Bea is up front with him. Sean and Joel are sitting together on seats near the front, and Hailey and Lily are at a booth with a table. Hailey's glued to her phone, like Lily isn't even there. At least Lily doesn't seem to be taking it too personally. She's staring out the window.

Fortune gets a good look at their latest cast member. Lily's pretty but she needs to stop eating dairy. Her hair looks flat next to Hailey's. Hailey has a more platinum shade, and she always wears a piece to fill it out—but she'll punish you for bringing it up by, say, filming a scene with you where you go shopping and she conveniently "forgets" her credit card and turns to you and says, "Do you mind getting it this time, darling?" and making you look totally uncool because you never pay for it because you can't afford to pay for it and she knows it! Fortune had to admit on camera that he didn't have the money to foot the bill they racked up at Kitson. Hailey ended up charging it to her mother's account, like Fortune knew she was planning to from the start. She just wanted to humiliate Fortune first.

Fortune doesn't envy Lily's position. If Hailey wants her taken out, then Lily doesn't stand a chance. Fortune has nothing against the girl personally, but she's standing in the way of his contract to become a full-time cast member on the show.

"Hey, Lily, I brought you something." Sean leans over from where he's sitting and passes Lily a multicolored stone—different shades of gray, red, and beige swirled together.

"Wow," Lily says, turning it around between her fingers. "So pretty. What kind of stone is this?"

"Agate. It's supposed to be a stabilizing and strengthening influence. It harmonizes the yin and yang of things . . . the negative and positive. I carry one in my pocket." Sean shrugs. "Just thought maybe you could use some positive vibes joining this group."

Fortune notices Sean's eyes flicker on Hailey for a second. Oh, the subtle shade of it all!

Joel laughs. "I'm not sure if a stone is going to cut it."

"This is really sweet of you, Sean." Lily closes the stone in the palm of her hand. "Thank you."

For some reason Sean thinks it's a good idea to pull out his phone and start playing some of his and Joel's old YouTube videos for everyone to watch. They had a channel in junior high.

"I totally remember that one!" Hailey laughs. Joel is cringing and pulls his HUF hat over his face.

In the video, filmed with a handheld camera, Joel and Sean douse a mattress with gasoline, light it on fire, and roast marshmallows in the flames. They throw it into Sean's pool to douse it and then take turns jumping on the seared mattress. It kind of put them on the map because Sean's dad Shared it.

"We've had some good times with that pool, man," Sean says, exiting out of the video. "Remember when we filled it with a million Lucky Charms?"

Joel does his best Irish accent. "They're magically lit!"

"We should make another vlog," Sean says. "How long has it been? You OOC?"

"OOC?" Lily asks.

"Out of content," Hailey answers.

"That's it! Either this hatbox gets chucked out the window or Idris does!" Greta comes storming out of the back room interrupting everyone and holding a piece of hatbox luggage threateningly. "I can't breathe in this RV!"

"Maybe you just need to get into the spirit of it," Hailey says. "Do you have a selfie stick? We should do a group photo."

Fortune grabs the hatbox out of Greta's hands before she can chuck it at Hailey. He holds it to his chest protectively. "Sorry, Idris," Fortune says, "it was nice knowing you."

Greta sits alone on a seat and puts in her AirPods, crossing her arms as she stares out the window at the passing highway.

Fortune squeezes past Idris into the room at the back to tuck away his luggage. Idris follows him, fuming as he flops onto the bed.

"She destroyed my Lambo, and you don't see me holding it against her, do you?"

"Do you even like Greta?" Fortune asks. "I always thought you saw her as a stepping stone to Hailey."

"What does Joel Strom have that I don't?" Idris asks bitterly.

"Integrity. And a Disney prince jawline."

Fortune sits next to Idris on the bed.

"If you want Hailey to notice you," Fortune says, "you have to get her the one thing she can't get for herself." Fortune motions with his head to the front of the bus. Idris looks in that direction.

"Joel?" Idris asks. "How will pushing Joel and Hailey together help *me* rebound with Hailey?"

"She wants Joel to take her to the season 2 premiere at the Sofitel and walk the red carpet with her. If you can help me make that happen, then I bet I can convince Hailey to let you in on the virginity storyline. Think about it—after Patrick Paley and Hailey took that vow of abstinence at Hillsborough? You'd be a legend!"

"No way will Joel go along with it," Idris says. "Hailey's gone against Greta too many times. Joel doesn't forgive you when you mess with his sister, believe me."

"Maybe it'll never be real love between Hailey and Joel," Fortune says. "But it doesn't matter what's real."

He nudges Idris's shoulder.

"It only matters what people think is real."

Idris smirks. "What do you have in mind?"

"Here's the deal," Fortune says, keeping his voice low enough so no one else in the RV can hear them. "You help me get Joel to take Hailey to the premiere and you get to be Hailey's official first. Think of the coverage. You'll have more screen time than Joel come season 3."

"What are you getting out of it?"

"Hailey's going to help me make permanent cast member status on *Platinum Triangle*."

Idris laughs. "And how exactly are you going to convince Joel?"

"Oh, I'll just blackmail him."

"Squeaky-clean ad-friendly YouTube star Joel Strom?" Idris asks.

"Everyone has a secret, even Prince Charming. I'll find a way to get it out of him." Fortune drags a nail down Idris's cheek. "Leave it to me."

Fortune turns and looks across the RV. Hailey's up at the very front with Brandon and Bea now, and Lily and Joel are sitting on the same side of the table, close enough that their arms are touching.

"The real challenge is keeping Lily away from Joel," Fortune says. He sizes Idris up. "But I'm sure you're up to it."

"Me?" Idris asks.

"Distract her. Think about how epic it will be if the virginity storyline ends with a screen grab of Idris Morcos 'checking in' to Hailey Paley."

Fortune knows it's sick enough to pique Idris's interest. And it's just the kind of scandal Sam and the network heads drool over. It'll be an Idris versus Patrick showdown over Hailey's purity. Hailey can turn on the waterworks and pull off her ring, like, legit "Daddy, I'm in love with danger!" How can Idris resist? He's always wanted to be a Marvel villain.

The bus comes to a sudden, lurching stop. Fortune peers out the window. They're in the parking lot of a supermarket. Brandon wants to do a beer run. Thank God. Even if he's just shopping for cheese puffs and hot dogs, Fortune needs some retail therapy if he's going to make it through this trip!

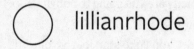

lillianrhode

44k followers

camillanicolamarie BEAUTIFUL QUEEN U DESERVE EVERYTHING

pilettacarozina_ @lillianrhode I love Jailey not you

pwnimma You look like a little boy who got into his mom s makeup

bartakatiz Ölürüm öldürürüm

akirailyas Fake

officialcatriana You can never outshine hailey and stop being a stalker 🔥🔥☺

carolcaldner Keep that pretty head in tune with your heart 🖤

They pull up to the Ventura Ranch KOA campsite on the top of the Topa Topa mountains, with breathtaking canyon views. There are seating areas, a firepit, a grill, and trails leading to the safari tents and teepees where they'll be sleeping.

Brandon steps off the RV carrying a case of beer. They spent $1,500 on junk food at the supermarket. Lily noted Hailey's enthusiasm. She loaded a cart full of cinnamon buns and pie and cookies from the bakery.

"There are three safari tents and two teepees," Brandon says. "We all have to double up."

The pairings happen automatically. Brandon and Bea want one of the teepees, Sean and Joel take the other, Hailey and Fortune claim one of the tents, which leaves one for Idris and Greta and one for Lily and Valeria when she shows up. Valeria sent Sean a text saying she got backed up and is going to drive straight to the campground.

"No way," Greta says. "I am *not* sharing a tent with Idris. I'd rather sleep out in the open and let the wildlife get me."

"Then Idris can bunk with Lily, and Greta and Valeria can share," Brandon says.

Lily sees Joel open his mouth to object, but before he can, Bea speaks up. "*I'll* sleep with Greta," she tells Brandon. "And you and Idris can share a teepee. You boys deserve each other."

Lily gives Bea a smile of gratitude, but Bea just looks away. Lily doesn't know what she did to offend her but it's obvious the Getty heiress is #TeamHailey, like so many of Lily's followers, who keep trolling her. Does it have to be a competition? Lily doesn't know if she can survive in the wilderness with these girls. She can't wait for Valeria to show up.

"Then it's settled," Joel says quickly, before Brandon can complain.

"Fine." Brandon sighs. He nuzzles Bea's neck. "I'll just have to take you out into the woods . . ."

"Let's go see if the tent has WiFi," Hailey tells Fortune. She leaves him to deal with their mountain of bags.

They all disperse to check out where they'll be sleeping and to unpack. Lily doesn't know if you can call her accommodation a "tent." It has a queen-size bed, two chairs, a couch, and a table.

The furniture is in earthy tones, with a zebra-skin rug on the floor. It's bigger than the trailer where Lily grew up!

As Lily is putting away the few pieces of clothing she brought in one of the dresser drawers, there's a tap on the screen door.

"So, what do you think?" Joel asks, stepping inside.

"Not exactly what I was expecting." Lily fluffs her pillow. "But I think I'll survive."

"The teepee where Sean and I are sleeping is sick," Joel says. "And there's a bunch of trails, apparently." He passes her a pamphlet with a map. "You wanna meet up tonight? The views are supposed to be insane."

"I'm in." Lily smiles. "But I don't want everyone to know about it. Things are still kind of tense between me and Hailey . . . I just want to avoid drama this trip. If it manages to stay out of the press, I'll consider it a success."

"We'll go separately, then." Joel points to a spot on the map, just off a trail and next to a stream. "Meet you there at midnight?"

"I can't wait," Lily says, leaning in for a kiss.

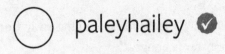

paleyhailey ✓

1m followers

leodragon1313 Lily and Joel look cute but not similar as hailey n Joel 🖤 🖤 🖤 they'd be perfect together 😣

alesxisandrorocchi @missemmyy Still no JAILEY 😂

rose.pellegrino @mariataff9 Haileu is obsessed with him but he's was seen with @lillianrhode her COUSIN

mariataff9 @rose.pellegrino TF?? Where? 😣

rose.pellegrino @mariataff9 The beach...... They're filmingg together

mariataff9 @rose.pellegrino NO!!!! I've been waiting for Jailey to get together literally my whole life 😭 😭 😭

ailey steps away from the door to Lily's safari tent when she sees Lily and Joel kissing through the screen. She saw Joel sneaking up the path to Lily's tent and followed him. She wanted to see for herself if her followers are right and Joel and Lily are together. . . . Hailey almost trips on a tree root sticking out of the ground as she turns and runs back down the trail toward where the RV is parked.

Hailey screams when a peacock comes out of nowhere and crosses the path she's on. Random peacocks roam all over the campground. She almost crashes into Idris at the end of the path.

"Woah!" He holds out his arms to stop her. "Sasquatch after you or something? Brando says you can take guided tours to try and spot one. You up for it?"

"Why don't you take Lily?" Hailey asks, pulling away from him. "Hopefully the monster is hungry."

While they were unpacking, Fortune had filled Hailey in on his conversation with Idris on the RV. Hailey isn't exactly thrilled about giving Idris bragging rights over her highly coveted virginity, but it's not like she'll actually have to go through with it. And it would certainly be ratings gold if Hailey and Idris had a storyline for season 3. Hailey can't cling to Joel for too long. It's starting to look pathetic. The key to longevity on a platform like reality TV is to keep evolving. Hailey's always known she'd have to orbit around Idris eventually.

"I don't see why you want Joel to take you to the premiere anyway," Idris says. "If you ask me, we look much better together . . ."

Hailey starts walking away. "Tell that to your girlfriend," she calls over her shoulder.

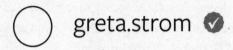

greta.strom ✓

725k followers

magarsabnan So disgusting ew

itsmehillary99 U have a mental issue.

itsmehillary99 Psycho

laura.gough1 Get help

meg_baked1217 @itsnotbritneybitchitsmimi yeah ikr she has 'human feeling' 😂 nah man people hate each other it's just human nature get over it

They need wood for the firepit. Brandon bought an ax because he's basically Patrick Bateman from *American Psycho* and Idris is being a misogynistic jerk saying the guys will go get it and so Greta grabs the ax and starts a revolution.

"Um, Greta . . . ," Joel calls after her but Greta is already walking toward the woods. She lifts her hand in the air and gives the boys the middle finger.

"Come on, girls!" she yells.

Lily is right behind her, and Hailey and Bea follow them into the woods. Greta wishes Hailey wouldn't. It's not like it's the first time they've played dirty in the press. That was basically

173

them all season 1. But Greta's sick of it. She wants only real relationships from now on.

Greta leads them deeper into the woods, gaining some satisfaction from Hailey screaming at every bug she sees and crying about "furry spiders." Greta knows this is torture for her. Hailey is afraid of everything. She has to take Xanax before she'll fly anywhere. On the cast trip to the Bahamas, Hailey had to hold Greta's hand as the private jet took off.

"Does anyone know how to chop wood?" Bea asks. They all stop walking and look at each other.

"How hard can it be?" Greta asks.

"I think we're lost," Hailey says. She holds up her phone. "I'm not getting a connection."

"I am," Lily says. She's looking up how to split firewood on Google. "There's a website called 'The Art of Manliness' with a step-by-step guide. We might need a chopping block . . ."

"The Art of Manliness?" Greta shakes her head. "The fucking patriarchy. I'd like to chop off its dick!" She lets out her rage by bringing the ax down on the stump of a tree that has fallen over. It doesn't exactly split it but she keeps hacking at it until chunks of wood break off. Who says they have to be logs?

"Or you could just do that," Lily says, putting away her phone.

"Watch it!" Hailey gasps. "You're swinging that thing like a maniac!"

Greta stops hacking at the tree stump and spins around to face Hailey. It's like the forest becomes still as Lily and Bea and the animals in the woods wait to see what Greta will do next. Greta backs Hailey against a tree and lifts the ax, holding it to Hailey's neck. Hailey swallows nervously.

"I'd chop off your head if I didn't think two more would pop up in its place," Greta says.

"Back off, creep!" Hailey pushes Greta. Greta throws the ax into the woods. She doesn't need it. She pushes Hailey back and Hailey goes flying into the tree.

"You bitch!"

Hailey lunges at Greta.

"Stop!" Lily tries to take a step forward but Bea holds her.

The revolution has gone a bit sideways. There's hair-pulling and they're rolling around in the mud. Greta has Hailey pinned.

"What kind of a friend are you?" she asks.

"You're the one who tried to make me look bad by planting the story on Radar about Joel and Lily!" Hailey says through gritted teeth. She uses all her strength to get free from Greta's restraint, then pushes her off. They stand and face each other.

"You're right," Greta says. "I did plant that story. I know how to get you where it hurts."

"Why would that hurt?" Lily asks. She looks at Hailey. "I thought you told me you weren't interested in Joel?"

"Are you kidding?" Greta laughs. "She'd kill for him."

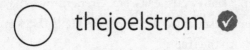

thejoelstrom ✓

1.8m followers

annadudley HOW DO WE BECOME FRIENDS?!?!

"You want to fight me?" Brandon tosses his ping pong paddle on the table set up outside. "I'll fight you right now, you little bitch!"

Joel stands his ground. He's not scared of Brandon Cadogan or his infamous temper tantrums. Brandon's brother, Conrad, got all the good genes. Brandon's the black sheep of the Cadogan family, especially when he starts drinking.

"What happened?" Sean asks. "It was going so well!"

It was, too. After they started a fire (by "We'll go get firewood" Idris meant they'd go to the office and check in and pick up a stack there, one of the amenities of the campground) and cracked a few beers, Brandon and Idris started playing a game of ping pong. Joel called winner.

Joel is already tired of this fight with Brandon—sometimes the only thing you can do is move on. He can't just cancel Brandon, though. The Cadogans are family friends. Joel surfs with Conrad when he's not off saving third world countries. If Joel could, he'd cancel both Brandon and Idris. He's never believed that Idris treats Greta right, and he's glad that she finally seems to be done with him. But Joel's had his hopes up before. He knows how things can change in a heartbeat.

"It was going fine until this bitch started flinging the ball at my face!" Spit flies out of Brandon's mouth.

"It's not my fault you can't hit it," Joel says.

"That's it!" Brandon comes around the side of the ping pong table and swings at Joel. He misses, and Joel trips him, sending Brandon falling to the ground and landing on his back.

Sean and Idris circle around, and even Fortune puts away his phone long enough to watch. Brandon bounces back up.

"You're probably a faggot," Brandon says. "That's why you won't give it to Hailey. Who turns down Hailey Paley?"

"No kidding," Idris says.

Joel drops his paddle on the ping pong table. "Unlike you, Brando, I don't have anything to prove."

"You almost broke my nose, Strom!" Brandon is about to blow. The vein in his neck is starting to pop. "How dare you touch my face with your dirty peasant hands!"

"He was just protecting his sister," Sean says calmly. "You can't hold that against him."

"Whose side are you on, anyway?"

"No one's. I'm just saying—"

"I'm gonna smash this pretty boy's face in!" Brandon grabs Joel by the collar of his tee-shirt and shoves him against the side of the RV.

"You really want to settle this?" Sean runs over and breaks them up. "What about a race?"

"Oh my God, yes!" Fortune's eyes light up.

"A drag race?" Brandon asks.

"What's the matter?" Sean taunts. "Scared?"

"Set it up." Joel doesn't miss a beat.

"Yeah." A smile spreads on Brandon's face. "Set it up. Of course, I'll have to buy a new car for the occasion . . ."

They're interrupted by the sound of a car pulling into the camping lot. Valeria parks her BMW behind the RV and steps out.

"What'd I miss?" she asks.

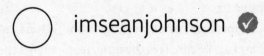

imseanjohnson ✓

1.5m followers

ayecandy13 @riprakash if I could I would eat him

simonregan @christianrdouglas he's goals man

reelinevisca dope

ines.rebel Você não é bom o suficiente para Valeria

debsterbanx @raven.ly i have to fuck him by next summer too :(

After all the drama, everyone goes rock climbing to blow off some steam. Valeria and Sean decide to go off on their own. Sean wants to check out the trail where the camp gives guided group tours in search of Sasquatch, aka Bigfoot. Sean believes Sasquatch is real but he doubts you'd spot one on a group tour. They steer clear of human beings. They must know better.

"Don't you think there would be some kind of evidence?" Valeria says as they walk down the trail.

Sean stares down at her Golden Goose metallic leather platform sneakers.

"Like a corpse or something?" she goes on. "Not just grainy photos and videos that are probably people walking around in ape costumes."

"What if it's not from this dimension?" Sean looks up at her. "Like, what if when it dies, it just, like, disappears and goes back to wherever it came from?"

"You have quite the imagination, Sean Johnson," Valeria says. She reaches for his hand. Sean likes the intimate moments they share when it's just the two of them.

Valeria means a lot to him. She knows what his dad is like and she's tried to make things better for Sean at home. Valeria goes out of her way to charm Christoph. Sean's dad thinks he's all right so long as he has a girl, which is why Sean let Sam and her henchmen at the network push him into this relationship in the first place. Sean has come to depend on Valeria. Sometimes he thinks she's the only one who really knows him, aside from Joel. Fortune doesn't know him—but Sean wishes he did. They've been exchanging secret texts since arriving at the campground, planning to meet in the woods late at night. He knows that for Fortune it's just a thrill, and that it's dangerous to want it to be anything more. Fortune loves only himself.

"For me it's not a matter of whether they're real or not," Sean says as they continue walking. "I already know you can be both."

Last season, when Sean was doing press for *Platinum Triangle*, hair and makeup descended upon him before the camera started rolling. Sean felt them smoothing his hair and straightening his shirt and brushing his eyebrows with that small, ticklish brush. His eyes closed as they powdered his face to hide the sheen under the glare of the lights. It took only a few seconds, but as the hands moved over his face and body, it was like he stopped belonging to himself. He experienced this strange phenomenon where it was like he had disappeared, like he was hanging suspended between dimensions, and his life was just a dream.

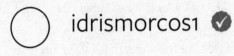

idrismorcos1 ✓

573k followers

larayasser33 Are u sure that u r Muslim!!

stevensko2 @larayasser33 what do you mean?

larayasser33 @stevensko2 He is said to be a Muslim ... but all he does is vice versa 😵 😵 😵 unfortunately there are many people like him 😖

stevensko2 @larayasser33 but that doesn't actually mean that he is a bad muslim... ig you are a good person inside, than you are a good human being... which makes him a good muslim

larayasser33 @stevensko2 I didn't say he is a bad muslim! Only God knows if he is a good muslim or not.. I'm just talking about his doings which are clear for all 😑

Idris is going to drive Lily and Joel apart. No problem. If he can just find a way to get Lily to spend some time with him, he knows it'll drive Joel crazy. Joel Strom hates Idris's guts. They were friends before Idris and Greta started dating, but then Joel decided Idris was a bad influence on Greta, even though anyone who knows Greta knows she can't be controlled.

It's dark out and they're all hanging around the firepit and everyone's having a good time; even Hailey's getting into it. She brought out the marshmallows for them to make s'mores.

Greta's still ghosting him. Brandon pulled out a beer bong from the RV and Greta chugged a six-pack by herself. Shit's about to get crazy and Joel looks like he knows it. Lily and Joel are sitting next to each other.

All Idris has to do is make Joel *think* that Lily is interested in him by getting her to hang out with him. That'll be enough to piss Joel off and cause tension with Lily. Fortune's plan is a little bit of entertainment if nothing else.

Idris gets the plan in motion later on. He meets Lily when she's coming back to the campsite from the bathrooms.

"Yo, Lily," he says. "Can we talk?"

Lily stops walking. "What can I do for you, Idris?" she asks. Lily's no innocent fawn in the woods. She looks at him suspiciously.

"Greta's still ghosting me," Idris says.

"Good. She shouldn't waste her time on you."

"Not gonna lie; that hurts. But I respect you for saying it to my face. You're *real*. No drama. Like, grand theft aside. What I'm trying to say is that you seem like the kind of girl who knows what other girls want. So, tell me how I make it up to Greta?"

"How about trying *not* to be a douchebag? If I were Greta, I would never forgive you for that video."

"Not my finest moment. Admittedly. Obviously, the situation demands a big gesture. I was thinking I'd charter my dad's jet, right, and take her to SF for a romantic dinner, maybe get her a diamond. . . . But then I was, like, can I really just splash money to show her how sorry I am? Like, will that even work? Greta can charter her own jet if she wants, and she's not impressed by diamonds . . ."

"You're right," Lily says. "Greta deserves a genuine apology."

"That's what I'm thinking. So, like, what about a love letter? Like, handwritten and shit."

Lily tries to keep a straight face because she wants to be hard on Idris, but he sees her softening up.

"That's not a *terrible* idea," she says. "Try writing from your heart. Greta may decide that you don't deserve hers, but at least you'll have tried."

"There's just one problem." Idris lowers his voice and leans in. "I don't know how to write cursive."

"Didn't they teach you in elementary school?"

"At my school? We had our own iPads in kindergarten. That's why I need your help. I can't ask anyone else; it's too embarrassing. Will you teach me?"

They hear laughter from over the crackling flames of the firepit down the trail.

"I'm sorry, Idris," Lily says. "I can't help you. . . . I don't think Joel would like it very much if I helped you get back together with his sister after what you did."

"What do you care what Joel thinks?" Idris asks.

Lily can't hide her emotions. It's written all over her.

"Oh, I get it," Idris says. He shakes his head. "I gotta hand it to the guy. Joel Strom's playing two cousins and *I'm* the pig?"

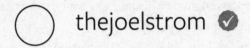

thejoelstrom ✓

1.8m followers

tan_cao21 What's the song you put in your story while you were in the Bahamas

tan_cao21 Pleassse I need to know

larapescoast WHat?!! I thought you were with hailey now you're with lily is that true?

miss_strom_ Hello Joel I love you you my passion I'm ready to sacrifice for you, the same who breathe it's true you don't know about me but thank God I got to know you you're the only one who lived for this life despite the hardness of her but I loved her thanks to you because you've lived it 🥺 💔

At midnight, Joel's about to sneak away from the campsite and go to the stream where he promised he'd meet Lily when he hears Hailey calling out his name.

She's running down the trail as Joel steps out of his teepee. So much for being discreet.

"Joel! You have to help!" Hailey catches her breath. "It's Greta. She's so drunk, and I think she took something. I don't know what. Some kind of hallucinogen. She's totally out of control. She took off all her clothes and she's running through the forest."

"Where?" Joel asks. He knew something like this was going to happen when Greta started beer-bonging. Why does she always have to take things to the extreme? He'll be angry at her later—for now he just needs to find her and make sure she doesn't hurt herself.

"This way," Hailey says. She turns and runs, leading Joel down the path.

They seem to be running for a long time, or at least it feels long for Joel, when suddenly they hear screaming echoing in the distance. Hailey stops abruptly.

"I think this is where she veered off."

Another scream. It's deep and scary, like an animal, but not exactly of this world. Like Bigfoot.

"Follow me," Hailey says. She pushes through the bushes. Joel's right behind her, feeling the branches scratching against his skin.

Hailey leads him to a clearing in the woods. They look around.

"This is where I last saw her," Hailey says. She looks at Joel. "I'm sorry. I never should've left her by herself!"

"It's okay," Joel says. "You did the right thing by finding me."

They both freeze when they hear the echo of another guttural scream.

"Greta," he says, running in the direction of the sound, shoving branches out of the way as he pushes through dense trees. He hears Hailey's panting breath behind him.

Joel stops running when he reaches the end of the woods and approaches the cliffside. Greta is standing there naked, screaming just to hear the echo reverberate through the mountains. She turns and looks at him, and her eyes are completely black. There's mud streaked across her cheeks.

Joel opens his mouth but he doesn't know what to say. He's paralyzed, just like he was when Greta slit her wrists on camera. There was blood everywhere. The camera operator didn't react; he just kept filming. Kathy was screaming hysterically and calling an ambulance and their dad tried to stop the bleeding by wrapping a towel around Greta's arm. Greta was laughing in the face of death. And Joel just stood there. He couldn't move.

The memory plays over in his head sometimes on a loop, usually in the middle of the night when he can't sleep and he's staring up at his bedroom ceiling for hours. He becomes as paralyzed as he was in that moment.

Hailey slips her hand into Joel's. It helps him unfreeze.

"Please, Greta," Joel says. "Let's go back to the campsite."

He puts out his other hand for Greta to take. Greta smirks and looks back out at the mountains. She takes a step forward, like she's about to leap off the cliff. Rocks and dirt fall down below.

"Greta!" Joel gasps. He lunges forward but Hailey holds him back.

"I'm sorry," Hailey says to Greta. "It's all my fault."

Greta turns back in surprise.

Hailey lets go of Joel's hand and takes a cautious step closer to the edge.

"All the games in the press, all the bitchy things I've said in my confessionals, all of it," she continues. "The truth is, I'm not confident enough to just be myself on the show." Hailey pauses, holding Greta's feral eyes. She takes another step forward. "I'm not like you, Greta. I've never admitted it because it isn't easy for me to admit to being anything less than perfect, but the truth is that if I could switch places with you, I would. I'd give anything to feel as deeply a you do and not be afraid to show it."

She puts out her han .

"You know I'm all for Free the Nipple but let's get some clothes on you, girl."

Greta looks down at Hailey's hand. Joel thinks he sees some life returning to her eyes. Come on, Greta . . . Joel hasn't taken a breath since Hailey took the first step forward. He finally breathes when Greta takes Hailey's hand.

"You're my ride or die," Hailey says. She pulls Greta into a hug.

Joel takes off his Palm Angels hoodie and passes it to Hailey, who helps Greta put it on. It's big enough that it covers her down to her legs. Hailey and Joel each link one of Greta's arms and lead her back to the campsite.

The fire has almost burned out in the pit when they get back. Everyone's sleeping. The last piece of wood is burning. It cracks, and sparks shoot into the air. Joel stares into the red and orange embers while Hailey takes Greta to her tent.

When Hailey gets back, he's still standing in the same spot.

"Bea promised to make sure Greta doesn't get out of bed," Hailey says. "I don't think we have to worry. She was out like a light."

Joel doesn't say anything. He just reaches for Hailey and they hug. None of the fake shit matters. Hailey proved her loyalty to his sister tonight. Joel will never forget it.

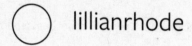

lillianrhode

46k followers

_lavish_bohemia_ Who the hell do u think you are?

Lily comes down the trail to the campsite after waiting nearly an hour for Joel at the stream where they planned to meet. She stops when she sees Hailey standing in Joel's arms by the fire.

The stars had been so bright and felt so close that Lily couldn't help but lift her hand up as if she could pluck one out of the sky. She sat on a rock listening to the water flowing in the stream and waiting. She sent Joel a pin drop in case he was having trouble finding her spot, but she was close to the opening of the trail so she didn't think he could miss her. It was creepy sitting in the dark by herself. She heard the echo of a scream ringing through the mountains.

When Joel didn't show up, she walked down the dark trail by herself back to the campsite, using the flashlight on her phone to guide her, telling herself there must be a good reason for him to have not shown up or even texted. Another fight with Brandon? Not exactly a good reason but a probable one. The more beer Brandon drank the more he was taunting Joel around the campfire about their drag race.

Now Lily turns and runs away from Joel and Hailey before they see her standing there. She doesn't stop until she reaches the safari tent she's sharing with Valeria. Valeria's sitting up in bed reading a script when Lily enters.

"You okay?" she asks. "Lily?"

Valeria puts down her script when Lily just stands there.

"Where were you?"

"Stargazing," Lily says. She blinks and shakes it off. "New script?" she asks.

"A sitcom." Valeria flips through the pages.

Lily kicks off her shoes and sits on the edge of the bed, staring across the tent.

"Are you sure you're okay?" Valeria asks.

"Fine." Lily nods. "Just tired."

"The extended trailer for *Platinum Triangle* dropped tonight," Valeria says, reaching for her phone. "You made the cut."

Valeria shows Lily the trailer. Lily's really in it. Just for, like, half a second, along with audio of Whitney telling Hailey that her cousin is coming to stay with them after her arrest. The trailer cuts to Lily's mugshot.

"Get used to it," Valeria says. "They'll probably cut to your mugshot ten thousand times this season."

There's another scene that's like a kick in the gut. It's during the cast trip to the Bahamas. Joel and Hailey are lying in a hammock together on the beach . . . and then the trailer cuts to the next scene: Hailey's milli party. Joel and Hailey kiss, and then the screen smashes to black. End of trailer.

"Joel knows what he's doing." Valeria looks up from her phone and meets Lily's eyes.

"What do you mean?" Lily asks.

"Well . . ." Valeria pulls out a licorice from a bag open on the bed next to her script, one of the many things they bought during their supermarket stop. "Maybe I'm wrong and Joel really is over the show," she says, pulling the licorice between her teeth, "but I don't really believe it. Maybe that's because I don't believe you *can* be over it. Once you're infected, it's for life. With Joel, it's, like, okay, so maybe the YouTube account got tired. Maybe he's not as obvious about it anymore. But Joel likes the attention. He lives for it. Just like we all do. Joel runs the game almost as well as Hailey does. And you being Hailey's *cousin*? It practically played itself."

realvalerialeon

3.3m followers

constant.kermit I post the same picture of Kermit the frog. Every damn day. 🐸

Valeria has no choice but to board the RV for the drive back to L.A. Her car is missing. And so is Greta. She must've woken up in the middle of the night and slipped away without anyone noticing. Bea took two Ambien and didn't hear her leave. Everyone's worried, especially Valeria. She doesn't tell anyone how much she's freaking out—her mom stopped paying insurance on the BMW months ago; if Greta totals it like she totaled Idris's Lambo, Valeria can't just go out and buy a Rolls-Royce as a replacement. Valeria had been planning on selling the car. Before the Panthère de Cartier earrings, it was the one thing she wouldn't let her mother touch. She kept holding on to the belief that she would need it to take her to auditions.

On the ride home Valeria sits next to Lily and goes over her script for *Almost Everything*. She's going to wear the Cartier earrings to her audition this week for a good-luck charm. Valeria gets her old confidence back when she's wearing the earrings. She remembers she's a star.

Lily is staring out the window. Joel and Hailey are across from them. Joel went quiet when he learned Greta was missing. Hailey has been trying to comfort him but keeps going off on tangents about the Dress for Success show at the Beverly Hilton.

"What's the script for?" Sean asks Valeria when he sees her practicing her lines. He's sitting with Idris and Fortune at the table playing cards.

"A sitcom. The audition's Friday."

"That's the night of the fashion show!" Hailey says.

"Don't worry; I'll be there," Valeria promises.

"Good." Hailey's eyes land on Lily. "It'll be a night to remember."

"Runway models and drag races," Brandon yells back at them from the driver's seat. "End of summer's gonna be lit as fuck."

A ping comes into Valeria's phone. It's a message from her mom. Patrick wants to see her at the Montage tonight.

"It's the worst drug out there," Valeria hears Hailey telling Joel. Hailey holds up her phone. "This is what Greta is really addicted to. The more time you spend reading the comments the more you start to feel like there's only one mind, like everyone thinks the same and there's this single idea of who you are." Valeria knows Hailey's sudden philosophizing is as fake as her tan. She's just trying to impress Joel.

"Then why do we keep coming back for more?" Joel asks.

"People say that you can manipulate your image on social media but really you can only *feed* your image," Hailey says. "At least once it's been established, once people think they have you figured out. You're trapped by their idea of who you are, and if you're not careful . . . you become it."

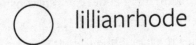

lillianrhode

53k followers

uguguyfdesxunx Hailey's so much prettier than u

uguguyfdesxunx Hide ur face pls

marsprobe52337 @uguguyfdesxunx - what a loser you are. Stay off Lily's page. Advice: get a life.

marsprobe52337 @uguguyfdesxunx - I see you just created this account probably b/c you got bounced off another one. Get ready to bounce again. The pro-Lily groups are all reporting you.

The week they get back to L.A. from the camping trip, Joel texts Lily that he wants to hang out but she tells him that she's busy, which isn't a total lie. She has a couple lifeguarding shifts, and *Platinum Triangle* production is keeping her occupied with a filming schedule to shoot final footage to be edited into the end of season 2. Filming will officially wrap tomorrow, after the Dress for Success fashion show.

Sam convinces Lily to film a scene in the pool house where she calls her mom in Reno to talk about what it's been like living with the Paleys and to share her concerns over her upcoming court case. Lily reluctantly agrees to the call. She doesn't know what to say to Erin. Thanks for selling me for a handbag? Are you still with the same guy or have you updated your profile? But there's a part of Lily that misses her mom. Especially while trying to navigate the minefield around Hailey. Maybe Lily's mom can relate and tell her something about her relationship with Whitney that will help Lily understand Hailey better. Despite it all, Lily still wishes they could be friends. Lily's followers keep pitting them against each other, and it's just worsened since the extended trailer was released.

Lily takes a deep breath before she calls her mom on camera. She puts her phone on speaker and lets it ring. When no one answers, Lily wishes she could hide her face from the camera filming her. Sam speaks up from the corner of the room, which she almost never does when they're rolling.

"Try again," she says.

So Lily makes another call. It rings again.

"At least it's not going straight to voicemail." Lily shrugs, trying to make light of this situation. When the voicemail does pick up, Sam motions for Lily to leave a message, but Lily hangs up. She isn't going to let the first time she talks to her mom in weeks be through a voice message.

Lily regrets filming the scene and wants to ask Sam to not use the footage. But she knows it's out of her control. It says so in the fine print of the contract that Lily's mom signed. *Platinum Triangle* and MKTV literally have a clause that says they are allowed to humiliate her on television and there's nothing she can do about it.

Later, Lily shoots another scene. She and Whitney take a conference call with the Paleys' lawyer. At least Shapiro answers. But he's frustrated. Chris is sticking to his story. Apparently he's hoping to do a sit-down TV interview but no one will touch it because he's asking for so much money.

"The good news is, we got a court date," Shapiro says. Lily's surprised by how soon it is. Two weeks away.

"Just before the premiere," Whitney says. "Won't it be such a relief to put this behind you once and for all, and in time for photos?"

"I pulled a favor to get us in before the school year," Shapiro says. "I don't want this hanging over your head, Lily. It won't be easy with Chris Taber refusing to co-operate, and the court might make an example of you because of the high-profile nature of the case, but I'm still confident that you'll get off with community service."

School. Lily's been so caught up in adjusting to life in Beverly Hills that she hasn't really considered where she's going to school in the fall. Ever since Joel brought up New Beverly High on the beach, it's been in the back of Lily's mind.

"We have time to go shopping for the perfect dress," Whitney says. "You should wear white. White on a pretty blond girl really says it's the illegal immigrants you should be worrying about."

Lily cringes. It's one of those moments caught on camera that Whitney will never be able to live down. It's almost like she can't help herself, but Lily knows the truth. Whitney doesn't want to help herself. The whole point is to shock and offend.

After the scene, Lily is alone in the pool house. She knows she's not supposed to contact Chris but she's determined to get him to confess and help her get out of this mess. Lily unblocks Chris's number and calls him. He answers on the first ring and doesn't sound at all surprised to hear from her.

"I wondered when you'd come running back to me."

"Get over yourself," Lily says. "I only went out with you because I was desperate and you had wheels. You said you were taking me to a party in Malibu."

"Technically, I said I knew *of* a place to party in Malibu."

"I am not doing this with you!" Lily snaps. They were bickering even as the police put them in handcuffs on the PCH. Lily takes a deep breath through her nose. "I'm just calling because I want you to do the right thing, Chris. Tell the police the truth! That I was just along for the ride and I had no idea what was about to happen!"

"Are you sure that's the truth?" Chris asks.

Lily remembers Chris calling the Lalanne her ticket out of the Valley. He was right.

"Hey, if that's the story, then I'm happy to go along with it," Chris says. "I'll play the bad guy. Anything you say."

Lily waits for it.

"There's just one thing."

She closes her eyes and tries to stay calm. "And what might that be, Chris?"

"I want you to do an interview with me on *Access Hollywood*. They're offering me double if I can get Patrick Paley's niece to sit down with me!"

This was a mistake. Lily thought she could reason with Chris but he won't be satisfied until he's milked this for everything it's worth.

"You know what?" Lily says. "You are not worth my time."

She hangs up and is still staring down at her phone in a rage when a DM comes into her phone from Idris. He reminds her that they're supposed to start their cursive lessons today and asks if he can come over now. Lily forgot. She got caught up in the shooting schedule and then Chris. . . . Lily blocks Chris's number again.

After Lily caught Joel and Hailey holding each other at the campground, Lily sent Idris a DM and told him she would help him learn how to write after all. It was a knee-jerk reaction. Lily wants to make Joel feel as jealous as she does.

Lily replies to Idris, telling him to come over whenever, and heads to the main house to ask Ana for some snacks to help them practice. Patrick's sitting out by the pool with his *Avengers* script.

"Hey, Lily." He smiles at her from behind his dark-lens Ray-Bans. "I haven't seen you since you've been back. These hours on set are killing me. How was the camping trip?"

"Whirlwind," Lily says.

"You have some time to help me run lines?" Patrick asks. "Hailey usually helps but she's at a production meeting for her fashion show."

"A friend's stopping by, but I have a minute." Lily accepts the script Patrick passes her and sits on the chaise across from him, scanning the page.

"Kang and Enchantress?" She gasps. She's not a huge *Avengers* fan but she's seen on gossip blogs that Enchantress is being played by Margot Robbie. "That's an unlikely duo!" Lily laughs.

"It's not exactly as it seems," Patrick says.

"Is it ever?" Lily's eyes flicker up from the page.

They run lines. Kang's monologue goes on for most of the scene. Lily prompts him with Enchantress's one-liners. She's no Margot Robbie but this is fun. Enchantress has Kang under some kind of love spell.

Patrick finishes his last line in the monologue and Lily stares at the page. The action line calls for Kang and Enchantress to kiss.

Lily can feel Patrick staring at her and she looks up from the script. Patrick raises his arm and tucks a strand of hair behind Lily's ear. The sun beating down on them is so hot that Lily's mouth has gone dry and she feels a bead of sweat dripping down her back. For a second Lily thinks Patrick is actually going to lean in and kiss her. But then he retracts his arm. The script almost slides off Lily's lap. Patrick catches it, his hand grazing her bare legs in a way that makes Lily jump up from the chaise and smooth out the creases in her skirt.

"You read well," Patrick says, leaning back in his chaise and adjusting his sunglasses. "Have you ever thought of acting?"

Before Lily has a chance to answer, they're interrupted by Idris coming around the side of the house.

"I was in the neighborhood," Idris says, "so I thought I'd come right over." He looks from Lily to Patrick. Lily's staring at the tile around the pool. When she looks up, she sees Patrick flash Idris an easy, charming smile.

"Good to see you, Idris," Patrick says, diving back into his script.

Lily motions for Idris to follow her into the pool house.

"Thanks for agreeing to help me with this," Idris says as they enter. He sits on the couch. "I really want to do right by Greta."

"Have you heard anything?" Lily asks. She takes a seat next to him.

After the camping trip, Greta was MIA for a few days. Valeria reported her car as stolen and some headlines popped up. Then Lily saw on Instagram that Greta was back home. Without the car. People are saying Greta's strung out. Lily doesn't know what to believe, but the comments make it sound like she was on a nonstop bender.

"She's ghosting me," Idris says. "But I'm going to win her back. With your help."

"Well, I'm glad to help you learn how to write cursive. If you depend on technology for everything, then what separates you from a robot? Writing by hand is a part of your humanity." Lily looks out the window at Patrick by the pool. "You don't want to lose that."

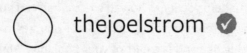

thejoelstrom ✓

1.8m followers

allalone311 PROMO FAKE LOVE 😂😂😂😂

Joel still hasn't explained to Lily why he didn't meet her at midnight during the camping trip like he promised. How does he explain what Greta was like that night? Joel's scared of Greta when she's manic. He was in shock and praying the entire RV ride back to the city that Greta would already be home by the time they got there, but she wasn't. She didn't come home for a couple of days. It's not the first time she's disappeared. Joel's biggest fear is that one time she won't come back.

Once Greta was home and Joel stopped feeling so anxious he reached out to Lily but she's been avoiding him. Joel couldn't believe it when he saw on Instagram that Idris posted a Story of him and Lily together. Joel didn't see that one coming.

On Friday, he sends Lily a DM asking if he can pick her up and bring her to the Beverly Hilton for the fashion show. He tells her they need to talk.

Lily's waiting for him in the Paleys' driveway when he gets to Trousdale. Near the same spot where he first met her staring up at the house. The sun is starting to set and it glows around Lily's blond hair as his Targa pulls up.

Joel can see himself reflected in Lily's polarized sunglasses when she gets into the car and looks over. "I missed you," he says, pulling out of the driveway. On the way to the hotel, Joel tells Lily what happened the night he didn't show up to meet her. He turns to face her at a stoplight and gets honked at by the car behind them when it turns green and he doesn't move fast enough.

"It's a messed-up time for my family," Joel says as they drive. "I don't know if you want to be with me right now." He glances over at Lily. The breeze is making her hair blow around her face. "I don't know if I can be with anyone. It's just going to get worse once the season starts. I wouldn't blame you if you didn't want to be around that."

"I'm not afraid of your life," Lily says. "And you don't have to face it alone."

At the next stoplight Joel leans over and kisses her.

"I thought maybe you were moving on with Idris," he says when they pull apart.

"Idris?" Lily asks.

"I saw his Story. I didn't know you guys hung out."

Lily sinks back in her seat. "I guess I owe *you* an explanation," she says as the light turns green. "I'm teaching Idris how to write cursive."

Joel laughs. "That troglodyte can't learn new tricks."

"You should probably know *why* he wants to learn how to write," Lily continues. "He wants to write a love letter. To Greta. Apologizing for #selfiestickgate."

"And you're helping him?" Joel asks. "After what he did to Greta? After what he did to you?"

"I know." Lily sighs, staring out at the street. "I guess I'm just a hopeless romantic."

She looks back at him. "I'll stop if it bothers you."

"No." Joel smiles at her. "I like that you have a big heart. I like that you think redemption is possible. Even for someone like Idris."

"What about someone like Hailey?"

Joel looks over at Lily blankly.

"I saw you and Hailey hugging at the campsite," Lily blurts out. "When I got back after I'd been waiting for you. I saw you two hugging."

"I told you, she helped me with Greta. Hailey was almost her old self again. I gave her a hug to thank her for being there for my sister."

"And the hammock?"

"Hammock?"

"In the extended trailer."

"I haven't seen the extended trailer." Joel tightens his grip on the steering wheel. He doesn't want to talk about the show. He doesn't want to be held to whatever images of him are out there in the world. He doesn't want to be reminded that he has no control.

"During the Bahamas trip," Lily says. "You and Hailey looked . . . close."

Joel pulls up to the Beverly Hilton and stays idling in front of the entrance. "It was just a stupid hammock, Lily. It was before I met you. We were drinking all day and had gone out on a boat, in the sun . . ."

"And the kiss at the milli party? I don't want to be played, Joel. Or pitted against my cousin. I'm not into games."

Lily steps out of the Targa. Joel's right after her, tossing his keys to the valet. He follows Lily into the Beverly Hilton.

"She kissed *me*," Joel says as he chases after her through the lobby. "She did it on purpose to get it on camera."

Lily spins around to face him.

"I just don't know what's real and what isn't anymore. I'm scared this *isn't* real. That it's just some storyline. And I don't know who's writing it!"

"But I'm telling you, this isn't scripted," Joel says. "No one's writing anything."

"Are you sure?" Lily asks. "Sometimes I think *I'm* the one writing it. Seeing you and Hailey kiss in the trailer reminded me of what it's like being a viewer of the show. I knew Hailey wanted you. But it didn't stop me from giving myself a starring part in your life."

"Life is not a reality show," Joel says. "The whole reason why I liked you in the first place is because you reminded me of that."

He takes a step closer to her.

"If you did write yourself in, I'm glad, because the cast list was seriously starting to bum me out before you showed up."

Joel sees a *Platinum Triangle* camera on them from across the lobby. He forgot the show is filming tonight.

"Last shoot of season 2," Lily says, noticing the camera at the same time.

"So what's your Hollywood ending?" Joel asks.

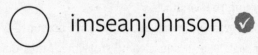

imseanjohnson ✓

1.5m followers

nadia.meyers Tell your dad I said hi

daneryspaul7679 Gay

buffy_dj ICON

lameier1998 Cool

jacquimclenne King

saaashha reciprocate all that energy 👏

yeshidab AHHHHHHHHH 🌟 🌟

Sean puts on a dress. He's backstage in the ballroom at the Beverly Hilton. Fortune is styling him with clothes donated to Hailey's Dress for Success fashion show by @dollskill. Fortune is featured on their website as one of their "dolls."

Fortune chooses this weird parachute-like dress for Sean to wear and puts him in the kind of platform boots that Fortune wears all the time. Sean checks himself out in one of the mirrors where models are getting their hair and makeup done. Fortune texted Sean to come early so he could dye Sean's shaved hair pink.

"Is this me?" Sean asks, looking at himself in the mirror. Sean's always wearing baggy shirts and sneakers, sometimes a chain. He's never worn what he wants to wear.

"It could be," Fortune says, taking a photo of them in the reflection.

It makes Sean nervous, thinking about walking down the runway in front of everyone. *Platinum Triangle* is filming.

What if he just ended the season as a completely different person?

paleyhailey ✓

1m followers

tellme.what.u.think I hate jailey @paleyhailey I'm a Jily fan.

saraneg8 مصمم امريا عليك

roben_damie Nose surgery gone wrong

britt_scholte_zayn_fan_x Hailey have you ever thought of modeling you are so pretty and i think the fashion show fundraiser could be the start of something really big for you you are so pretty

yunhiekim Photoshop queen

A runway has been erected down the middle of the ballroom at the Beverly Hilton and there's a curtained-off backstage area where the models are getting ready. Volunteers are running around with garment bags. A *Platinum Triangle* crew is filming.

Hailey's going to make sure that Lily Rhode's runway debut is one no one will ever forget!

"Greta's not here," Hailey says. "And neither is Valeria."

"Remember she said she had an audition," Bea says. She's sitting in a chair backstage getting her hair and makeup done.

"Why doesn't she just go whore herself to sheikhs in Dubai like a respectable former Disney star?" Hailey asks. "Her entitlement is really sad. Like, no one gives a shit. Sorry!"

Bea laughs as Hailey checks her phone to see if there's a text from Valeria, but there's nothing. Nothing from Joel or Lily either, but Sam promised she'll let Hailey know as soon as Lily arrives. Sam and Hailey are working with Bea to take Lily down tonight . . . and it's almost showtime! If Lily wants to be a TV star, it's time she learns the price of fame.

"Don't forget your accessory," Hailey tells Bea, passing her a large aquamarine cocktail ring with jagged edges.

Bea slides it on her finger and holds it up.

"Stunning," she says, winking at Hailey through the mirror.

Hailey's phone pings with a new DM.

princepaley You are the absolute best Hailey, there will never be another legend or anyone else more amazing than you, you are the most natural super star that keeps shining perfectly like pure gold that glitters!

She's killing it. Hailey just needs to remember that. She clicks on @princepaley's handle to scroll through his photos and fan art of her. It's a good ego boost before hitting the runway!

Hailey clicks on a recent photo. It's a candid of her at the campground. She's coming out of the public bathroom (she is *never* going camping again!) after purging all the junk food she ate. Hailey doesn't remember anyone taking her photo. Was there someone hiding in the bushes?

"Where did this photo come from?" Hailey flashes her screen at Bea, who gives her a shrug from the makeup chair.

"So creepy," Hailey says.

It's not the first time she's been photographed without realizing it. During her father's most scandalous moments there were paparazzi hiding in the bushes and ducking low in cars, with their camera lenses sticking out the window. But why would there be paparazzi all the way in Ventura County?

@princepaley's profile photo is from Hailey's *Paper* magazine shoot. "I stan @paleyhailey!!!" is all the bio says. Before she can give it much more thought, she sees Joel and Lily entering backstage together, and she lowers her phone.

"Got my car tuned up for the race," Joel tells Bea as he and Lily approach. "Brando ready to pick a date or is he still stalling?"

"Brandon's going to leave you in the dust," Bea says. "He's a motherfucking Cadogan."

Hailey passes Lily a garment bag. "Let's get you in this," she says. "Then straight into hair and makeup! Make sure Fortune looks you over before you dare step on the runway. He's my eyes."

Hailey starts tugging on Joel's shirt, lifting it up and flashing his abs.

"And let's take this off of you, mister."

She pulls the shirt over his head as Lily heads to get changed.

"Oh, and Lily," Hailey calls over her shoulder. Lily stops and looks back. "No bra. We can't have straps showing."

Lily's cheeks turn slightly red but she doesn't put up any resistance. Hailey smiles at the back of Lily's head as she walks off.

"*These* are for you, Joel!" Hailey passes Joel the swim trunks he'll be modeling. It's not an episode of *Platinum Triangle* without a scene where Joel's shirtless. "You're staying for the after party, right?"

"Maybe." Joel scratches his bare chest. "I'll see how Lily feels."

Joel walks off. Bea purposely avoids looking at Hailey as she recovers from the snub. They're interrupted by Valeria, who comes bustling backstage just then, out of breath.

"Sorry I'm late," she says. "I had an aud—"

"Why don't you just wait for the phone not to ring and save yourself the trouble?" Hailey cuts her off. "Quick! Get into this Alexis." Hailey thrusts a garment bag at Valeria. "The show's about to start!"

"Those Cartier earrings are gorgeous!" Bea exclaims to Valeria, spinning around in her makeup chair.

Hailey drops her phone. She bends over to pick it up and as she stands back up, she moves Valeria's hair to get a better look at the Panthère de Cartier earrings.

"Are they on loan?" she asks.

"Fakes," Valeria says quickly.

lillianrhode

60.5k followers

Lily is nervous right before she steps onto the runway. The ballroom is full; all of Whitney's rich Beverly Hills friends are in the audience lending their support to Dress for Success. Not to mention the *Platinum Triangle* cameras filming it. The Nicholas The Label dress she's wearing is pink chiffon. It's beautiful, with a long train that flows as she walks. It has string straps and feels like it could slip right off her.

She hears the screaming of girls in the audience when Fortune ushers Joel onto the runway. Fortune is running the show and seems to enjoy treating them all like cattle. Joel is modeling swim trunks, his bare pecs glistening under the runway lights. Lily peeks around the curtain to watch as Joel poses at the end of the runway. Fortune gives Bea a nod and she starts walking next as Joel turns to walk back. Bea walks with such confidence.

"Knock 'em dead," Joel tells Lily as he steps off the runway backstage. Fortune grabs Lily's arm and sends her down the runway with a little push before Lily can even gather her breath.

Lily can't see the audience; the lights in her eyes cast them all in shadow. She loves the power the anonymity gives her, like she can ride the wave of shadows and exist as high as they're willing to hold her up.

Bea poses with one hand on her hip at the end of the runway and then turns around, the train of her dress lifting in the air behind her. As Bea turns around, Lily takes her first step. She tries to stand as tall as Bea. Bea is smiling at her and reaches out for Lily's hand as they pass each other at the middle of the runway. Lily takes Bea's hand and flashes her a smile. It's so surreal. Like being in the Victoria's Secret fashion show or something. Lily's so caught up in the moment, she doesn't even realize what's happening. At a certain point she registers the gasps from the audience.

Lily's dress rips open down the front and her bare breasts are exposed. Bea's ring got stuck in the chiffon, and when she tried to pull her hand away, the dress tore. Lily is left standing topless in the middle of the runway, cameras flashing around her. She doesn't know what to do. The lights are shining right in her eyes and Lily winces.

Bea turns and keeps walking down the runway like a pro. The show must go on. Lily looks toward the shadowy audience. They're not holding her up anymore. She's hanging suspended in the air and they're all waiting to see if she'll fall flat on her face.

Lily manages to hold the dress up and cover herself. She walks the rest of the way down the runway cautiously but also fiercely. The audience applauds when she reaches the end and poses, smiling as the applause grows louder.

Backstage, Lily still clings to her dress.

"Sorry, sis," Fortune says. "But at least now everyone knows you don't have implants."

"Oh my God, Lily!" Bea comes rushing over. "Are you okay? I'm so sorry, my ring! It got caught and—"

"It's okay," Lily says. "Not your fault. Just an accident." She swallows, determined to hold back her tears. Lily has never felt this humiliated. It's even worse than when she was the joke of Brandon's party.

"You didn't miss a beat," Joel says when Bea gets shuffled off by Fortune to change into her next look.

"I can't believe that just happened." Lily cringes. "Did everyone see?" She stops herself from asking what she fears the most—was it caught on camera? Will it be on the show? Will Lily make her arrival in the Platinum Triangle with a mugshot *and* a topless scene? Lily feels her eyes tear up and she can't bring herself to look at Joel.

"Hey," Joel says, gently lifting her chin. "I was watching on the monitor. You recovered faster than Bea, and she does this for real. No one saw anything."

Lily isn't convinced. Joel hugs her.

"What would you say about driving up to Malibu with me sometime?" he asks. "I want to introduce you to my dad."

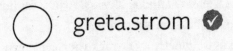

greta.strom ✓

728k followers

ernandares.ro__ Maybe there are no aliens because we are the aliens. We just don't know how to trigger our powers yet, or we forgot. Who knows what's life and what happens after death. Every thing, is nothing

"Rosé all day! Rosé all day!" Greta chants. She didn't make it to Hailey's fashion show but she made it to the after party in a suite at the hotel.

Greta showed up drunk to the Beverly Hilton after sneaking out of her house. She didn't steal a car this time. She was a good girl and took an Uber. Her mom has had her pretty much on lockdown since she finally came home after disappearing for a few days. She hasn't told anyone the things she's seen. Maybe Greta will write a book one day.

Valeria comes up to her and asks her where her car is. Greta vaguely remembers the BMW running out of gas and abandoning it somewhere in Silver Lake. But she might've set it on fire. Valeria is angry at her for driving off with it and keeps trying to get Greta to tell her its location but Greta can't remember.

"Did you check your pool?" She laughs.

"You know what, Greta?" Valeria snaps. "Fuck you!"

Greta's never seen Valeria so angry. It sobers Greta up and makes her feel instantly guilty. Valeria gets self-conscious when people look over. At least *Platinum Triangle* isn't filming. Cameras weren't allowed into the after party.

"I'm sorry," Greta says quietly. "I'll track your car down, I promise."

"You just don't understand," Valeria says. She gets flustered and storms off, leaving Greta standing alone in the middle of the party with all eyes on her.

"What are you looking at?" Greta asks the crowd. "Are my boobs hanging out or something?" She stumbles off to the suite's bedroom to do some coke.

Greta closes the door and walks over to the bed. She sits on the edge and pulls out a bag from her Louis Vuitton Da Vinci Montaigne purse. She cuts a huge line on the nightstand using her credit card, and snorts it with a rolled-up bill. Greta feels like she enters the Jeff Koons artwork on her handbag. She feels as enigmatic as the Mona Lisa.

The bedroom door opens and light and music from the party spill inside. Greta forgot to lock it.

"Well, well, well," Greta says, rubbing her nose. "Look who it is. The new train wreck of the Platinum Triangle."

Greta holds out the rolled bill for Lily.

"I don't want your drugs," Lily says, closing the door behind her. "I followed you in here to see if you're all right. You may be trying to play it off as a big joke, but I know how it feels to be the center of attention for all the wrong reasons."

"This is my second season," Greta says, dropping the bill into her handbag. "I don't feel anything."

She looks across the room at Lily, narrowing her eyes.

"I saw a video on Instagram of your little wardrobe malfunction," Greta says. "It was interesting the way the dress tore. I mean, you'd think that Bea, who, like, slayed Paris Fashion Week not that long ago without any problem, would be able to handle an amateur charity fashion show."

"What are you saying? You think she tried to rip my dress on purpose?"

"I think it was already partially ripped. And that Bea is one of those models who will probably try to be an actress one day and it will be really funny because she can't act. Like, at all. When she's being such a dumb slut on the show? That's real. And that look on her face when your dress ripped . . ." Greta laughs. She pulls the rolled bill back out of her purse. She always wants more. "It was like she knew that if she stepped on the train, it would tear right off of you," Greta says, cutting another line and snorting it. "It was a fake-surprised look, you know?" Greta does her best imitation. She does a few. Gasping and widening her eyes, becoming increasingly dramatic with each take. Lily actually cracks a smile.

"If it was a setup," Lily says, coming over to the bed and sitting, "then I doubt she did it alone."

Greta rubs some coke along her gums.

"I overheard Joel talking to Sam before production left the hotel," she says. "It was heated. They were in the lobby and Joel was saying how the footage of your dress ripping on the runway can't make the air. He threatened to quit the show if it does." Greta smiles at Lily. "He's obsessed."

Lily blushes.

"He'd do the same for you," she says. But Greta has to look away.

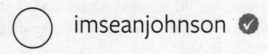

imseanjohnson ✓

1.5m followers

tala_rokdi_ I love how unique you are more like this please!!!

dlewaa @tala_rokdi_ if being unique means looking like a complete idiot or means losing your mind in the near future then fuck veing unique.but ur a fucking fanpage so there s nothing for u to understand

tala_rokdi_ @dlewaa that's my Main lmao being unique means being urself that's all First off if u really think he's losing his mind by putting grillz on or dying his hair pink or wearing dresses ur absolutely wrong. There are people that look like fkn business-men but are fuck heads it's not about looks it's about actions

Sean and Valeria come down from his room to grab some breakfast. Valeria slept over after the fashion show. Sean knows she's waiting to hear back about her audition and she doesn't want to be home because it's too much pressure—the anticipation, the fear of being rejected.

As Sean and Valeria reach the bottom of the stairs, Christoph calls out to them from the game room, where he and his squad are hanging out.

The guys are all staring at Valeria. There's a part of Sean that wants to tear their eyes out for objectifying her, but he's also grateful that they want her—that they respect Sean for having her as his girlfriend. Valeria is his shield, she's a living *Platinum Triangle* billboard that Sean can hide behind.

Sean's dad would be merciless if Valeria weren't over, if they weren't dating. He'd be aggressive, possibly violent. He'd tear the dress off him, even though Sean isn't wearing it now. Christoph would tear off his soul.

It's back to the oversize tee-shirts and the chains, like the collars for the dogs in the cages downstairs, which Valeria doesn't know about, which no one knows about except Joel because Sean broke down and cried about it to him once when they were skating at Venice Beach Skate Park and he thought he was going crazy because all he could hear was the savage barking.

There's a fight coming up. Sean wants to ask Valeria if he can spend the night at her house but his dad won't let him miss it.

"What the fuck, bro?" Christoph laughs, showing off the photos of Sean modeling the dress. "What were you smoking before you let them put you in this shit?" he asks.

Sean had so much anxiety when he posted the photos of him on the runway—he didn't know how people were going to react—but he knew how his dad was going to react and that's why he invited Valeria over.

"You like your boy in a dress?" Christoph asks Valeria.

Some of Sean's dad's squad stop playing at the pool table and look over at Valeria.

"I styled him," Valeria lies flawlessly. "Sean wasn't into it but I thought it was cool."

Sean looks up and meets Valeria's eyes, trying to convey his gratitude while keeping his face expressionless. He doesn't want to show his dad what he's hiding.

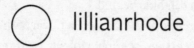

lillianrhode

69k followers

funhazy.blur Couple anthem @lillianrhode @thejoelstrom

masterkelly37 U and Joel make me believe in love! @lillianrhode @thejoelstrom

rsister11 Lily and Joel are my favorite couple I cannot WAIT to see them togetherr on the show! 🖤 💯 🖤 💯

The Paley family dinner Lily was hoping for never happens. Lily even gets Ana to pick up the ingredients she'll need to make her risotto on a night when she thinks she can get everyone in the same room long enough to enjoy a meal. But then Patrick calls from set and says that the shoot is running late, and Hailey say she's meeting Fortune and takes the opportunity to get out of Dodge. It's Whitney and Lily alone for dinner, but Whitney only wants Ana to whip her up a celery juice. Lily goes to bed hungry. She's lost five pounds at least since she started staying at the Paleys'.

Things may still feel forced with the Paleys, but they go back to being chill with Joel in the days after the fashion show. Lily and Joel hang out on the beach, and Lily's with him for an outdoor movie night at Hollywood Forever Cemetery when Sean texts in the middle of *Lolita* that Brandon's ready to set a date for the drag race. They agree on the end of the week.

"Why don't we go for dinner with my dad first?" Joel asks. "I'll need a distraction before the race."

Lily's glad she can help Joel escape the same way he helps her. When Lily's with Joel, she isn't thinking of the wardrobe malfunction at the Dress for Success fashion show, even though the comments are endless. When she's with Joel, Lily doesn't care.

On the night they're planning on driving up to Jessica's beach house, Lily can't help but let it slip to Hailey that she's going to Malibu with Joel. After the fashion show fiasco, the gloves are off. Lily doesn't trust Hailey. And she's done trying to be allies. If Hailey wants a nemesis, then she has one.

Jessica's Malibu house is amazing. It's obviously her dream bachelorette pad. It was just barely spared by the Woolsey fire and sits perched on a hill overlooking the ocean. Jessica has carved out this space in the world just for her. Every room has a crystal chandelier—"earrings for a room," Jessica says as she gives Lily the grand tour.

The house is decorated in shades of pink and light grays. In the foyer is a Roy Lichtenstein painting: furrowed pop art eyebrows over a set of intense eyes with a speech bubble that says, "What? Why did you ask that? What do you know about my image duplicator?"

As they sit at the dining table and eat dinner, Lily thinks how Jessica is happier and lighter than Lucas ever seemed on the show. He was always so quiet and irritable. Lucas and Greta were especially close, but he and Kathy clearly had marital problems long before the secret was out.

"You two just look so cute over there. Excuse me while I take a photo." Jessica lifts her phone and takes a shot of Lily and Joel sitting next to each other behind the candelabra. Joel's arm is around the back of Lily's chair and Lily is laughing as Jessica tells them a story about how she was locked out of the facial recognition on her phone after she had her face contoured.

"God, I was so happy," she says. "I'll send you the photo." Jessica winks. "For posterity."

"I'm stuffed," Joel says, jumping up and clearing the table. Lily can tell he's embarrassed. "That was delicious, Dad."

"My pleasure. You'll have to come over more often. And bring your sister!"

"Yeah," Joel says evasively over his shoulder as he takes dishes to the kitchen. "Soon, I hope."

Jessica sips her wine.

"So, Lily," she says, switching gears, "what do you say I show you embarrassing childhood photos of this son of mine?"

"Oh my God, yes, please!" Lily laughs.

"Please don't." Joel gives Jessica a warning look as he comes back to the table.

"Don't worry, darling, I won't totally humiliate you. Like, say, by telling Lily about your early dream of being a boy bander . . ."

Lily laughs again. "A *what*?"

"There were five of them. They performed at my fiftieth birthday party. They had choreography and everything. Wade Robson helped them with their routine."

"Who?"

"Michael Jackson's, er, protégé," Jessica says.

"He's a choreographer," Joel explains. He's blushing.

"What was the name of the band?" Lily asks.

"Don't you dare!" Joel juggles the salt and pepper shakers.

Jessica blurts it out. "LOML!" And she throws her head back with laughter.

"I think I'll go in the kitchen and wash the dishes by hand now," Joel says.

"Love of my life?" Lily giggles. "It's cute!"

"If by *cute* you mean mortifying, then, yeah, let's go with that."

"You're having quite the effect on him." Jessica smiles at Lily. "I've never seen him clear a table in his life."

"I cook, Greta cleans," Joel says. "In theory. She doesn't come down for dinner most nights."

"Since when do you cook?" Jessica asks.

Joel goes quiet. Lily's quick to fill the silence.

"I *need* to know more," she says to Jessica. "Did they record anything?"

"Like an EP? Yes, darling. Joel's mother was very invested. She thought her son was destined to be a star."

"Please tell me there's a music video out there somewhere?"

"Almost! Kathy wanted to go all in. But then Joel realized he liked surfing better than learning choreography."

"And that he can't sing," Joel adds. "Or dance. Like, at all."

Jessica gets up to help Joel put away the food in the kitchen. "Do you still remember some of your old moves?" she asks.

Lily offers to help but Jessica insists she sit and relax. Jessica plays a LOML demo while Lily takes a sip of her wine and leans back, smiling to herself. This is just like the family dinner she wanted to have with the Paleys. She makes a Story for Instagram.

Just then, Joel's phone lights up on the table. It's an incoming call from Hailey. Of course it is. Lily stares at the screen. No way is she letting Hailey ruin this moment.

Lily leans forward and double-taps the power button to make the call go away. Her heart starts racing but it's such a satisfying feeling seeing Hailey's name disappear from the screen. She leans back in her chair just as Joel returns to the dining room.

"I totally would've thrown my panties at you on stage," she says.

They hear Jessica cackling from the kitchen. "I like her!"

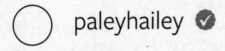

paleyhailey ✓

1m followers

paleyhailey followed @christaber02

"Come on, Joel, pick up."

Hailey is on her phone at Poppy, a nightclub in West Hollywood. She's out with Greta and Sean and Valeria. Straight to voicemail. Hailey hangs up. She can't get over Joel taking Lily to Malibu to meet Jessica. That's sacred ground, and Lily knows it. Lily posted a Story of Jessica playing a song off her phone and Joel burying his face in his hands. Hailey recognizes the song in the video. She knows all the lyrics. LOML were truly the love of her life in junior high.

During the camping trip Hailey thought she was getting somewhere with Joel. When he hugged her . . . it felt like she wasn't going to need Fortune's or Idris's help. Like she could get Joel all on her own.

Hailey regrets setting up the wardrobe malfunction. While it obviously humiliated Lily, it also appears to have brought Lily and Joel closer together. Hailey should've known Joel would feel protective. He probably finds it endearing, considering his sister's public antics.

Speaking of skid row . . . at the wood-paneled bar, Hailey orders a double vodka and writes Joel a text telling him to call her right away. Greta's wasted.

Hailey looks around the club. Where'd Greta go now? Hailey needs her to stay put and hopefully become increasingly messy until Joel shows up! But Hailey does not want to have to chase her around all night. Babysitting Greta in West Hollywood is so eighth grade.

Sean and Valeria are sitting alone in the booth, under whimsical lanterns. Poppy throbs around them in gold and amber. Hailey goes up to the booth and asks where Greta disappeared to.

"You were on the phone," Valeria says. "Idris showed up and gave Greta something. A letter, I think."

"She ripped it up and stormed off to the bathroom," Sean adds.

"Need any help with her?" Valeria asks.

Looks like Saint Valeria Leon is back. Her car was finally found and it's in one piece. She and Greta hugged it out earlier. Not that Greta seemed emotionally invested. Hailey's noticed Greta's been grinding her teeth and chain-smoking all night.

"Thanks, babe. I've got this." Hailey smiles at Valeria, suppressing tremors of rage as she heads in the direction of the bathroom. Her mother is devastated that her dad didn't give her the Cartier earrings for their anniversary. Valeria having the exact same pair can't be a coincidence . . . that whore! Hailey never shows her hand. But Valeria is *dead*.

So many lives to ruin, so little time.

"Greta?"

When Hailey pushes open the bathroom door, she finds Greta on the floor, her head slumped forward. Oh, this is awesome. Hailey steps over Greta's legs with two clicks of her Dries Van Noten snake-embossed leather pumps. What a fucking victim. She bends down and checks for a pulse. It's faint.

Hailey reapplies her 999 lipstick by Dior in front of the mirror. 911 or Joel? It's a real emergency.

drewisplastic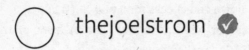

little.kaelly I'm so scared right now I literally can't type.
@thejoelstrom be safe!!!

julia_lachowski Jily! 😍😍😍 @thejoelstrom @lillianrhode

_viki__xo You got this bro !! @brandocadogan @thejoelstrom

When Joel posts the photo that Jessica took of them to his Instagram, it's his way of telling the world that he and Lily are official.

"It means a lot to me that you came out with me tonight," he tells Lily on the drive back to the city.

"Your dad is the coolest person ever," Lily says. "I'll never forget tonight. It was the perfect distraction. I didn't think of my court case all night. It's just a week away."

"I'll be there," Joel says, reaching over and taking Lily's hand. He smiles. "In case you need a getaway car. Once I leave Brandon in the dust, that is." Joel pulls away his hand to reach for his phone in the pocket of his Fendi varsity jacket. He checks to see if Sean has sent him the location of tonight's race.

"I wish you wouldn't go through with this," Lily says. "Brandon isn't worth it."

Joel isn't scared. He's looking forward to the thrill. When he's driving fast enough, it's like he's lifting out of his body.

"A declined call from Hailey." Joel checks his phone as he drives. "I didn't ignore a call." He opens his messages. "She sent a text, too. Something about Greta . . ."

Lily stares out at the coastline as the highway weaves.

"Everything okay?" she asks.

"She says it's an emergency. It's about Greta—Hailey called the paramedics."

"What?" Lily looks back at him. "Joel, I should've told you earlier—after dinner, while you and Jessica were in the kitchen, I saw on your phone that it was Hailey and I ignored the call. I thought she was up to something and—"

Before Joel can call Hailey back, his phone starts ringing in his hand. It's his mom.

"Joel," she says as soon as he's answered. "Greta's in the hospital!"

Joel tries not to run as he and Lily arrive at Cedars-Sinai. He's trying to stay inside of himself. Hailey is in the waiting room. She jumps up from her seat and tells them that Kathy is with Greta now.

"Where were you?" Hailey asks. "I tried calling but it went straight to voicemail."

Joel looks over at Lily. Her eyes drop to the linoleum floor.

"What happened?" Joel can't control the panic in his voice. "Is Greta all right?"

"She's going to be fine. I found her slumped over in the bathroom at Poppy and couldn't wake her. She was acting crazy again all night. I was so scared that what happened at the campsite was going to happen again." She touches Joel's arm. "I called 911 as soon as I found her. The doctors say she's dehydrated."

Joel falls into a waiting room chair. Hailey sits next to him.

"Why didn't you answer when I called?" she asks.

A ping comes into Joel's phone. Sean texts that he was at Poppy and saw what happened with Greta; he's going to tell Brandon the race is canceled. Joel stares down at his phone without really seeing it. He stands up and starts backing down the hallway.

"Where are you going?" He isn't sure if it's Hailey or Lily asking; they're both staring at him.

It doesn't matter.

Joel takes the stairs and runs out of the hospital, jumps into his car.

Don't cancel, Joel texts Sean back. *Location?*

The siren blue of Joel's Porsche Targa and empty cans of Modelo and Corona bottles on the street, the smell of marijuana hanging in the air as a crowd stands outside their cars to watch the race. A slow-burning end of a cigarette. They're in an industrial area of the San Fernando Valley. Joel is in the driver's seat, staring straight ahead.

The races bring out a diverse crowd, super-rich kids with high bets and white-trash smoking blunts and listening to rap music from the stereos in their Dodge Neons.

Joel's trying not to think about Lily, or about Hailey, or Greta, or anyone. He's trying not to think. But why did Lily have to mess with his phone? That's a Hailey play.

If he'd got Hailey's call sooner, maybe he could've got to Greta before she OD'd. He could've stopped it.

Joel opens Instagram and looks down at the photo he posted of him and Lily. It's blowing up with Likes.

Headlights shine in Joel's rearview mirror and he hears a car engine rev. Brandon pulls up beside him in a Hennessey Venom GT. A chrome-wrapped car for a chrome-wrapped heart. Brandon opens the passenger window and looks over at Joel with a cocky smirk.

"You ready for this, pretty boy?"

"Just because you have the car," Joel says, "doesn't mean you know how to drive it."

Joel is going to win this for his sister.

He deletes the photo of him and Lily from his account and tosses his phone on the passenger seat.

Through his rearview mirror Joel sees Hailey's Mercedes pull up, and Hailey and Lily step out together. He looks away. In his peripheral vision he can see Bea run up to Brandon and give him a kiss through his open window.

Sean comes up to Joel's window.

"You sure you wanna do this?" he asks. Sean looks worried.

Joel nods at him and stares straight ahead.

"All right," Sean says. "You got this, bro." He taps the top of Joel's Targa and joins the crowd.

Ready, set . . .

Joel cancels out the sound of the crowd and blaring rap music. He syncs his mind. Fortune runs over from the crowd to wave the flag, standing between the two cars, wearing an oversize Balenciaga sweater. The crowd starts roaring and Fortune waves the flag. Instinct takes over Joel's body.

Go.

The Hennessey is the fastest-accelerating car in the world. Brandon gets in front of Joel right away. But Joel is a smarter driver. Brandon is anarchistic, tearing up the road. Joel's little Porsche sneaks up on him but Brandon doesn't let him get past. Just as Joel is inching ahead, Brandon jerks the wheel of the Hennessey and taps the side of the Targa. Just a tap. And then another. Joel tries to keep control of the wheel. Brandon's out of his mind.

It happens both fast and in slow motion. Brandon taps Joel's car again just as they're approaching a bend in the road. It rocks the Targa so hard that Joel loses control of the wheel. He feels his wheels lift off into the air, still spinning so fast it's like his Porsche has antigravity properties. Like he's going to fly up into the sky and never come back.

Joel's phone lifts in the air. It hangs suspended, and there's this single moment when everything is paused and clear.

Then the screen cracks and Joel is hanging upside down. Through the shattered window he can see the crowd in the distance holding up their phones. His eyes close. Smash to black.

lillianrhode

72k followers

bk40041 Duck quack quack quack quack quack quack quack quack quack quack quack quack quack quack quack quack

wave_a_flave You always was obsessed with Joel chasing him even when he was with Hailey, you still pay dearly for dating Joel for interest, everything that starts badly ends badly, I do not need to be a fortune-teller to know that This relationship is a farce, a business, you date him for his millionaire heritage and to forget the former I do not continue to try to conquer Hailey's place in the hearts of Joel's fans because you're never going to be like Hailey Paley… 😣😠😣

yeshii99 You're body is fine 🔥 but can't deny your face kinda look like a man!

katee.erin Joel can do so much better now fall off into obscurity and die

auckland5 Why'd Jole delete the photo of you ? @lillianrhode @thejoelstrom

jenegreen358 You look OLD af!!! You're going to age young and not good. Then your future husband (not joel 😂😂😂) will find a new and younger wife. They always do, so dont get mad at me!

t's the worst moment of her life when Joel's car flips. Lily has never been so terrified or felt so helpless. She and Hailey

231

speed after the ambulance in Hailey's Mercedes. But when they get to the hospital, they're turned away for not being family.

"You don't understand," Lily tries to plead with the nurse. "It's . . ."

She can't bring herself to say it, but she can tell by the way Hailey is looking at her that she's thinking it, too.

It's all Lily's fault.

If she hadn't ignored Hailey's call, then Joel would've found out about Greta sooner and he wouldn't have been so angry before he raced. Lily made it so much worse. Joel was too agitated and worried about his sister to race.

Hailey is silent most of the drive home. They're both in shock. Lily checks Instagram for any updates. She can't keep track of all the notifications. The photo Joel posted of them at dinner got his fangirls riled up; they've been sending her death threats all night. There are also countless references of the drag race crash. There are videos and photos. It's in the press.

"I'm scared," Lily says. She fights back tears.

"Don't say that," Hailey says. "There's nothing to be scared of. Joel's going to be fine. He was conscious when they put him in the ambulance." Hailey takes a deep breath. "He's going to be fine. He has to be."

Through her tears, Lily reaches over and takes Hailey's hand. Hailey actually gives Lily's hand a squeeze. In their shared worry over Joel, they've been brought together. Or at least that's how it feels, for a fleeting moment.

"Because if anything happens to Joel," Hailey says, pulling her hand away, "it's on you."

When they get home, Hailey follows Lily into the pool house.

"I just can't believe you hid that I called Joel from him,"

Hailey says, slamming the door behind them. "He deserved to know that Greta needed help!"

"Don't you think I know that?" Lily spins around to face Hailey. But she doesn't have the energy for a fight. On the drive to the drag race, Lily admitted to Hailey that she ignored Hailey's call. It was so obvious why Joel was upset, and Hailey wouldn't stop pushing until Lily told her what had happened.

"You're lucky Greta's going to be all right!" Hailey says. She won't drop it. Lily snaps.

"If you were so concerned about Greta, then why didn't you call her mom? Why didn't you get someone from the bar to help? Why did you keep partying with her? Why were you enabling her? Is it because you wanted her to OD so that you could call Joel? You knew that we were in Malibu and you wanted to ruin it!"

"Are you out of your mind? The world doesn't revolve around *you*, Lily. Tonight was about me and my best friend and her brother. In case you haven't realized, we have a whole history that doesn't involve you."

"What is that supposed to mean?"

"You don't belong here. The longer you try to exist in this world the more harm you'll cause! Greta's going to be okay, but if anything happens to Joel . . ."

Lily shakes her head. "You're never going to accept me, are you?" She looks searchingly in Hailey's eyes. "I hoped that this rivalry wouldn't last forever. That the Hailey on-screen and the Hailey in real life would meet and I'd get a whole human being. But that's never going to happen, is it? To you I'll always just be a piece of trash from the Valley."

"Do you know *why* I hate you?" Hailey asks. "It's not just because you're tacky, or even because of Joel. It's because you've acted so innocent all this time. Like you didn't know there was something between me and Joel? Like you didn't purposely go after him?"

"I didn't *go after* Joel. And he didn't go after me. We just . . . happened."

"Yes, Lily. I know. Things just *happen* to you. You're just, like, fated. Right? That's how you ended up living my life." Hailey glares at her for a second and then goes on. "The real difference between us isn't just economics. It's that I know who I am. You talk about on-screen Hailey versus off-screen Hailey like I'm not consciously uncoupled. I'm a two-faced bitch, Lily. I like it that way! But you? You're not even aware of your own duality. You think you're simply good. And those are the worst kind of bad people."

As soon as she regains consciousness and learns that Joel's been in an accident, Greta insists on seeing him. When the nurse won't let her, she rips the IV out of her own arm. They're giving her fluids because she's dehydrated, which is what made her overdose. There's a sick video making the rounds of her foaming from the mouth.

Joel's in bed with his arm in a cast when Greta enters his room. His eyes are closed, and even though Greta tries to shut the door softly, it still wakes him up. He looks directly at her, pressed against the door, mascara running down her cheeks and her head pounding. She's not dead yet.

Joel smiles. Greta can't meet his eyes. She's so ashamed. Joel knows her better than anyone. He knows her better than she knows herself.

"Joel . . ." She doesn't finish.

"No big deal," Joel says. "Just a few cuts and scrapes. They're keeping me here for observation to make sure I don't have a concussion. My Porsche got the brunt of the damage. Poor baby."

Greta bursts into tears. She can't control it. She sits next to the hospital bed and buries her face in Joel's chest.

Joel puts an arm around her back. "I didn't realize you cared," he says softly.

Greta was born two minutes after Joel. But it might as well have been two years judging by how protective he's always been of her. And sometimes two lifetimes, by how distant they can be. Greta knows that no boy has ever loved her as much as her brother.

When she was nine years old and anorexic, she refused to take off her coat in class and her teacher started yelling and threatening to send her to the office. All the kids in the class chimed in. "Just take off your coat already!" Greta started crying. It wasn't that it was a new Burberry. They didn't understand. She *needed* her coat. She hated herself less when she was wrapped in her coat. The teacher told her to go to the office, and when Greta stormed out, Joel leaped from his desk and followed after her, even when the teacher called him back. The next day he refused to take off his own coat. And Joel was the most popular kid in class. Suddenly, everyone was wearing their coats in class. It became a trend for the rest of winter and the teacher was just, like, FML.

When the first season of *Platinum Triangle* aired and Greta was insecure because Hailey, Bea, and Valeria got so many more followers than her, it was Joel who took her phone out of her hand and said they're more popular only because they're not as honest. That it's easy to get followers when you're willing to manipulate them into believing an idea of who you are. When you're selling them what they want.

And when Joel caught on that Hailey wasn't a true friend to Greta, he stopped crushing on her like he had been since they were kids.

Greta lifts her head from Joel's chest. He wipes a smudge of mascara off her cheek and looks down at his black thumb.

"How are you doing?" he asks. "I tried to see you before the race."

Greta gives a little laugh. "Both Strom kids in the hospital *and* disasters behind the wheel." She makes Joel smile. "Twinning."

She puts her head back down on his chest. "Thank you for defending me against Brandon and Idris. I was too embarrassed to say it before. But you wouldn't be here if it weren't for me."

"I want you to go to rehab, Greta. Please?"

Before Greta can answer, they're interrupted by voices outside the door.

"Which room is he in?" Jessica asks. "This one?"

Greta lifts her head.

"He's resting," Kathy says.

"You are not stopping me from seeing my son!"

Greta stands up so fast she almost knocks the chair back. Jessica and Kathy burst into the room. They just stare when they see Greta with Joel. The room goes quiet and it's like everyone's holding their breath, until Joel says from his hospital bed, "Looks like the gang's back together."

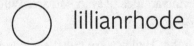

lillianrhode

75k followers

jaden_199969 Hailey wannabe

jaden_199969 U wish u were Hailey

jaden_199969 U just wanted Joel bc of his name not him

jaden_199969 U even use Hailey quotes

jaden_199969 Duck

jaden_199969 Ur racist too

jaden_199969 No one likes u

Lily puts a few celery sticks in the Breville blender on the kitchen counter in the Paleys' main house. Ana is watching from the other side of the island like she's sure Lily's going to cause an explosion.

It's not Lily's usual breakfast, but she just wants to take something to go this morning so she can head straight to the hospital and see Joel. She wants to talk to him before he's released. She has to explain why she ignored Hailey's call last night.

Lily likes the sound of the blaring blender. It feels like she's letting out what's inside of her. She's especially agitated because, for some reason, Sam wants "Real Home" footage of Lily this morning. Sam didn't give her a shooting schedule. She just showed up.

"I thought the fashion show was the end of filming?" Lily asks.

"We want to check in with you," Sam says, "see how you're doing after . . ." Sam waves her hands around her chest.

Lily pours the celery juice into a plastic bottle. "This really isn't a good time, Sam." But *Platinum Triangle* will not be deterred. There's a camera, and Lily has a mic wire dropped down her back while she takes a sip of her juice.

"Seriously," Lily pulls away. "I just called an Uber."

The doorbell rings. Ana goes to answer it and comes back into the kitchen to tell Lily that it's for her.

"A boy," Ana says.

Lily can feel the camera zooming in on her. She glares at Sam. What kind of a setup is this? Lily is so not in the mood! She starts pulling out her mic-pack as she walks down the hall to see who it is. Idris? What would he want? He gave Greta the letter last night, and from what Lily has heard in her Mentions, it did *not* go well.

When she sees who is, in fact, standing in the middle of the Paleys' foyer, Lily stops dead in her tracks. She lets go of her mic-pack in surprise.

"What are *you* doing here?"

Chris picks up a framed family photo of the Paleys from the front table, next to a fresh bouquet of flowers.

"How'd I not know you were related to Hailey Paley?" he asks. "I follow her. Think I have a shot?"

Lily's eyes automatically land on the camera that has followed them into the foyer. Hailey is still sleeping. At least, she hasn't come downstairs yet. Or did she have the same idea as

Lily and go see Joel early? If she is home, the last thing Lily wants is for Hailey to see her with Chis and go running to Joel, making it seem like something it isn't.

"Come with me." Lily grabs Chris by the arm, pulling him past the camera.

"Are we on TV?" Chris asks, almost dropping the frame as he replaces it on the table.

Lily leads him out back to the pool. The camera operator tries to follow them out.

"No way!" Lily gives a warning look to Sam. "You're not shooting this!"

"Okay, okay!" Sam holds up her hands. "We'll back off." Sam motions for the camera to stay inside the house. Lily sees that the camera is still filming them through the glass door and she remembers her mic-pack. But instead of pulling it out, she decides that this is her opportunity to get a recording of Chris admitting that he was behind the break-in.

"Not happy to see me?" Chris asks. "Too much of a big-shot Beverly Hills princess now?"

"Nope," Lily says. "Still just me. The same girl who sees through you."

Lily pulls out her phone from her jeans to check the time.

"Somewhere you need to be?" Chris asks.

Lily just slides her phone back into her pocket.

"Joel Strom?" Chris asks. "I saw the photo he posted, and deleted, last night."

"You don't know anything," Lily says.

"I know that I hope it works out. You've got a good thing going here, babe. The last thing I want to do is mess it up for you."

"What *do* you want? I already told you I'm not interested in a publicity tour."

"Come on; you gotta help me out! I already have a record and I'm not a minor like you. I'll probably end up serving time over that fucking sheep."

"And? It's what you deserve. Time for you to grow up."

"Say it was your idea to do the Malibu house. You *were* the one holding the Lalanne."

"Because you made me! I tried to shove it out the window. You're crazy if you think I'm taking the fall for this."

"You'll get no more than a slap on the wrist." Chris waves her off. "I've been appointed a state attorney, some jerk-off with a hundred other cases. He doesn't give a shit about me! But you have your fancy Beverly Hills lawyer, right? Patrick Paley hooking you up or what? No way you're going to serve time."

"You're a real piece of work, you know that?"

"I'm not going anywhere until you agree to help. You owe me!"

"Owe *you*?"

"It wasn't exactly a *satisfactory* date, you know what I mean?"

"That's it!"

Lily shoves him into the pool.

And *scene*.

paleyhailey ✓

1m followers

paleyhailey Surround yourself with people who allow you to blossom. ✿

She only wishes she could be there to see Lily's face when Chris shows up at the house. But the whole point is to keep Lily distracted while Hailey sneaks away to visit Joel at Cedars. And of course to make Joel think Lily is a cheating ho! Hailey tipped off Sam, who was all for resuming production to get footage of Lily and Chris before the trial. It'll bookend her storyline fabulously.

It was oh-so easy to manipulate Chris. Hailey slipped into his DMs and convinced him to come pay Lily a visit. She won't ever need to stick a finger down her throat to barf again after he sent her a dick pic in response.

She thought she was going to have to pay or play him, and was willing to do it, but in the end, a follow and the invitation to Patrick Paley's house was enough to win him over.

Hailey parks her Mercedes outside the hospital. She pulls out her phone and shoots Valeria a text.

Hear anything about the audition?? Fingers crossed!!

She follows it up with another text, asking Valeria to come over later.

Isn't it crazy about Greta? Straight to rehab this morning. Could really use some girl time!!

It was reported on Reality Tea that Greta checked into Cliffside Malibu. Joel's car crash and her OD were the wake-up call she needed. Hailey's *so* relieved. One less bitch to pose next to on the red carpet for the premiere.

She checks her reflection in the rearview. Time to visit her guy!

Joel is asleep in his hospital bed when Hailey enters his room. There's a bottle of painkillers on the table next to him. She sits beside Joel's bed, brushing a strand of hair off his forehead. He stirs and opens his eyes.

"Hey, you," he says, reaching for her hand. His eyes are droopy.

"How are you feeling?" she asks.

"Better now."

She lets him pull her in for a kiss.

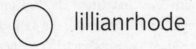

lillianrhode

75k followers

Lily drops the bouquet of flowers she had quickly bought in the hospital floral shop. She had rushed to the hospital after pushing Chris into the pool, promising her Uber driver a big tip if he got her to Cedars fast.

It hits her so much harder than seeing them kiss in the extended *Platinum Triangle* trailer. There's no way to trick her mind now. Joel's arm around Hailey's back, pulling her closer to him as he lies in his hospital bed and kisses her: it isn't a part of the show. Joel and Hailey aren't characters. They're real people. With a real story.

The rose petals squish on the soles of her shoes as she runs down the hospital corridor and outside. She calls an Uber and tries not to cry in the backseat, staring out the window at the palm tree–lined street, the razor-sharp fronds blowing in the wind like they might come flying loose and slice off your head.

She gets her Uber driver to take her to the beach so she can clear her head. She stands at the edge of the water and remembers the night after Brandon's party, when she and Joel ran into the ocean together, kissing for the first time, their lips salty from the water and from Joel's tears. Lily tips her face up to the sun and closes her eyes. Sometimes she wonders if she'd be happier if she had never come to Beverly Hills.

But when Lily gets back to the Paleys' house an hour later, she knows it wouldn't be any easier if she were still on her own, struggling to pay rent on the trailer, with no one to love or love to hate her. She'd rather have had this brief romance with Joel that made her feel so happy to be herself than fall asleep every night wishing she could be someone else.

Lily goes straight to the pool house, closes the door behind her, and leans against it. She buries her face in her hands. She's about to let herself break down and cry when a voice across the room surprises her.

"Hey, you okay?"

Lily drops her hands. Idris is sitting on the couch flipping through the Bettina Rheims book on the coffee table.

"What are you doing here?" Lily asks.

"I know we're done our lessons. But I miss hanging out with you." Idris looks shyly at Lily.

"You okay?" he asks again. "You look kind of pale. Maybe you should sit down."

Lily collapses next to him on the couch.

"You wanna talk about it?" Idris asks.

She opens her mouth but no words come out. Her mind is spinning.

"No." Lily slowly turns her head toward Idris. "I don't want to talk."

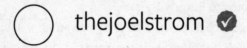

thejoelstrom ✔

1.8m followers

jkleejk (931) 320-8171 Joel's number has been exposed!! Call him and ask how he's doing!!

londonboy99 @thejoelstrom I unfollowed @brandocadogan

raeanne_silvvaaaa Sending you love bb

mscdeb I could be your nurse…

alessiaxtilliana PLEASE lb before you're dead

mdihx @thejoelstrom Our poor husband!! 😭 @staciewasneverhere

annayesir Hope your face isn't fucked up man! You don't have nothing else @thejoelstrom

Joel's doctor prescribed him OxyContin for the pain. Gotta love Hollywood doctors. Joel is lit AF. Joel's mom wants him to go straight home but he insists on taking an Uber to see Lily.

"I'm fine," Joel tells his mom. "I've taken falls on my board worse than the crash."

"Your car flipped over!" Kathy cries. It's been an emotional roller coaster since Greta overdosed. At least some good came of it. Greta's in rehab. Joel's too numb from the meds to process it all.

The crash definitely looks worse than it was. He watched a time-lapse video on his phone of his Targa flipping. So crazy. He doesn't care about the car. It can be replaced. He's just not so sure about him and Lily.

Joel regrets deleting their photo. He's still mad that she went on his phone, especially because it kept him away from Greta, but now that Greta's entered treatment, Joel's not going to hold on to his anger. It's over now. And everything turned out all right. Brandon's getting trolled online and people are saying he's finally gone too far this time . . . that's all the justice Joel needs.

Now what he wants is to see Lily. After almost losing everything, he knows what matters. Lily didn't mean for any of this to happen. Her only fault is letting Hailey get in her head, but they're all guilty of that.

Joel had thought it was Lily who came to visit him in the hospital and who he was kissing. He was so out of it from the pills that he only realized it wasn't Lily mid-kiss when he opened his eyes and his vision cleared. But then the meds took full effect and he passed out. Joel woke up with so much anxiety, knowing something was wrong.

When he gets to the Paleys' house, Joel doesn't ring the bell at the front door. He wants to avoid seeing Hailey in case she's home. He goes around the side of the house and over to the pool house.

He stops when he sees Lily and Idris through the window, kissing.

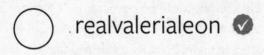

realvalerialeon ✔

3.3m followers

iamnicola_ Wish I could be u... @realvalerialeon 😍 👑

Valeria sits on Hailey's bed next to Hailey, who is recounting how she found Greta at Poppy and saved her life. The way Hailey is martyring herself you'd think she'd given Greta a piece of her liver or whatever Selena's friend did for her. Doesn't Hailey know that no one's watching? But maybe that stopped mattering a long time ago. Valeria drowns her out.

She thought she would've heard back from the producers of *Almost Everything* by now. She nailed the audition. It had been just like she remembered when she was a kid, that intuitive feeling that she was everything they had dreamed she would be.

"I'm just glad Greta's in rehab now," Hailey says, feigning concern. "She's at Cliffside Malibu. It burned down in the Woolsey fire and they rebranded."

"I hope she's doing okay," Valeria says.

"Oh, she'll be fine. You get your phone back after seventy-two hours."

Hailey sighs, shaking her head. "All of this could've been avoided if Lily hadn't tried to keep me away from Joel. She's *so* insecure."

Valeria listens as Hailey fills her in on how Lily purposely ignored Hailey's call.

"She could've saved *two* lives," Hailey says.

"Well, Joel's being discharged today and Greta's safe," Valeria says. "In a weird way, everything worked out for the best."

Valeria wants to know if anyone has asked Hailey how she really feels about Joel and her cousin getting together. Has Greta? She's supposedly closest to Hailey—but even now, sitting on Hailey's bed with her, Valeria knows what it means to be both close and miles away from Hailey at the same time. It's unlikely anyone has asked Hailey how she feels. What are they so afraid of? Hailey has a way of making you feel like talking about emotions is lowbrow, that it's embarrassing to even admit to having them.

"Remember last year when you accused me of only wanting to hang out with you on camera?" Hailey asks.

Valeria doesn't remember. She doesn't think about the past. It causes her too much anxiety. But she does vaguely recall a particularly icy period in her friendship with Hailey last year when she called Hailey out one episode. That had been fun. And like all things, it had passed.

Valeria used to think she was morally superior to Hailey. Is she being punished?

"So I thought we could hang out today," Hailey says. "Just the two of us, no cameras. Like old times. We could hit Anastasia. Or we could stay in and eat ice cream in the theater while we sexually exploit Armie Hammer and Timothée Chalamet."

Valeria smiles. Guy-on-guy fantasies did bond them one Oscar season.

"That sounds fun," Valeria says. But she's suspicious. The way Hailey is watching her, Valeria feels like she's under a magnifying glass. Like Hailey is holding it angled at the sun and trying to set her on fire.

Valeria's phone rings. It's her mom. Valeria can barely make out what she's saying she's talking so fast. And then all of a sudden Valeria hears it, the words she's been waiting for. The words that mean so much.

You got the part!

paleyhailey I can make grown men follow me to hell.

As soon as Valeria leaves, Hailey removes a bottle of Klonopin from her Benedetta Bruzziches minaudière and swallows a pill dry.

Such a busy schedule of destroying lives to maintain!

First, a text to Fortune. Her patience has worn thin. Time to play hardball.

Lock down Joel as my date this weekend for the premiere or I will still use the Paley power to influence the producers to have your broke ass fired!!

And look good doing it.

Next, an appointment with Nurse Jamie. While getting a Platinum Lift facial, she reflects on recent events. Joel kissed her, and at first Hailey was so happy, nothing could've made the moment better—except maybe if it had been on camera. But halfway through the kiss, Joel murmured that he "forgave" her for ignoring Hailey's call, and Hailey realized he was out of it from his pain meds and thought she was Lily.

Third on the agenda: dropping a nuke.

But first, snack time! Two dozen chocolate bouchons from Bouchon Bakery. Followed by a good fifteen-minute purge.

Ah.

Now she can decimate Valeria Leon.

Hailey comes out from the back of the house wearing a Milly ruffled bandeau striped bikini top and bottoms.

Patrick is sitting in a chaise lounge next to the pool with his *Avengers* script. He looks at Hailey through his black Ray-Bans.

"Hi, Daddy," Hailey says as she sits at the edge of the pool.

Patrick lowers his script.

"Hey, princess," he says. "Heard about the Strom twins. They going to be all right?"

"Oh, they'll survive." Hailey dips her toes in the water. Her iridescent pink nail polish sparkles under the sunlight.

"And how's Lily doing?" Patrick asks. He looks at her intently.

"I'm kind of worried about her, to be honest," Hailey says. "Fame really goes to some girls' heads. And it's all happened so fast for Lily . . ."

"She isn't being a negative influence on you, is she?" Patrick asks vaguely. He's back to his script. Sometimes Hailey pretends she's an *Avengers* character so that her father might pay attention to her. She's Enchantress.

"Oh, Lily's harmless," Hailey says. "She's just trying to fit in. If anything, I hope to be an influence on *her*. I feel really protective of Lily."

"That's great, sweetie." Patrick doesn't look up from his page.

Hailey glides into the pool and does a few languid laps before climbing out and wrapping a towel around her waist. She comes up to the end of Patrick's chaise, blocking the sun with her head. It casts a shadow on him.

A bead of water drips from Hailey's hair onto the script. Patrick looks up from the wet spot.

"Daddy, I've been thinking about getting into the industry. There's this part on a sitcom that I think I would be *perfect* for."

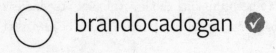

brandocadogan ✓

333k followers

Brandon's dad isn't screaming at him. There are no threats of military school. No comparison to his older brother, who happens to arrive home from Chile just in time to throw Brandon's latest controversy in his face. "Still a homicidal maniac, I see," Conrad jokes when he sees him. "Some things never change."

L.Y. sighs and rubs his eyes as Brandon sits across the desk from him in the home office. Brandon keeps waiting for it, the guilt trip—how he's killing his mother, how it's all his fault. But it doesn't come. It's better when his dad is yelling at him. The silence is worse. It's the unspeakable.

"Our lawyers are dealing with the police," L.Y. finally says. "It'll be a miracle if there aren't charges brought against you.

And you'll be lucky if the Stroms don't sue. You know how shameless that family is."

Morgan hasn't said anything about the drag race. Brandon's been holed up in his room, drinking whiskey and smoking Spice all day. His mom is out with Conrad. She's feeling better today. Before Brandon left for the drag race, he overheard his mom crying to his dad about how selfish he is for not taking more time off of work to be with her while she's sick. She was acting like she doesn't have much time left.

The only person Brandon has reached out to is Bea. But she's ghosting him. She wrote a post about "eliminating toxic people from your life." Brandon knows she doesn't have a choice. Her followers are turning on her, trying to force her to take a stand against Brandon. She has to protect her brand.

Brandon's entire body is kind of trembling and he can't stop. He thinks he hears someone whispering behind him. *You are a very evil person. Despicable.* But when he turns around, no one's there.

The truth is, Brandon choked. He was racing against Joel Strom. *The* Joel Strom. And Brandon was intimidated. That's why he kept pushing back the date of the race. He said it was to customize his new wheels, but it's really because he was afraid. Brandon didn't try to cause Joel to crash, no matter what people think. Brandon lost control of the wheel. It wasn't just the possible humiliation of losing. He could've handled that. But there was this moment while they were racing when Brandon caught his own eyes in the rearview mirror and saw his mom's face.

L.Y.'s office phone rings. Brandon sees the name on the call display: Dr. Rick Bancroft.

"I have to take this," L.Y. says. "It's your mother's doctor." He gives Brandon one last tired look before answering the call.

Brandon slips out of the office but leaves the door open a crack as he listens in on his dad, who has put the caller on speaker.

"What's the diagnosis, Rick?" L.Y. asks. "Has she lost her mind?"

"She's aware of what she's doing, L.Y. She doesn't believe her own lies . . ."

"Why the hell is she lying in the first place?"

"She's lonely. She likes the attention you've been giving her. She talked about the trip to Switzerland for thirty minutes without once mentioning the treatments she was supposedly there for. She said it was the first time you two had gone away in years."

"It's the show," L.Y. says. "She was just fine before she got caught up on that goddamn show."

"The pressure to remain relevant and have an interesting storyline may be playing a part . . ."

Brandon steps away from his dad's office door. Rick Morton is one of L.Y.'s golf buddies. They play at the Bel-Air Country Club every weekend. He's not treating Morgan for cancer. Dr. Bancroft is a psychiatrist.

shelby.b.sanders you poor sick little idiot @brandocadogan

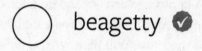

beagetty ✓

11m followers

directordiovoice Instagram models are trash.

The Mentions about Joel Strom are so hysterical. Bea doesn't care! She likes Joel and everything and she's glad that he's not dead but she's not, like, *outraged* in the way her followers want her to be. She's not joining the mob and tearing Brandon down. But there's no way that she can be associated with him right now. Brandon's not the look.

So Bea unfollows him.

Thank you. Next. Bea's moving on. Her career is heating up! Not only did she just launch her own clothing line for @prettylittlething, but her agent wants her to be Sam Mendes's new beard. It'll practically guarantee that Bea will be on season 3 of *Platinum Triangle*. Her role has been vulnerable ever since her mom quit. The show is built on the families. If Bea can bring in a high-profile romance as a storyline, not only will she secure a future on the show, she'll secure modeling work. Reality TV fame and her Instagram following are directly connected to editorial and runway interest in her. When they did their first campaign together, Marc Jacobs admitted he watches the show. It all started with a follow.

Bea's followers are trying to demand that she denounce Brandon. Unfollowing him isn't enough. They want to hear her loathe him. Joel Strom is America's golden boy and Brandon is, like, Darth Vader. It'll be interesting to see what route Brandon goes on as a character on the show. Will he take it as far as Spencer Pratt on *The Hills* and become a caricature of himself, becoming so much the villain that it's comical? Or will he get dark and become a Hollywood teen tragedy?

Bea's sitting alone at the bar at the Chateau Marmont drinking a martini; she hasn't eaten anything all week. When it's hot out, she doesn't have an appetite. While she's drinking, she comes up with a few things she could tweet in response to her followers' demands for a statement regarding Brandon and the drag race. She could send out her well-wishes to Joel. Thoughts and prayers!! Bea laughs out loud. Or . . . she could continue to remain silent. No comment. It's a bit cold, but Bea's heard rumblings that MKTV is booking some of the *Platinum Triangle* cast to appear on *Ellen* next week to promote the new season. Everyone is saying it's going to be Whitney, Kathy, Hailey, and Greta, but since Greta's in rehab and Bea is trending over her breakup with Brandon, she might be the right replacement!

Bea orders another martini and slips into Conrad's DMs. She heard he's back in town. He agrees to meet her at her bungalow. She's not contractually tied to Sam Mendes yet! Why not live a little?

Before Conrad arrives, Bea takes a few pills. The male model she was shooting with earlier gave them to her; she's not sure what they are. Bea is topless and clicking Like on all her haters' comments when Conrad shows up.

She's a pretty little thing getting fucked by her boyfriend's brother. For more, pick up the latest issue of *Vogue*!

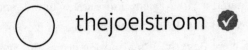

thejoelstrom ✓

1.8m followers

thejoelstrom My dad always told me "thoughts become things"

After catching Lily with Idris, Joel just wants to forget. He spends the next couple of days ignoring the doctors' orders for bed rest and escapes to the beach. He doesn't go to Zuma, to avoid running into Lily. She hasn't tried to get in touch since Joel's been out of the hospital.

When he's not surfing, he's skating. Joel's at Venice Beach Skate Park when Conrad Cadogan sends him a text inviting him to a poker game that night at the Beverly Hills Hotel. Conrad's back in town and offering to cover the six figures to get Joel into the game. Joel knows that it's probably L.Y. Cadogan's idea, his way of softening Joel up so that there won't be a lawsuit over the crash.

If Joel's being used, he doesn't care. He doesn't care about anything anymore. Not just because of the pills he's on, but because seeing Lily and Idris kissing in the Paleys' pool house flicked a switch in him. Is *everyone* fake? He thought he could trust Lily. He thought he was falling in love with her.

Joel arrives at the Presidential Suite of the Beverly Hills Hotel after dark. When Joel enters, his HUF hat pulled low over his eyes, there are eight players total—two Saudis, one of whom

259

Joel thinks might be royalty, a '90s child star who won an Oscar, a girl who looks like she could be a supermodel or a Russian spy, this socialite who dated a *Vanderpump Rules* star, Conrad, and his buddy who is coked out AF and who Joel recognizes as a former student at New Beverly. It's a motley crew, and Joel doesn't really know what he's in for.

As Joel sits at the poker table, he pulls out his phone and texts Sean.

Tomorrow night?

He adds, *I want to be there.*

Even if Sean doesn't think he can handle it. Even if Sean thinks he'll be haunted by it for the rest of his life, Joel doesn't care. He wants to see how ugly this world is so he can stop feeling so disappointed all the time. He wants to be one of those jaded Hollywood types who can't be phased by anything anymore. Nothing can hurt him.

There's a knock on the door of the suite. The actor is expecting a buddy, one last player for the game.

"Sorry I'm late, gents."

Luis Leon walks into the room, a Cuban burning between his teeth. He takes a seat across from Joel at the table.

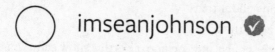
Fortune starts pulling on the drawstring of Sean's Yeezy
Calabasas sweatpants as soon as Sean steps through the
door. Fortune is house-sitting for a friend in the Bird Streets of
the Hollywood Hills.

Sean pulls Fortune's hands away.

"What's the matter?" Fortune asks. "Isn't this what you came
over for?"

It is. Or at least that's what Sean thought he wanted. A little
release to relieve him of the pressure. There's a dogfight tomorrow night at his house.

Now that he's here, Sean knows sex isn't distraction enough.

"I just thought we could hang out a bit." He breaks eye contact with Fortune and steals a quick look back up at him.

"You want foreplay?" Fortune asks. "When did the DL get
so intimate?"

Sean plays with his drawstring. "Netflix?" he asks. Fortune can't stop smiling. "What?" Sean shifts his weight on his feet. "What's so funny about that?"

"Well, come on, then."

They sit on the couch and Fortune picks this show called *Elite*. While he's filling Sean in on the premise of the show—working-class kids versus rich kids at a private school in Spain, which turns deadly—Sean is only half listening. He peers at Fortune through the corner of his eye, wondering what it would be like to take his hand. He bets it's smoother than Valeria's, which are dried up from all her tears. She's never cried in front of him; she doesn't really show much emotion around him ever. But Sean knows what's going on beneath the surface, just like he's pretty sure that she knows what's going on beneath his surface.

Fortune catches him looking and Sean's eyes land back on the screen.

"Are you in the mood now?" Fortune touches Sean's leg.

Sean takes a breath and reaches for Fortune's hand. "It doesn't always have to be about hooking up, does it?"

The way Fortune is looking down at their hands makes Sean self-conscious. Sean pulls away. "I just thought we were friends," he says.

A ping comes into Sean's phone. It's a message from Joel.

Sean closes his eyes and hears the barking in his head. He doesn't notice Fortune reading Sean's phone over his shoulder.

"What's happening tomorrow?" Fortune asks.

"Nothing." Sean holds his phone away. But Fortune will not be denied. Isn't that what Sean likes about him? His topknot and makeup and stilettos and faux furs and his crazy nails, each painted differently. His middle finger is painted like money, the pyramid and all-seeing eye at the tip. His nails are so long that Fortune wears diamond rings around them and not his fingers. Sean has always wanted to ask Fortune to tickle his back.

Fortune grabs Sean's phone with his extravagant hand. "Tell me, or you're not getting this back!"

"Oh yeah?" Sean tackles Fortune, pinning him to the couch. He knows this is what Fortune wants. It doesn't take long for Sean to get his phone back. He stares down into Fortune's eyes.

Maybe *this* is why he came here.

"If I tell, promise you'll keep it a secret?"

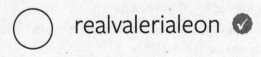

realvalerialeon

3.3m followers

cielspabh Kidchella! This is the cutest! HBD Sophia! 💕

therecessionista What an adorable theme! Loooooove the dreamcatcher cake!

tammyleejackson Oh my goodness!! Time is flying by so quickly! Cherish every single moment! Time goes by sooooo fast!!! @realvalerialeon @sophialeon1919

thetipinator Happy Birthday 🎂

moniquekingkearney My sweet Sophia, hope you had a wonderful birthday! 💕💕🎉🥹🥹💋

Nothing is going to ruin today.

When Patrick sends Valeria a text asking if she can meet him at the Montage, she ignores it. Valeria has to resist replying no; she'll never see him again. She decided as soon as she landed the part on *Almost Everything* that she's done with Patrick. This role is her one shot to remind the industry that she's still alive, to show them that just because she's growing up doesn't mean she has to be phased out. This is the start of Valeria's career as an adult actress. A *serious* actress.

The kids are having a great time. Especially Sophia. She's running around the backyard with her friends, shrieking with laughter. Valeria hired party planners bDASHd to help with the Coachella theme. Valeria came up with the idea because Sophia always loves watching Valeria get ready to go to the festival and asks if she can go with her. Sophia is in such a rush to grow up. Valeria wants to make sure she enjoys her childhood, that she actually *has* a childhood. Seeing her playing with her friends and being so carefree is exactly what Valeria wanted for her today. It's everything Valeria never had.

Valeria watched some YouTube video Sean showed her saying that until the age of seven, you're not really conscious, you're theta, which is a state of hypnosis and imagination. Your entire identity and how you see yourself is being built. The first seven years of your life is a period of programming. It's why rich kids stay rich and poor kids, no matter how talented, so rarely ever deprogram. When they try, the world asks them: *Who do you think you are?*

Sophia's programming has been different from Valeria's. Valeria is still stuck in her theta mind, still performing the same choreography and trying to make people love her.

When Sophia blows out the candles on her three-tier cake, which has a dream catcher made out of icing and a teepee on the top, Valeria knows what she's wishing for. Valeria saw some comments from her followers that say her dad has been spotted back in L.A. If he is in town, he hasn't let his family know. He hasn't even called Sophia.

Gloria is the only one who doesn't seem to be having fun. She disappears during cake time. Valeria takes two plates and goes looking for her. Valeria knows she's jealous. Her mother resents her for knowing how to take care of Sophia and Leo better than she does.

Since the day she was born, Sophia has been a threat to Valeria. Her mother always warned her that there was someone younger, prettier, and more talented right behind her. When Valeria reached the first grade, she saw the younger kids in kindergarten as her mortal enemies. She's always struggled to make friends.

Valeria refuses to let her mother's threats or the fear of looming competition affect her relationship with her little sister. It infuriates Gloria, their bond. Valeria's ability to love more than just herself.

She finds Gloria alone in her bedroom, sitting in a chair by the window and watching the kids playing outside.

"There you are," Valeria says. "Is everything okay?"

"Oh, Valeria," Gloria says in one breath.

Valeria stops in the middle of the room, the two plates balancing on her palms.

"What?" Valeria asks. "Is it Dad?"

"I didn't want to tell you this during the party. You worked so hard on it. I wanted you to be happy . . ."

"Mom, what is it?"

"I'm sorry, Valeria. The producers of *Almost Everything* called. They're giving the part to someone else."

Valeria doesn't hear the plates break when she drops them. *They told her they loved her. She was being sent the final script. There was a date for rehearsal, a filming schedule.* Now there's just icing and shattered porcelain everywhere.

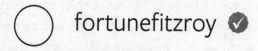
adhikari.rahul Doggy filter pls!! 🖤

Fortune has never understood the appeal of Joel Strom, why everyone's in love with him. Personally, he thinks Joel is too common a choice. He always thought it was kind of basic of Hailey to be so into him. But then Hailey has always seen herself as a Disney princess. She made her boyfriend in junior high get a tattoo of her name in Disney font on his arm! And Joel's the kind of guy who would, like, pull a sword out of a stone and chop down a fortress of prickly rose vines to reach the girl of his dreams. Too bad for Hailey that girl is Lily.

But Fortune is determined to change that. He *will* be made a permanent cast member on *Platinum Triangle*. It's his destiny to rule from his TV. Fortune knew that he just had to wait for the right opportunity to fall in his lap . . .

Fortune's Uber pulls up to the driveway of the Johnsons' house in Holmby Hills. The driveway is lined with parked cars. Sean is waiting for him out front and looks over at Fortune nervously as he steps out.

"Phones are checked at the door," Sean tells Fortune as he approaches.

"Got it."

Sean doesn't move. "Are you sure you're up for this?"

Fortune isn't totally heartless. His fur is faux, thanks! He finds it much more satisfying hurting people than animals. But when Sean told him that Joel was going to be there, Fortune knew he had to show.

"I'm morbidly curious," Fortune says. "And I got you." Fortune gives Sean his sincerest smile.

Sean is obviously gutted about the fights and needs all the moral support he can get. He gives Fortune a look of appreciation as they head into the house.

Down in the basement, the atmosphere is tense. There are a couple dozen people, mostly men, around the ring. Fortune sees the two pit bulls pacing in their cages, barking and growling. He watches as Christoph injects one of the dogs with a needle.

"Look, it's Greta," Fortune jokes. Sean doesn't crack a smile. Fortune's making bad jokes because he's nervous. Even he has to admit this is fucked up.

"Performance enhancement mixed with painkillers," Sean says under his breath. Sean looks away from the dogs.

Sean gets called over by his dad, leaving Fortune standing alone in the crowd. He tries to blend in. He dressed down for the event, all in black, with a hat covering his silver hair. The spectators are as hyped as the dogs. The testosterone and adrenaline are palpable. Fortune would be horny if he weren't so anxious. This is possibly the craziest thing he has ever witnessed, and Brandon once showed him a snuff film from his dad's vault.

Fortune looks through the crowd until he spots Joel, arms crossed over his Brooklyn Projects hoodie and his hat pulled low. But there's no mistaking him. Fortune's counting on it.

The crowd cheers when the doors to the cages are lifted. It's like the dogs slide into the basement from outside of this world. From one of the circles of hell. They bare their fangs and clash. Within seconds, blood is splattered across the cement floor. The fired-up crowd is louder than the whimpering of the dogs. Fortune winces, but he doesn't look away.

The dogs are moving so fast it's like Fortune is watching a time-lapse video. They're savage AF. Fortune isn't sure what he was expecting. Some kind of buildup? But the dogs go straight in for the kill. It's like the climax of episode 19 is happening in the first few minutes of episode 1.

It's the yelping that really gets you. The terror. Then there's the breaking of skin, fur shedding in bloody pools, fangs trembling in slobbery, red canine mouths.

Fortune feels a bead of sweat running through his foundation.

One of the dogs is down and the crowd collectively holds its breath. But then the dog struggles to a stand. Fortune wants to cry. It seems enlivened by the cheers of the crowd. The dog is Fortune.

"End it, Beelzebub. End it!"

Across the basement Fortune sees Christoph jumping up and down, screaming at his dog. Beelzebub is a thirsty follower. He just wants to be acknowledged. He just wants to make you proud. He bares his fangs as his eye hangs out of its socket.

Christoph is shaking Sean's shoulders with excitement. Sean isn't even looking at the dogs. He's staring at a bloodless spot on the floor.

There's a second phone strapped to a shirt garter around Fortune's thigh. He reaches through the hole he made in the pocket of his black jeans and pulls it out. With most of the phone concealed by his sleeve, Fortune surreptitiously records Joel watching the dogs.

Everyone around Fortune is too consumed by the last round of the fight to notice anything. Both the dogs look like monsters. Beelzebub's comeback has the crowd, especially Christoph, going wild. Beelzebub looks directly at Christoph with his one good eye before he uses a last burst of energy to rip the other dog's throat out.

Christoph picks up the dead dog by its practically severed head. The roar of the crowd is deafening.

Fortune sees Joel push through the cheering bodies and bolt upstairs. Fortune's right behind him.

Outside the house, Joel is leaning against a car parked in the driveway. He pukes.

"It reminded me of *Platinum Triangle*," Fortune says.

Joel quickly stands up and spins around to face Fortune, surprised to see him as he wipes his mouth with the sleeve of his hoodie.

"Tearing each other apart is all we've ever known."

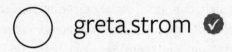

greta.strom ✔

733k followers

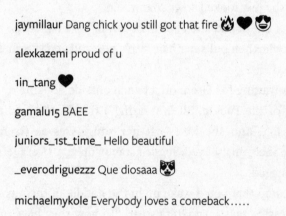

jaymillaur Dang chick you still got that fire 🔥🖤😍

alexkazemi proud of u

1in_tang 🖤

gamalu15 BAEE

juniors_1st_time_ Hello beautiful

_everodriguezzz Que diosaaa 😻

michaelmykole Everybody loves a comeback.....

Greta wakes up and for a second doesn't know where she is, but there's a familiarity in that. Through the open window she can hear seagulls and waves crashing. Malibu.

There's a knock on the door. One of the Cliffside Malibu staff tells her she has a visitor waiting for her outside.

She dreamed of her dad last night. It was more a memory than a dream. When she was little, she used to sit in his lap and drag her hand across the stubble on his chin, over and over again, in the same way she would touch the velvety ears of her teddy bear as she fell asleep. It comforted her.

It was seeing herself through Jessica's eyes that made Greta realize she needed to enter rehab. She hadn't really been seeing herself, but Jessica stood her in front of the mirror in the bathroom attached to Joel's hospital room and made her look at her reflection. She was so skinny, and there were dark circles under her eyes. There were still some scratch marks on her arms and legs from running through the forest. Her hair was greasy. And most of all, she just looked so goddamn sad.

Greta gets out of bed and slips on a pair of yoga pants and a cropped hoodie, then pulls her hair into a ponytail and splashes water on her face.

Jessica is waiting for Greta on a bench outside, looking out at the view of the Pacific. She's wearing a floral dress and a floppy sun hat, and she takes off her sunglasses as Greta approaches. She's misty-eyed. Jessica stands up and Greta lets herself be hugged.

"I was scared that you'd wake up in the middle of the night and run," Jessica says into Greta's ear. "I know they have an open-door policy here. I don't want to lose you ever again."

Greta pulls away from her dad's arms. "I didn't want to lose *you*," she says. "Sometimes we don't have a choice."

"You're right." Jessica sighs. "Sometimes we don't."

They stare into each other's eyes, communicating a million things without saying a word. Greta thought it would be so weird looking at her dad after all the plastic surgery and changes. She thought seeing her dad in a dress would scar her the way it did Joel when he caught Jessica in Greta's closet freshman year. Greta's clothes were going missing and she'd thought it was Hailey raiding her closet. When Joel told her what he'd walked in on, he'd seemed so disturbed by it, but Greta had just laughed it off. So Dad liked to play dress-up. She thought vaguely it might be some weird sex thing. Whatever. There were tons of weird things. Greta didn't think it was that serious. She didn't think it was going to lead to her losing her dad and hero.

Greta lifts her hand and touches Jessica's chin. Jessica lets her. She doesn't even blink. It isn't the same. Jessica's chin has been lasered, pulled, stuffed. It's so smooth, Greta's fingers slide right off.

"I hope you aren't thinking of coming to the premiere tomorrow night," Jessica says. "I think it's too much pressure too soon . . ."

"Don't worry, Dad. The show is the last thing on my mind."

Jessica nods with relief. She rubs Greta's cheek affectionately. And there it is. The familiarity Greta was hoping for. When her dad touches *her*, it feels the same as it always has.

"I'm so glad you're here," Jessica says.

Greta smiles. "I'm glad you are, too."

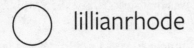

lillianrhode

79k followers

lillianrhode I'm more than just pictures.

The morning of her hearing, Lily wakes up early, does some laps in the pool, and makes herself a full breakfast before anyone wakes up or Ana comes in for the day (eggs, bacon, toast—she doesn't so much as look at a stick of celery).

After breakfast, Lily tries to keep herself calm as she showers and gets ready for court in the white Catherine Malandrino dress Whitney picked out for her.

Lily's ready too early, and then she doesn't know what to do with herself. She sits on the couch, taking a few deep breaths while holding the agate stone Sean gave her. But its calming energy doesn't seem to be working. Lily's so anxious she almost wants to ask Hailey for one of her Klonopin. She tells herself that it's going to be all right, Shapiro is a star lawyer. But what if they make an example of her? And what if the judge has been following all of the press about her? The runway wardrobe malfunction, gossip about the drag race crash . . . Lily hasn't exactly been keeping a low profile.

She's taking a break from Instagram. She's tired of all the negative comments about her and Joel and comparing her and

Hailey. Lily has wanted to reach out to Joel so badly since he checked out of the hospital but she hasn't let herself. Not after seeing him with Hailey. It might be the way she was brought up, the way her mother left so easily—but Lily feels so cold.

There's a knock on the pool house door and Whitney steps inside. She's wearing a suit with serious shoulder pads, as ready for her moment in court as Lily.

"Is it time?" Lily stands up and faces her aunt.

"It's a shame, really." Whitney's hand rises to her throat and she toys with her pearl choker. "Rather anticlimactic. I thought whatever the verdict was it would be a great pre-show before tomorrow's premiere . . ."

"What are you talking about?" Lily asks.

"Shapiro called. Chris changed his story this morning. He told the prosecutor that you weren't involved in the break-in or burglary and that you did indeed try to stop him. The charges have been dropped."

Lily's knees give out and she sits back down on the couch. "Why would Chris do that?" she asks. The last time Lily saw Chris, he was choking on a mouthful of chlorine and seemed determined to keep dragging Lily through the dirt with him. What changed his mind? Lily feels like she's missing something, like there's been some kind of behind-the-scenes play that she isn't aware of.

"It's already online," Whitney says. "I'll send you a link to the article in *OK!*"

Of course, the world finds out before her.

"There's nothing like a little vindication on a red carpet." Whitney winks at Lily. "You're riding in a limo with me and Patrick to the Sofitel tomorrow, by the way. Hailey's getting picked up for the premiere by Joel Strom."

Lily feels all of the air leave her body. And Whitney breathes in all the air in the room. Lily's about to flop to her side and start wriggling like a fish out of water.

Whitney smiles at her. "The tension between them has been building all season."

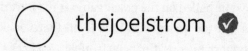

thejoelstrom ✓

1.8m followers

hilda__s @janavaphillip @calderoned37 STOOOP OMFG DO U HEAR THAT? it's the sound of my heart exploding

"Couldn't wait until the premiere?" Hailey asks, opening the door when Joel rings the bell at the Paleys' house.

"I'm here to see Lily." Joel wants to settle things with Lily before tomorrow night's red carpet. He's confused over why she hasn't been in touch since the accident, but he's starting to get the picture. There's more going on between her and Idris than Lily revealed. Joel was about to cave and send her a text but he wants to see her, face-to-face. No matter what, Lily deserves to hear it from him that he's taking Hailey to the premiere. He just can't tell her the real reason why.

"Sorry, Lily's not here," Hailey says. "You'll have to check to see when visiting hours are."

Joel feels his heart sink. Lily's court case.

"Don't worry," Hailey says, seeing the look on his face. "The charges were dropped. You just missed her. She went out to meet Idris and celebrate being a free woman."

Joel sits at the bottom of the Paleys' front steps. He rubs his eyes. He didn't sleep again last night. He's been going nonstop since he was released from the hospital. He's getting as bad as

Greta. Joel doesn't want to be home. He doesn't want to be inside of himself. He's been making bad choices. Like going to the dogfight. At least he bailed on the poker game at the Beverly Hills Hotel. It was just too weird with Luis Leon there. Joel's heard the gossip about the Leons' financial troubles. Joel has all these dark Hollywood thoughts swirling in his mind. He wants to unleash them. There was a part of him that thought seeing the fight would be cathartic. Like it would prove to Joel that he's not the only one who's sick.

Hailey sits on the stairs next to him and puts a hand on the back of his shirt.

"Poor baby lost his innocence," she says. "Careful, Joel. It's a slippery slope . . ."

Joel lowers his hands from his eyes and looks at her. "You know, I probably would've gone with you to the premiere, posed on the red carpet, bought you a new Judith Leiber . . . whatever you wanted. You may not always be the best friend to Greta, but you were there when it counted. More than once. I owe you. You didn't need to send your vapid little minion to blackmail me."

"What kind of a pet owner would I be if I didn't throw a stick for Fortune to catch and bring back to me every now and then?"

"I was barely conscious when you kissed me," Joel says.

Hailey flips her hair. "Start a hashtag about it."

"I hope it's enough for you." Joel pulls himself to his feet. "The image, I mean," he says, looking down at Hailey. "Because that's all it's going to be."

"Don't you get it yet?" Hailey stands up and faces him. There's a new look on her face Joel doesn't recognize—pity. "That's all it *can* be."

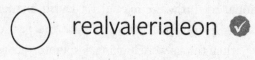

realvalerialeon I'm not sure why my mind went there?

"A hundred dollars for these?" Valeria is trying to control her voice as she lifts up a pair of round-toe Chanel pumps and a Balenciaga purse. "Do you know how much they cost?" But the owner of Wasteland won't budge, and Valeria ends up leaving with considerably less money than she'd expected.

She needs a hundred *thousand*. That's how much the IRS wants in back taxes the Leons owe. It's like the walls are closing in on them. Luis is still MIA, Valeria lost the part on *Almost Everything*, the mortgage is due, and now they owe all this money to the government. What were her parents thinking? The money owed is from one of Valeria's highest-earning years.

Gloria broke the news to Valeria after she told her that her part had been recast. It was almost too much for her to take in at once. Valeria felt herself about to shatter like the cake plates. She didn't know why she was dropped or who was replacing her. It almost didn't matter.

Valeria wasn't going down without a fight. She sprang into action, and she's been collecting clothes from her closet and from Gloria's closet to sell. She drove to Melrose in her BMW, which will be going up for sale by the end of the day. She'll take the bus to her damn auditions.

It was delusional to throw Sophia such a lavish birthday party. Valeria started planning it before she got the part on *Almost Everything*, when things were looking desperate. She felt as phony as her mom parading around with her glam squad like she doesn't have a care in the world and has endless money to spend, but she was doing it for Sophia. She was doing it to compensate for everything that Sophia won't have because of Valeria's failures, their father's absence, their mother's denial . . .

Valeria still has the Panthère de Cartier earrings from Patrick; she hasn't been able to part with them. She's an idiot for clinging to them, for believing they bring her good luck. They're probably cursed.

As Valeria leaves Wasteland, she pulls out her phone and texts Patrick.

Now?

lillianrhode

8ok followers

silvia_strom_paley You know the truth @lillianrhode The heart
doesn't lie

Lily's thinking about Joel as she sits in the passenger's seat of
Idris's Rolls-Royce. She was about to call him before Idris's
name appeared on her screen. Lily wanted to talk to Joel about
her case being dropped and hear it from his own mouth that he's
taking Hailey to the premiere. And just when she was about to
call him, her phone rang and it was Idris's voice on the other end
saying his followers had filled him in on the good news about
the charges being dropped and they should go out and celebrate.

They go to The Bar at the Montage Beverly Hills and sit on
the terrace overlooking Beverly Cañon Gardens. Idris orders a
bottle of Dom Pérignon. Lily hasn't talked to him since their kiss
in the pool house and she isn't sure how to break it to him that
she doesn't have feelings for him; she was just reacting to seeing
Joel and Hailey kissing at Cedars.

"I was going to make #FreeLily tee-shirts if you were sent to
jail," Idris says.

Lily smiles. "It's all over. And I have no idea what's coming
next . . ."

"What do you mean?"

"Summer's almost over. School will be starting soon. I don't know where I'm going to school, where I'm going to live . . . I've been so wrapped up in the show and Joel and the newness of everything, I haven't been thinking about the future."

"You're not going to stay with the Paleys?"

"They haven't said anything. And now with the new season of *Platinum Triangle* about to start airing . . . I feel like I've served my purpose."

"Well, I hope you stick around. The cast needs someone like you. Someone to remind us what the world's like on the other side of the screen."

Lily lowers her Champagne flute. "Idris, there's something I have to say—"

"No, you don't." Idris stops her. He fusses with his La Californienne Rolex watch. "It didn't mean anything." He finishes his Champagne, refilling the flute from the bottle in the ice bucket at the end of their table.

The fact that he looks so heartbroken doesn't give Lily any satisfaction. She used him to help herself forget about Joel, and she told herself it didn't really matter because it's not like Idris has real feelings for her, it's not like he's *capable* of real feelings— but maybe she read him wrong.

"You're really hung up on Joel, huh?" Idris asks.

"I'm sorry," Lily says.

"You have nothing to be sorry about. *I'm* the one who should be sorry."

Idris takes another big sip of Champagne.

"I can write cursive," he says.

"You can?" Lily asks. "Then why would you pretend you can't?"

"To keep you away from Joel."

Lily lowers her Champagne to the table, giving Idris a look.

"It was all Fortune's idea."

"Fortune?"

"I guess he made a deal with Hailey. If Fortune could get Joel to take Hailey to the *Platinum Triangle* premiere and pose with her on the red carpet like a real-life Barbie and Ken, then Hailey would help make Fortune a permanent cast member next season."

"So you tricked me? What was in it for you?"

"If I distracted you from Joel so Hailey and Fortune could make their moves, then Hailey was going to let me boast that I . . ." Idris actually blushes. "You know the saving-herself-for-marriage storyline from the first season?" he asks. "Let's just say I was going to get to be in the last scene."

"That's disgusting!"

"That's reality TV."

Lily is furious. Hailey's not a bitch, she's a psychotic bitch! How far is she willing to go to keep Lily and Joel apart?

"I wanted to tell you right after we kissed," Idris says, but Lily's already getting up. "I haven't been able to stop thinking about you. It all became real to me and I realized that I like you, and—"

"Drop dead!" Lily says, storming out of the bar and into the hotel lobby.

She comes to an abrupt stop when she sees Valeria stepping into the elevator, dark sunglasses concealing her face.

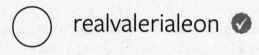

realvalerialeon ✓

3.3m followers

_casparandrey @soh.fys Her sis is way cuter than she was
@sophialeon1919 @realvalerialeon

selgforever0758 @realvalerialeon Broke ass bitch

rob_in_tribeca Ur my dream girl to have sex with

lola.asl No one likes talking about death.

shitfaced_pony Will you EVER be in another movie?!

Valeria lies on her back on the bed in Patrick's suite at the Montage Beverly Hills. She let herself in. Patrick is in the shower. She can hear him singing to himself over the running water. The ceiling is so familiar. She finds the spot where she's going to be.

A ping comes into Valeria's phone. It's Sean. *Here if you need me* is all it says. She almost laughs. Did the IRS story leak? Or do people know that she's been dropped from *Almost Everything*? Both? No publicity is bad publicity. The only bad publicity is no publicity. Valeria's too afraid to look at her phone. It's this endless cycle of abuse. She gets so depressed and so she turns to her phone to distract her but it always leads her lower; she's going in circles, the comments are so mean.

Valeria replies to Sean with a heart emoji, dropping her phone to her side. It slides off the bed and lands on the floor with a thud.

Patrick stops singing in the shower.

"Valeria, that you?" he asks.

Valeria sits up.

No. It's not.

She gets off the bed and she's leaving the room, cutting across the suite toward the door, when she remembers her phone. She goes back and picks it up off the floor just as Patrick comes out of the shower with a towel wrapped around his waist.

"Going somewhere?" he asks.

Valeria turns without a word and walks to the door, sliding her dark glasses over her eyes as she swings it open. She isn't expecting it when she comes face-to-face with Lily Rhode standing in the hallway. Valeria sees Lily's eyes widen as she looks behind her to where Patrick is standing in nothing but a towel.

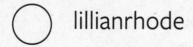
poppykd_ you actually kill me

L ily runs back to the elevator and presses the button frantically. Valeria's already gone. She bolted down the stairwell when she saw Lily.

"Wait!" Patrick runs out after her, holding up the towel around his waist. "Lily, please! I can explain. It's not what it looks like."

"It's *exactly* what it looks like!" Lily has to control her voice to keep from screaming. She presses the elevator button again. *Come on. Come on.* "How could you?" she asks, her voice shaking with rage as she looks at Patrick's dripping-wet face. "She's just a girl! She's the same age as your daughter!"

Lily knows immediately there must be money involved. All the press about the Leons' finances. The latest is that the IRS is after them.... Valeria would never do something like this unless she absolutely had to.

The elevator finally arrives but before Lily can step inside, Patrick grabs her by the arm and drags her back into his suite.

"Let go of me!" Lily tries to shove him off. Patrick closes the door behind them and locks it.

"Whatever you think you know—"

"Don't you dare!" Lily stops him. "Don't try to pretend like this isn't real life! Like this is just some scene I saw on TV, something I flicked past. I won't let you do that! Why does everyone think they can just do that?"

Lily sees remorse in Patrick's eyes, which she would almost believe if she didn't know he's a consummate professional.

"God knows I'm not perfect," Patrick says. "But I will not be demonized here. I'm not a bad guy, Lily. I've done a lot for you, haven't I? I gave you a second chance after you brought coke into my home—"

"You don't actually believe that and you know it! You're just as deluded about Hailey as you are about yourself!"

"You ungrateful little bitch!" Patrick raises his hand like he's going to slap Lily. She stands her ground and he draws back, trying to control his anger. "I gave you a place to live, paid off the credit card bill for an entirely new wardrobe, put you on TV . . . hell, I even paid off the hood rat you got arrested with to change his story and take the fall."

Lily's mouth drops open in surprise.

"You could show me a little appreciation!"

"This isn't about me!" Lily tries to steady her voice. "It's about Valeria."

"I should've gotten rid of you when I had the chance," Patrick says. "I knew you were going to be trouble."

"You're a monster!"

Lily turns and tries to unlock the door but Patrick stops her. The towel around his waist is slipping and Lily is suddenly terrified to be alone with him. Patrick grabs her arm and tightens his grip.

"Don't be such a consciously naive little bitch!" he hisses. "Do you have any idea how good you have it?" He lets go of her arm with such force that Lily is flung against the door. "Do you have any idea how hard people have to fight to end up where you've just landed? You went from a trailer park in the San Fernando Valley to Trousdale Estates in Beverly Hills. You think there isn't a price?"

Patrick laughs. It's a Marvel super-villain laugh, and it gives Lily chills.

"How do you think it happened, Lily? Luck? Fate? The goodness of your family's heart?" Patrick shakes his head. "Face it, kid, your soul was for sale and we bought it. And what's more, you wanted us to. You wanted to be one of us more than anything in the world. Like a lamb to the slaughter."

"You're wrong." Lily steps away from the door, right up to Patrick's face. "I'll never be one of you."

She looks into Patrick's eyes.

"*I'm* going to be a different kind of star."

○ **paleyhailey** ✓

1m followers

paleyhailey At 10, rocking my Chanel suit planning world domination like a #boss

Hailey posts a throwback photo as she tries on her premiere dress—a Marchesa Notte sweetheart illusion Mikado ball gown with a 3-D floral-embroidered bodice.

It's going to be fun thinking up a way to punish Joel. Now that she's so close to finally getting what she wants from him, she'll have to start moving her attention to the next chapter of their little storyline.

Season 3, baby!

Joel's going to get what's coming to him. He could've seriously hurt her brand by rejecting her. After they pose together on the red carpet tomorrow night, Hailey will have all the validation she needs and she'll be able to kick Joel to the curb.

As a part of his agreement to take Hailey to the premiere party, Joel insisted Fortune delete the video of him at the dogfight. Fortune sent it to Hailey first. She's keeping it as collateral, and when the time is right, she'll send it to Sam and they'll plot the takedown of Joel Strom.

Hailey does a little twirl in her dress, looking down at her recent throwback post. The Likes are blowing up.

She opens a new DM.

princepaley YES QUEEN

princepaley Born to rule!!!

princepaley You are my life.

princepaley I'd go to the moon and back for you Queen!!

Aw. So cute. Hailey replies to @princepaley.

paleyhailey What if I asked you to go further? 💋

She drops her phone on her bed and steps into her closet, trying to decide which Judith Leiber clutch she should hold on the red carpet, when there's a knock on her bedroom door.

Lily pokes her head in.

"Can we talk?" she asks.

They haven't been alone together since the blowup in the pool house. As far as Hailey is concerned, it's all been said.

She'll have the last word tomorrow night.

"You look beautiful," Lily says. "Is that the dress you're wearing to the premiere?"

Hailey's smile is as cold as ice.

"Have you seen Joel since he's been out of the hospital?" she asks, allowing Lily into her room. She knows Lily hasn't seen him and just wants to rub it in. She's disappointed when Lily doesn't react, not so much as a blink. Her face remains that Beverly Hills blank. The girl's learning.

"It's such a miracle that he wasn't seriously hurt," Hailey goes on. "And Greta's in rehab. Looks like the Strom twins are both going to bounce back. I'm sure you're relieved."

"Yes," Lily says. "I would never have forgiven myself if it had been worse."

Hailey eyes her suspiciously. Here we go. Lily's back to the victim narrative.

"Can we sit?" Lily asks. She motions to Hailey's bed. Hailey nods and they take a seat on the edge.

"I want to say I'm sorry," Lily says. "Everything you said in the pool house was true. I haven't wanted to admit it but I *am* jealous of you."

Hailey fingers the appliqués on her dress. *Yes?* she's thinking. *And?*

"Not just of your Beverly Hills lifestyle or your fame," Lily continues, "but of your family. I look at your relationship with your mom and you're so much alike and I wish I had that. And your dad . . . he's *such* a good guy."

Lily smiles at Hailey.

"He's been so generous to me, and he obviously *adores* you. I've never had that, and I guess I just wanted a piece of the pretty picture for myself. And that's why . . ." Lily takes a deep breath. "This isn't easy for me to say. But that's why I tried to steal Joel from you. Can you ever forgive me?" She legit has tears in her eyes.

"Oh, Lily." Hailey takes her hand. "Wow. Of course I forgive you. I know how hard it must be for you to admit all that."

"I didn't even realize what I was doing," Lily says. "But after the charges against me were dropped, it's like I dropped all my illusions, too. I've literally been the worst cousin in the world and I understand if you just want, like, some space, but I really want to hit refresh with you. I'd love nothing more than to start over. Maybe one day we can even be friends."

"That's all I've ever wanted, Lily." Hailey hugs her. "I hope you know that. Girls have to support other girls. We're so much stronger together!"

"Agreed." Lily smiles at Hailey as they pull apart. "Which is why I'm hoping you'll go shopping with me tomorrow before the premiere and help me find a dress. I'm struggling to keep up with life in Beverly Hills in a lot of ways—obviously that includes shopping. And you have *the* best style!"

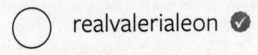

realvalerialeon ✔

3.3m followers

realvalerialeon Last night I couldn't sleep so I drove to East L.A. to visit my childhood home where I lived from birth to age ten (no one was home when I knocked lol). It's been a long time since I've been back. Sometimes I wonder if it might've been better if we'd never left, but I'm grateful for every opportunity, every challenge… Even if I don't know how to do it and I'm not sure if I even want it anymore

Valeria stares at the *Did I Ever Tell You How Lucky You Are?* poster on her wall. A film by Disney, adapted from the book by Dr. Seuss, starring Valeria Leon and Patrick Paley, in theaters everywhere Thanksgiving 2014.

It's the morning of the *Platinum Triangle* premiere. In her hand is the latest issue of *US Weekly*. Lily, Joel, and Hailey are on the cover with the headline "PLATINUM LOVE TRIANGLE!" A photo of Lily takes up the bottom third of the cover—it's of her lifeguarding, her blond ponytail blowing in the wind and the beach behind her. The middle section is of a shirtless Joel surfing and looking his most gorgeous. The top tier is a photo of Hailey sunbathing in a bikini. The bar code is covering her left eye. She's the capstone on top of the Young Hollywood pyramid.

The article is all about the drama between "rival cousins" Lily and Hailey that's been happening since Lily moved into the Paleys' pool house and caught the eye of Hailey's romantic interest, dream guy Joel Strom. The sub-headline is "TV's Hottest Teens Duke It Out!" The inside sources are definitely the *Platinum Triangle* producers. They always do a big PR push before the season premiere. It's crazy how much they know. Sometimes Valeria feels like they're in her mind, like the powers that be know her better than she knows herself.

Valeria puts down the magazine and goes into her mother's bathroom. She opens the medicine cabinet and stands back as she appraises the bottles of pills. She just wants to hold them. She just wants to know that she could.

She hears Leo crying in his room and goes to check on him. She's babysitting Leo this morning while her mom takes Sophia to get headshots and then goes for a facial ahead of the premiere. At first Valeria thought her mom was joking. Gloria had always threatened Valeria with Sophia, but Valeria didn't think she would actually go as far as pushing Sophia into the industry just to spite her. Maybe it isn't spite, though. Maybe it's necessity. Valeria hasn't come up with a way to save her family from their impending doom, and the Leons are running out of options.

Valeria lifts Leo out of his crib and cradles him in her arms. He stops fussing and cuddles against her chest.

"Did I ever tell you . . . ?" she whispers, smelling his head.

The *US Weekly* article mentions Valeria by announcing that Hailey is replacing her on *Almost Everything*.

Hailey Paley in her acting debut.

Valeria knows she used Patrick's influence to steal the role out from under her feet. Valeria just doesn't know why. Is it just because she was there when Valeria got the call and she knew how happy it made her? Or . . . Valeria walks with Leo back to her bedroom and pulls the Panthère de Cartier earrings out of her pillow case and holds them in the palm of her hand. Does Hailey know her secret?

The doorbell rings.

Valeria puts the earrings away and goes down to answer it, balancing Leo on her hip as she swings open the door.

"I've been expecting you," she says when she sees Lily standing on the doorstep, weighed down by Neiman Marcus shopping bags.

"I just got away from Hailey. We went shopping for the red carpet tonight and got a bit carried away. I've been wanting to get over here all morning. Can I come in?"

Valeria was hoping Lily would just forget it and pretend like she'd never seen her coming out of Patrick's suite at the Montage. But Lily's too good not to be shocked by bad things; she hasn't been around them enough to know to keep quiet. Valeria's ready for whatever explanation Lily demands of her.

"Come on." Valeria leads Lily into the living room. "Do you want something to drink?"

"Please don't do the whole I-don't-feel-a-thing-therefore-I-can't-be-fazed thing," Lily says, dropping the shopping bags. "It's so overplayed. I saw *US Weekly*. I know Hailey stole your part."

Valeria puts Leo down so he can play with blocks on the floor. She and Lily sit on the couch.

"I'm not pretending. I'm fine. It doesn't matter what Hailey tries to do to me . . . she can't hurt me where I live." Valeria shoots Lily a look. "Do you know who told me that?" she asks. "Elizabeth Taylor. Elizabeth fucking Taylor!" Valeria doesn't admit that it's something she only heard Elizabeth say in a video she watched under the covers late at night.

"I respect your strength so much, Valeria." Lily glances over at Leo on the floor. "I know you'd do anything for your family."

Valeria remains silent. It's like when she would give interviews as a kid and the reporter would ask a question that intimidated Valeria, a question that was leading or trying to trap her—trying to get her to say something bitchy about another child star or give away something about her dad's rumored gambling with the money she was making. Valeria would just freeze up. She wouldn't say anything. She would just stare at the reporter, politely but firmly. She wouldn't give anything away.

"Here's what we're going to do," Lily says. "Patrick's paying off your mortgage."

Valeria blinks.

"What?"

"That was the deal I made with him. He pays off your mortgage and he never sees you again. I told him I would go to the police and the media if he didn't. He said no one would believe me, and he seemed so sure of it I was scared he was right. So I figured I would need proof."

"Proof?" Valeria asks.

"Something to hold against him and threaten him with, something to keep him in his place. So then Patrick was putting on his clothes in the bathroom and telling me how it was going to be: he was going to drive us both home and we were going to act like nothing had happened, raise absolutely no suspicions with Whitney or Hailey. And while he was talking, I went on his phone. The passcode is the day he won his Golden Globe; I overheard Hailey teasing him about it once. I had a feeling there would be some kind of evidence, something between you two that I could use. A text, anything. That's when I found the photo you sent him."

Valeria swallows.

"We can go to the police if that's how you want to handle this," Lily says. "I think you should, but I understand if you don't want to. It's your choice, Valeria. I'll stand by you no matter what. I have the phone."

"No police," Valeria says, her mouth dry. It's all she'll ever be known for if the truth comes out. The girl who was raped by Patrick Paley. Valeria refuses to go down in history as a footnote in Patrick Paley's Wiki. Even if the courts don't name her because she's underage, it'll spread through the industry. Valeria knows how it works. Hollywood never forgets.

"Patrick's going to pay off the house and help your family financially," Lily says.

The house. Her true Hollywood house. Valeria can't believe it.

"You don't have to worry about the IRS anymore. And Sophia's going to go to the most bougie private elementary school in Los Angeles. And whatever else you want. Patrick's not getting away with what he's done to you. From now on, *we're* calling the shots."

Lily smiles at Valeria proudly. "You're looking at the new executive producer of *Platinum Triangle!*"

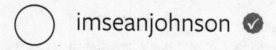
ofri_platt Take out of your life the people who make you feel like there is something wrong with you, friends and even family because those people don't know how special you are. And if you feel alone or that life can't get better I promise to you that it will get better. I hope you will find your happiness because you deserve it 🐾 🖤 👑

As the sun starts to set, Sean and Joel come out of the water with their surfboards tucked under their arms and sit on the beach. They've been at Zuma all day ignoring the inevitable—tonight's premiere.

Sean lights a joint. An outline of a surfer cuts across the sun, which has just set far enough to hit the water, creating a smudge of light that ripples across the horizon.

They sit in silence, exhausted, and it's exactly what they both wanted. They're so drained they'll just be on autopilot tonight at the premiere, just going through the motions. And since they've let all of their emotions wash away with the waves, it won't be so bad. They'll be as two-dimensional as the photos of them on the red carpet. But Sean hasn't been able to cancel *all* of his emotions. He's been in a trance state since the dogfight. He doesn't think he can live through another one.

Sean passes Joel the joint.

"We could skip the red carpet," he says.

"We could start a wildfire," Joel says.

Sean catches Joel glancing over at the lifeguard tower, like he's hoping to see Lily. Sean doesn't know the details of what happened to make things implode between Joel and Lily but he knows it's bad by the violent way Joel surfed today, treating his board like a weapon against the water. Joel hasn't mentioned the US Weekly cover story but it's hard to get away from that kind of coverage. Sean noticed paparazzi earlier, shooting them out on the water from the beach. If they thought season 1 of Platinum Triangle was intense, they might not yet know what's in store for them. Sean has this intuitive feeling that things are going to change this season and their lives will never be the same.

"Why was Fortune at the fight?" Joel asks, taking a pull and passing the joint back to Sean. "He recorded me at the fight, bro."

"What?" Sean looks at Joel through the smoke.

"He and Hailey are using it to blackmail me into going with Hailey to the premiere."

Sean just lets the joint burn between his fingers. The sunset is killing him.

"There's a part of me that doesn't want to go through with it," Joel says. "I'm so done with the games. If Hailey and Fortune want to try to ruin me and my family, they can go ahead and try; I won't let them control my life. We can handle it. The Stroms always bounce back." Joel looks over at Sean. "But I won't do that to you, bro. I promised you that your secret is safe with me, and it is. If you want to protect your dad, I understand. I don't think he deserves it, personally. But I respect your loyalty."

Sean is dazed. His mind is like a GIF of a hot guy with smoke blowing in and out of his mouth over and over again and you can't look away.

"There's video?" he asks.

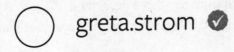

greta.strom ✓

735k followers

greta.strom We have calcium in our bones, iron in our veins, carbon in our souls, and nitrogen in our brains. 93 percent stardust, with souls made of flames, we are all just stars that have people names. #NikitaGill

Greta spends the day of the premiere doing yoga on the beach, followed by a little equine therapy, and then role-playing during her psychotherapy session at Cliffside Malibu. It reminds her so much of being on the show—dramatizing scenes from the past and the future. Stick a camera on her and it's *Platinum Triangle*.

It's not 100 yet but Greta's leaning toward leaving the show. She's going to see once she finishes treatment, but there's a part of her that already knows if she really wants to get healthy, then she can't keep putting herself in unhealthy environments. The show is toxic. She'd be glad if it were over and she could have a normal life. It's definitely better being rich than famous. It's definitely better being a family.

She imagines her friends getting ready to hit the red carpet and feels sorry for them. All that pressure . . . Greta wants to flip the page. She sits on a chaise lounge out by the pool and watches the sunset, a copy of *US Weekly* on her lap. She opens it to the story about Hailey, Joel, and Lily.

It's kind of nice being on the other side, being a follower. For the first time in a long time Greta can't wait to see what happens next!

realvalerialeon ✓

3.3m followers

sophialeon1919 my mama said i'm a good role model

"Valeria, can you help me practice my lines?"

Sophia comes into Valeria's bedroom as she's sitting in front of her vanity dressed in the ruffled Retrofête dress she's wearing to the premiere. Sophia shows Valeria the script she's holding.

Gloria moves fast. The headshots haven't even been printed and she's already got Sophia an audition. It's for a show on Nickelodeon. Gloria and Sophia have been out all day. After getting Sophia's headshots and facials, they stopped by Sheldon Bell's office at CAA. He had just the right part for Sophia. He thinks she's going to be "the next big thing."

"Valeria?" Sophia blinks at her and smiles.

"Of course I will." Valeria lowers her makeup brush. She takes the script from Sophia and they run through it.

Sophia reads well, but she's rigid. Her performance has already been crafted. Valeria remembers all too well practicing with Gloria over and over again and taking her direction. Gloria had very strong ideas about Valeria's scripts and thought her directors were all idiots. She'd make Valeria recite her lines as she instructed, adding gestures and inflections where she

303

thought appropriate. "Like this," she'd tell Valeria, making her repeat the line exactly as she had.

Valeria would go along with it during the endless rehearsals with her mom to keep her happy, but on her very first movie, her idiot director gave her some great advice. He told her to try memorizing all her lines by rote, without any emotion. Just simply learn the lines so well you know them better than the back of your hand. Because you won't know what you're feeling—and so how the lines should come out of you—until you're in the scene and the emotions are real.

"Can I give you some advice?" Valeria asks. "Live in the moment. Do you know how to do that?"

Sophia shakes her head. Valeria smiles.

"I'm not sure anyone does anymore."

They hear a throat clear and look up to see their dad standing in the doorway.

"This is what I like to see, both my girls together." Luis smiles at them.

He showed up at the house shortly after Lily left. Valeria wants to hate him. She wishes she could. But when she saw him, she burst into tears and hugged him. It's been the same cycle all her life, and Valeria wishes it were a different ride but knows she'll never get off it. She's loyal to her family. Family is the one thing that's more important to Valeria than being an actress.

Sophia was ecstatic when she got home with Gloria and saw Luis sitting with Valeria in the living room. Her happiness lessened the blow when Valeria found out about Sophia's audition. Poor Leo is shy around Luis. It's been that long.

"Hey, Sophia," Luis asks, "why don't you go downstairs and play with Leo for a while? I need a minute alone with your big sister."

"Okay," Sophia says, jumping off Valeria's bed and telling her they can "live in the moment later."

Valeria laughs.

Luis closes the door behind Sophia and turns to Valeria. She knows that look. Valeria doesn't wait for him to ask.

She goes over to her nightstand, puts her hand in her pillow case, and removes the Panthère de Cartier earrings. Valeria drops the earrings in her father's palm. She's not a character anymore, an idea of who Valeria Leon is supposed to be. She's determined to find out who she really is.

Luis whistles. "I'll tell the guy at the pawn shop to hold off on resale. I'll buy these back for you, superstar. I just need a little help paying off a hotel bill . . ."

"I don't want them back," Valeria says. "They're not my style."

Luis pockets the earrings and kisses the top of Valeria's head. He notices Sophia's script on the vanity and picks it up, waving the pages around.

"Cute kid, but she doesn't have *it*. I saw her rehearsing with your mother and it wasn't the same."

"I hope not," Valeria says.

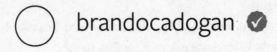

brandocadogan ✓

336k followers

dietsodabish Brat af

Brandon is totally medicated and he's also been snorting rails and smoking Spice and he hasn't had anything to eat in forty-eight hours. Who isn't on something? Who doesn't pop a Xanax or Adderall every now and then? He pulls into In-N-Out in his dad's Bentley for some Roadkill Fries and eats them as he continues driving around, the dashboard specked with cocaine and palm trees through the windshield.

He goes to The Nice Guy for a drink and they let him in even though he lost one of his Gucci Princetown slippers. The Nice Guy got its name because someone told the owner he was too nice to make it in this town. No one has ever told Brandon that he won't make it in this town. He drinks and hits on a girl who reminds him of Bea, but he knows that a Bea look-alike won't be the same as the real thing.

Brandon leaves and stops at a convenience store and picks up a bottle of vodka and some cigarettes. He's drinking from the bottle as he drives to the Chateau Marmont. He has to see Bea before she leaves for the premiere. Brandon's not going. He has no interest in standing there and being all, like, *What is even life?*

as people take his picture and reporters ask him how he's coping with his mom's cancer.

The first thing a child learns in this world is that when the mother lowers her hands in the game of peekaboo, her face is meant to be there.

Brandon needs Bea. She's the only one who understands. He loves her. He really loves her. She's the billionaire boy's girl. The it girl and the heir. It's the new '20s, old boy. It's Brandon's decade.

When Brandon gets to Bea's bungalow, he knocks. Maybe they'll sit out by the pool. He'd like to put his head in her lap. He'd like her to run her hands through his hair and tell him about when they're going to rule the world.

The door swings open and Brandon is confronted by his shirtless brother. Conrad looks surprised to see Brandon. Bea, standing behind Conrad in nothing but a pair of Louis Vuitton bunny ears, doesn't.

"Coming up this season," she says, raising a martini glass to Brandon and taking a sip.

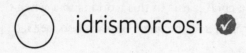
idrisregal OMGGGG

idrisregal MIRROR SELFIE

idrisregal I MISSED THISSSSS

Idris and Fortune get ready for the premiere over at Idris's house. Idris is wearing a metallic Dolce & Gabbana tux but he's not as flashy as Fortune, who is wearing thigh-high sparkling Louboutins, with his hair in side-braids and a smoky eye, a faux fur draped over his Moschino shirtdress.

"Tonight is a new beginning." Fortune looks at his reflection in Idris's bedroom mirror. "From this point forward I'm a star on the show."

Idris fusses with his bow tie. "So how'd you finally get Joel to agree to go with Hailey to the premiere?"

"Let's just say he's a total dog." Fortune smirks. "Sam and I are already talking about possible season 3 storylines. Like, she literally wants to throw me into Sean and Valeria's relationship to expose that it's fake as fuck and Sean is on the DL. Can you imagine? And you know I'll do it."

"Why do you want to be on the show so badly?" Idris asks. He gives up on his bow tie. Fortune comes over to do it for him.

"I don't really have a family of my own," Fortune says. He doesn't meet Idris's eyes. "The show is kind of like my family."

"You know I've got your back whether you're on the show or not, right?" Idris turns to look at the finished result in the mirror. Fortune never talks about his past; he pretends he doesn't have one, that his life is only what he's posted. "I just want you to remember that," Idris tells Fortune through the reflection. "No matter what happens."

Idris checks the time on his phone.

"I've gotta make a quick stop before the red carpet. See you there?"

Fortune hangs his fur off his shoulder as he poses in front of the mirror.

"Front and center."

"Dapper as fuck, bro," Idris says.

Joel's wearing a Tom Ford tux. He looks at Idris coolly as Idris stands at the doorway of the Stroms' Mediterranean mansion. Joel's expecting him—the guard at the Beverly Park gate called to ask if Idris could be let in. Idris wasn't sure if Joel was going to allow him to pass. But then the guard nodded his head and Idris slid past in his new $2.2 million Devel Sixteen hypercar.

"Drink?" Joel asks as Idris follows him into the living room.

"Sure, bro," Idris says.

Joel pours them each a tumbler of whiskey and they sit in two brown leather upholstered chairs near the fireplace, which is on, despite the end-of-summer heat. It's probably always on. Ambience.

Idris takes a sip of his drink.

Things are awkward AF between him and Joel. They weren't always. They had some good times. Legendary beach parties. Joel used to be a clown. Now he's moody and suspicious and hiding behind his 1.8 million followers like he knows he could flip the switch and sell himself out and get maybe 10 million, maybe more, enough to bury them all. And maybe Idris is just waiting for that Joel to come out.

"So?" Joel sips his drink. "Why are you here?"

"I have some things I have to get off my chest," Idris says. "First off, I'm sorry about Greta, man. I didn't treat her right. I respect your loyalty to your sister. I hope she finds a better guy than me."

Joel stares through him.

"That it?"

"I told Greta all this in the letter I wrote her. Not that she read it."

"The letter Lily helped you write?" Joel asks.

"Which brings me to the other reason I stopped by," Idris says. "You're a fool if you lose a girl like Lily. She's crazy about you." Idris swallows the rest of his whiskey. It hurts being honest. But this is something Idris knows he has to do. For Lily.

"Before you take Hailey to the premiere, there's something you should know."

◯ lillianrhode

birdymayjohnston Infection - everyone get your shots

lauragough1 Horse jawline, duck lips, body of man.... seriously wtf

selenamariegeorgia Jailey is really best 🖤 and joel strom is really cute couple than lily rhode and joel strom @paleyhailey @thejoelstrom @lillianrhode 🖤 🖤

hailay.paley Aceita que ele ama a Hailey

jazmynruiz2001 At least Hailey can dress better than you

"Do you know what this means?" Hailey holds the latest issue of *US Weekly* to her chest. "We are officially connected by something that runs *much* deeper than blood!"

Hailey's been reading the article to Lily up in Hailey's bedroom as they get ready for the red carpet together. It's not exactly the Paley family dinner Lily had been hoping for, but getting ready for a red carpet seems to be a ritual that brings the Paleys together. Hailey offered to let Lily use her glam squad. Hailey has finally achieved a lifelong ambition—to appear on the front cover of a tabloid—and with her ascension, lingering resentment and bitterness between her and Lily has faded away.

Or so Hailey thinks.

"What color do you want to do your lips?" Hailey's makeup artist asks Lily.

"Red," Lily says. To complement her pink sequin Monique Lhuillier gown. She steals a look at Hailey in the mirror, who's back with her nose in the magazine. "Maybe Housewife by Priscilla?" Lily asks the makeup artist.

"Classic." Hailey looks up from the tabloid and gives Lily an approving smile. A *real* smile.

"Listen to this . . ." Hailey reads aloud. "'Lily Rhode's arrival in the Platinum Triangle shakes up the new season of the hit reality show, shifting the dynamics between the teen cast of celebrity offspring and #richkid train wrecks. This season Lily moves in with the Paleys and joins Hailey's ranks as a Beverly Hills princess—but only one of them can be queen!'"

Hailey throws her head back in laughter. "This is so epic!" She comes up behind Lily sitting in front of the mirror and presses her head against Lily's as they stare at their reflection. Lily smacks her Housewife lips.

"You and me, girl," Hailey says. "The dream team. We're ratings gold!"

Patrick tried to fight Lily on the EP credit. He said there was no way. But Lily insisted it was the only way she would keep his secret. Patrick finally agreed to try to pull some strings.

This season Lily may be introduced as a pawn to Whitney and Hailey, a device to make them look sympathetic, but come season 3 not only will Lily be a permanent cast member, *she'll* be the one pulling the strings. And the whole world will finally see @paleyhailey for the fraud she is.

"Let's take a photo," Lily says, lifting her phone and snapping a pic of her and Hailey posing in front of the mirror.

Getting ready together for the premiere reminds Lily of when she and Hailey got ready for Brandon's party. It was only a month ago but it feels like a lifetime. It's so clear to Lily now that Hailey was just disarming her before going in for the kill. Now it's Lily's turn.

"I hope the *US Weekly* story isn't going to come between us now that we've decided to start over," Hailey says, glancing back down at the magazine in her hands. "Joel's picking me up for the red carpet . . ."

"No more competition," Lily says. "It is a new season after all. My first. And I want to start it off with good vibes only."

Hailey may not realize it yet, but the competition is over. Lily won. Why isn't it enough, though? Lily doesn't feel like she won anything. She hates how things ended with her and Joel. That's one storyline even her EP credit can't rewrite.

Lily runs her hand down the bodice of her dress, checking her angles in the mirror. Hailey's glam squad went all out. Her hair is curled and she's wearing mink eyelashes from Hailey's favorite brand—appropriately called Lilly Lashes. She and Hailey have never looked more alike.

"All that's missing is my new clutch," Lily says. "I left it in the pool house." She used her lifeguarding savings to buy a Judith Leiber Crystal Swan minaudière while she and Hailey were out shopping. She'll have to remember to put some candy inside before they leave, in case she gets a craving . . . .

Coming down the stairs on her way to the pool house, Lily sees Patrick talking with Sam in the living room. They grow quiet when they see Lily approaching.

"You look beautiful, Lily!" Sam says. She leans in. "And I'm so excited to hear we'll be seeing a lot more of you."

Lily looks from Sam straight at Patrick. He takes a sip of his drink.

"And soon, I hope," Sam says. "We still need to schedule a date to shoot your confessionals. The editors are piecing together the last episodes of the season, right when you make your grand arrival. The highlight of the season, if you ask me! You up to shoot over the next couple of days?"

"Oh, I think so." Lily's eyes stay on Patrick. "There's so much I could say . . ."

At the pool house Lily looks for her clutch in the bedroom. The blue neon *Land of Hopes & Dreams* sign is glowing and she stares up at it. She smiles to herself in the electric glow. Once upon a time in Hollywood.

"Lily, there you are!" Whitney steps into the bedroom dressed in a deep-V Balmain gown. She turns on the light. "I wanted to talk to you before we leave."

Lily picks up her clutch and turns to face her aunt.

"Now that your court case is behind you, and with the show premiering, it's time to think of the future. I've talked it over with Patrick and we would both love it if you would agree to stay with us. On a more permanent basis. Summer is almost over and school will be starting soon. . . . What do you think of joining Hailey at New Beverly? We want you to make Beverly Hills your home," Whitney says.

Lily knows that the real reason she's been invited to stick around is because of the *US Weekly* cover. She's proven to be a valuable investment. And she's just getting started!

"Home," Lily smiles. "That sounds really nice."

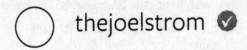

thejoelstrom ✔

1.8m followers

samijanwazir Seriously, haters, back off. Would you like it if people would kept commenting stuff like that on your pic? It's none of your buissness whether Joel love hauley or lily. It's his life... So back off. Lily is just as human as Hailey, she's also beautiful and nice. This isn't a reality show for you. You have no idea how much these comments hurt. So sad that people today are using social media to hurt other peoples' feelings.. @thejoelstrom @paleyhailey @lillianrhode

portersmania JAILEY! JAILEY! JAILEY!

hailey.exe I'm so sory but i'm not a long follower of Joel. I'm so sory Joel, I love you, but I can't support to say a photos you post with you and Lily. I remain a follower of Hailey Paley. 😔 🤦 😔

Joel sits as physically far away from Hailey as he possibly can in the back of the limo. He's on his phone reposting the photo of him and Lily that his dad took over dinner. Hailey's making him go to the premiere with her but she can't control his Instagram. Joel's making his own statement tonight.

Hailey opens a bottle of Cristal and pours herself a glass. She asks Joel if he wants one and he just keeps staring out the window. Hailey pulls out her phone and they ride in silence the rest of the way to the premiere.

Joel keeps going over what Idris told him. He wanted to go straight to Lily after he found out the lengths Hailey went to in order to force him to be with her at the premiere. But he knows that would mean exposing Sean and his dad, and Joel promised Sean he'd take it to the grave.

As the limo approaches the Sofitel, Joel sees the fans and press behind barricades and he feels his heart speeding up. He almost forgot what this feeling was like. The energy is unreal.

It's total pandemonium when Joel and Hailey step onto the red carpet. It's like stepping onto another planet. And as the fans scream and the cameras flash, it's not so bad up in the stars.

The step-and-repeat has the *Platinum Triangle* title and the spiral MKTV network logo, along with the ABC circle logo because it owns MKTV, and the Disney logo because it owns ABC, and if you look closely enough, you'll see your own DNA.

Some of the other cast members have already arrived and are at various stages of posing and talking to the reporters. Jessica looks like an Old Hollywood movie star in her mermaid dress and with her hair curled and to one side. She winks at Joel from the press line.

Joel and Hailey aren't the only couple making a debut. Bea Getty is posing with Conrad Cadogan. Brandon's nowhere in sight, and Joel saw on Instagram that he posted a photo boarding his dad's jet. No caption.

A surge of energy is directed toward Joel and Hailey as they pose. He keeps a hand on her waist and Hailey does her thing, posing from various angles while Joel just sort of stands there— he's just a mannequin for Hailey to hang off of. There's a group of girls literally crying behind barricades for Joel, and he goes over and takes selfies with them.

Hailey joins him over by the fangirls, who freak TF out as she approaches. One girl just wants to touch Hailey's hair and Hailey lets her, and then Joel and Hailey are being led by a publicist over to the press line. The Johnsons are doing an interview up ahead. Joel looks in Sean's eyes and sees a tortured look. Sean breaks away first, staring down at the red carpet.

A reporter from *E! News* interviews them. "It's so good to see you two together!" she exclaims into her microphone. "Does that mean that the rumors are true and there's a Hailey and Joel romance brewing this season?"

"Well, we did do a cast trip to the Bahamas," Hailey says. She looks directly into the camera. "It's hot over there . . ."

The reporter laughs.

"Just how hot?" she asks. "And how did Lily Rhode react? Are the rumors true about you and Hailey's cousin?" The mic is thrust in Joel's face.

Joel scratches his cheek. He doesn't know how to respond.

"I guess you'll have to watch," he says.

The paparazzi go wild as another car pulls up to the red carpet. The Leons show up as a family. Luis is with them. Valeria looks beautiful and her smile is effortless.

"Looks like the Leons have just arrived," the reporter says. She turns back to Hailey. "Is it true that you're replacing Valeria on the new sitcom *Almost Everything*?"

"I love Valeria," Hailey says. "She knows I'd literally do anything for her. But I've been thinking about acting and this opportunity came my way. I think the producers just wanted to go with a fresher look . . ."

317

Joel stops listening. He's distracted by the next arrival. The Paleys light up as they step out of a limo. Patrick and Whitney appear first, followed by Lily.

The roar of the crowd is so undeniable that even Hailey has to pause her interview. She looks down the red carpet and sees Lily's flashing arrival.

"Lily!" the paparazzi are screaming. "Over here! To your left!"

Lily's pink sequin dress sparkles in the lights. She puts one hand on her hip and looks directly in Joel's eyes as she strikes a pose.

lillianrhode

107k followers

The screaming of the crowd and frenzied clicking of the camera lenses go mute for Lily. The lights are flashing so rapidly that she sees a crown of white spots surrounding Joel's head as he stands on the red carpet next to Hailey.

Lily can hear her heart beating in her ears. A flashing light shines into her eyes and she blinks, the sound suddenly turning back on. The paparazzi are calling her name.

She looks back over at Joel and sees his profile as he talks to a reporter, a microphone suspended in front of his lips. The camera lights shine through his eyelashes and his eyes are brimming with something—it's like they're bugged out in a way, like he's high. It's a state that Lily finds herself experiencing for the first time. After Greta told her that Joel was threatening to quit the show if her wardrobe malfunction made the air, Lily was convinced that the warnings she's heard about him weren't true.

But maybe Valeria wasn't totally wrong when she said you can't get over it. Once you're infected, you're a fame junkie for life. Few ever manage to escape the pull that keeps them coming back for more of their favorite substitute for love.

The cheers from the fans suddenly stop and are replaced by gasps when a fight breaks out. Lily loses her pose as Christoph Johnson lunges for Sean and throws him against the step-and-repeat. Christoph gets Sean in a chokehold.

"You betrayed your own father? Your own blood?"

Sean manages to break free. He punches Christoph in the nose and Christoph goes flying back, crashing into the press line.

The lights flash even more rapidly. It's chaos, and everyone looks stunned as they watch Sean wring out his fist, prepared to hit his father again as Christoph rises to a stand, blood dripping from his nose. Shondra Johnson is pretending to hide her face from the cameras.

"It ends now," Sean says. "It ends tonight!"

Lily doesn't know what Sean's talking about. She looks over at Valeria, who looks just as shocked and confused.

Sean storms into the hotel. Christoph tries to go after him but security holds him back. The flashing lights are making Lily dizzy. She can't see anything. But she can hear.

"Joel! Any comment?" The reporters and paparazzi are all asking at once. "Is it really you in the video?"

paleyhailey ✓

1m followers

glowingrselle Stop insulting Lily. She's as pretty as Hailey. This is not what Hailey wants. They both deserves love and happiness. Nothing will change from your meaningless comments. Remember when Hailey said " kill people with kindness , and respect women. " why so many hate? You - Stop hate! More love! Be kind, please.

"Joel, what are you—" Hailey stops mid-sentence as she watches Joel offer Lily his hand. Hailey just stands there, with cameras flashing, as Lily accepts it. They escape the cameras and head into the hotel, leaving Hailey alone on the red carpet. Suddenly each flash feels like it's cutting into her.

"*What* is happening?" Hailey rushes up to Fortune in the hotel lobby, away from the mayhem outside.

"Like I know," he says. "Sean's dad just went, like, legit crazy."

"The video of Joel at the dogfight—you didn't send it to anyone but me, did you?"

Fortune looks at Hailey guiltily. "Sean asked to see it. I didn't think that he would—"

"No, you *didn't* think," Hailey says. "And now the photographers have a shot of Joel running away from the drama with Lily and *not* me. Say goodbye to ever being a permanent cast member!

By the time I'm through with you, my housekeeper will have a bigger role on *my* show."

Hailey turns and struts away, leaving Fortune in the lobby. She joins the cast and crew in the reception room for the party and goes right up to Joel standing in a group with Lily, Sean, and Valeria.

"I had to do it," Sean is saying as Hailey approaches. "I just couldn't live with the secret anymore."

"You did the right thing, bro," Joel says. "I'm proud of you."

"It was so brave, Sean," Valeria adds. "I'm proud of you, too."

Joel and Sean hug.

"I'll tell everyone that I dragged you into it," Sean says. "That I couldn't face it alone and you were a true friend. You stood by me. I'll tell them you encouraged me to leak it, to stop it. Because *that*'s who you are. You care more about doing the right thing than about your own image."

"Speaking of your image," Hailey butts in. "Joel, don't you think you should make some kind of statement to the press? I'll go with you." She tries to take Joel's arm but he pulls away.

"Don't act like you care," Sean tells Hailey. "You were using the video against him. That's the only reason he's here with you tonight."

"Is that true?" Lily asks, looking at Joel.

Joel's about to answer when a photographer gets past security and bursts into the party, lighting them up in the flash of his camera and taking a succession of photos. They're trapped.

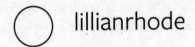

lillianrhode

107k followers

Lily and Joel run hand in hand through the hotel kitchen. They come flying out the back door, spilling into the alley. One of the hotel staff is outside smoking a cigarette, leaning against the wall. His eyes widen when he recognizes them and he asks for a selfie.

"You can't live your whole life on your phone, man!" Joel yells back at him as they run down the alleyway.

They come around the side of the hotel, approaching the parked limo that Lily arrived in with Patrick and Whitney.

"A limo?" Joel laughs. "This is your getaway car?"

"The driver's nowhere in sight and the keys are in the ignition," Lily says, pointing through the partially lowered window. "You have a better idea?"

"If by 'nowhere in sight' you mean on his way back with some street meat, then . . ." Joel looks at Lily. "Get in!"

Lily hops into the back and Joel gets behind the wheel. The driver sees and drops his food on the sidewalk. He chases after them as they pull away from the hotel. Lily sticks her head out of the sunroof and waves.

"My first stan!" She laughs.

Some of the paparazzi notice them driving off and join the chase down the street. Joel makes a turn and they lose their followers. The last shot the paparazzi get is of Lily blowing them a kiss.

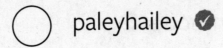

paleyhailey ✔

1m followers

paleyhailey I hate her!

paleyhailey She ruins everything!

paleyhailey That backstabbing bitch is after my life!

princepaley Omg!!! Who??

princepaley What's wrong Queen???

paleyhailey BRING ME HER HEAD.

lillianrhode ✔

108k followers

wearemily4 Make your story and love live forever

They go to Malibu.

Joel parks the limo on the PCH and they get out, running onto the beach.

"Lily, there's so much I want to say—"

"Save it for the confessionals," Lily says. "I don't want to think about the past. I don't want to think about the future. I just want to be *now*. Here. With you."

Lily drops her swan clutch into the sand and slips out of her heels, looking out at the water and smiling back at Joel as she lets the straps of her dress slide off her shoulders. Her dress drops to her ankles in the sand.

Joel's already kicking off his shoes. "How soon is now?" he asks. Joel whips off his tuxedo jacket and throws it behind him. Lily helps him unbutton his dress shirt, her hands shaking. She runs into the water as Joel hops out of his pants.

Lily dives under and when she breaks the surface, Joel is running into the water in his white Calvin Klein briefs. He swims over to her.

As they kiss, Lily remembers Joel standing on the street outside the Paleys' house, meeting her eyes through the window as the *Platinum Triangle* production SUV slowly drove past. She didn't know then what was going to happen to her, but she knew there was no going back. And from that first moment when she locked eyes with Joel Strom, she hasn't wanted to.

The facade of the house isn't real. A part of her must've known then, when Joel walked up to her on the driveway and saw her staring up at the Paleys' glass cage, that glass walls promoting transparency can become a labyrinth of mirrors.

Life on a reality show can make everything feel like a reality show, like the world is going to separate, as if it's an elaborately designed stage set, and you'll learn that everyone was acting and you were the only one who didn't know.

When they get back to the beach, Lily's phone is going off in her clutch. She pulls it out and looks up at Joel standing at the edge of the water and letting the waves break over his feet.

"I've been Verified," she tells him.

"Welcome to the club," Joel says, water dripping from his hair down his face.

Lily drops her phone back in the clutch. She's shivering, and it's not just from the cold. Joel comes over and retrieves his jacket, dusting off the sand, and he wraps it around Lily's shoulders.

"My dad's place is close to here," he says. "Why don't we go there? She'll probably still be at the Sofitel." He rubs Lily's shoulder. "We'll start a fire. Get warmed up."

Lily kisses him one more time.

"Last one to the limo has to perform an LOML number," she whispers in his ear, bending over to grab her shoes and dress. She makes a run for it across the beach toward the highway.

The sand kicks up around her as she runs. She can hear Joel running behind her and turns around to look at him as she reaches the PCH. Joel's not far behind, a big smile on his face. He stops running just as Lily turns and starts to cross, feeling the pavement beneath her feet.

"Lily!" Joel screams.

There's a car barreling down the highway straight toward her. Lily freezes mid-pose. The headlights are like the camera lights and she's nothing but a cover girl.

paleyhailey ✓

1.1m followers

kate_sara_ I'm gonna have nightmares after seeing this lol

Hailey is asleep on her bed and doesn't hear the window sliding open, or the person climbing on her roof slipping inside so quietly it's like he's not really there. But he's always watching.

She looks so beautiful, sleeping peacefully with her hair fanned out across her pillow. The ends twist to make perfect heart shapes. It's exactly how he always imagined she'd sleep. Like she's the most Liked photo in the world.

His face is distorted in her mirrored bedpost. He's a blurry image, not quite a whole person but more solid than a ghost—and certainly more influential.

If only he could touch her. He reaches out his hand . . . her skin! It looks so soft. He wants to wear it. But he won't. Not yet. It isn't time to wake her from her dream within a dream.

He knows she hears it all the time but he's her biggest fan!

She stirs and rolls to her side, breaking hearts as he takes a selfie with her sleeping behind him.

princepaley Queen Hailey Forever 💎 ✨